# MONTANA FIRE

A SMALL TOWN ROMANCE - BOOK 1

VANESSA VALE

Montana Fire

ISBN: 978-1-7959-0010-2



Cover design: Bridger Media

Cover graphic: Hot Damn Stock; Fotolia: chesterF

Edition 2: This book was previously published.

## GET A FREE BOOK!

JOIN MY MAILING LIST TO BE THE FIRST TO KNOW OF NEW RELEASES, FREE BOOKS, SPECIAL PRICES AND OTHER AUTHOR GIVEAWAYS.

http://freeromanceread.com

# 1

"I'm not sure which one I want. I didn't realize there were so many choices!"

The woman wasn't on the hunt for a new car or juice boxes at the grocery store. Nope. She wanted a dildo. I called her type a Waffler. Someone who contemplated all options before even attempting to make a choice. Because of Miss Waffler, I had ten different dildo options spread out across the counter. Glass, silicone, jelly and battery powered. She needed help.

That's where I came in. My name is Jane West and I run Goldilocks, the adult store in Bozeman, Montana, my mother-in-law had opened back in the seventies. Story goes she named it after the fairytale character when a mother bear and her two cubs strolled down Willson right in front of the store the week before it opened. She called it fate. Or it could have been because her name is Goldie, so it made sense. I started working for her when my husband died, a temporary arrangement that helped her out. Three years later, things had turned long-term temporary.

The store was tasteful considering the offerings. The walls were a fresh white with shelves and displays just like you'd find at the typical department store. Then tasteful made way for tacky. Gold toned industrial carpet like you'd see in Vegas, a photo of a naked woman sprawled artfully across a bearskin rug hung over the counter. A sixties chandelier graced the meager entry. Goldie had to put her unique stamp on things somehow.

It wasn't a big store, just one room with a storage area and bathroom in back. Whatever she didn't have in stock—although you'd be amazed at the selection Goldie offered in such a small space—we ordered in. Montanans were patient shoppers. With few options store-wise in Bozeman, most people ordered everything but the basics from the Internet. There's one Walmart, one Target, one Old Navy. Only one of everything. In a big city, if you drove two miles you came across a repeat store. Urban sprawl at its finest. Not here, although there were two sets of Golden Arches. One in town and one off the highway for the tourists who needed a Big Mac on the way to Yellowstone. The anchor store of the town's only mall was a chain bookstore. No Nordstrom or Bass Pro Shop out here. You shopped local or you went home to your computer.

In the case of the woman in front of me, I wished she'd just go home.

Don't get me wrong, I liked helping people and I was comfortable talking sex toys with anyone. But this time was definitely different. Big time.

Behind Miss Waffler stood a fireman. A *really* attractive, tall, well-muscled one wearing a Bozeman Fire T-shirt and navy pants. Can you say hot? A *hot* man in uniform? Yup, it was a cliché, but this one was dead-on accurate. God, he was literally heart stopping gorgeous. He'd made mine skip a beat. I felt all tingly and hot all over.

He'd come in while I was comparing the various dildo models before I went into the perks of having rotation for best female stimulation, and when I looked up...and up and he was there, I practically swallowed my tongue. I'd certainly lost my train of thought. I had no idea God made men like him. Magazines, maybe. Real life? *My* real life? Wow.

"Can you explain the features of each one again?" Miss Waffler had her fingers on the edge of the glass counter as if she were afraid to touch them. Petite, she was slim to the point of anorexic. Her rough voice said smoker, at least a pack a day. Her skin was weathered, either from cigarettes or the Montana weather, and wrinkles had taken over her face. She'd be pretty if she ate something and kicked the nicotine habit.

I gave her my best fake smile. "Sure."

I darted a glance at the fireman over the woman's shoulder. Sandy hair trimmed military short, blue eyes, strong features. Thirties. A great smile. He seemed perfectly content to wait his turn. If the humorous glint in his eye and the way he bit his lip —most likely to keep from smiling—was any indication, he was clearly enjoying himself. And learning something about dildos. Maybe he wanted some options for his girlfriend. He had to have some woman warming his bed. A radio squawked on his belt and he turned it down. Obviously, my lesson on sexual aids was more important than a five-alarm fire.

Miss Waffler was completely oblivious of, and unaffected by, the fireman. I now knew why she wanted a dildo.

I picked up a bright blue model. "This one is battery powered and vibrates. Ten settings. Good for clitoral stimulation." I put it down and picked up another. I was used to talking sex toys with people. Some guys, too, but I was dying of embarrassment having said *clitoral stimulation* in front of *him.* I just imagined this hot fireman stimulating my clit. I squirmed, cleared my throat and continued. "This one is glass. No batteries, so it's meant for penetration. The best thing about it is you can put it in the freezer or warm it and it provides a varied experience."

The woman made some *ah* sounds as I gave the details. I went through all the possibilities with her one at a time. I got to the tenth and final model. "This one is obviously realistic. It's actually molded from the erect penis of a porn star. It's made of silicone and has suction cups on the base."

Fireman peered over the woman's shoulder as I suction cupped the dildo to the glass counter. *Thwap.* He didn't seem too stunned by the size. Did that mean he was that big, too?

"You can...um, attach it to a piece of furniture if you want to keep your hands free."

Both fireman and Miss Waffler nodded their heads as if they could picture what I was talking about.

"I'll take that one," she said as she pointed to number ten. The eight-inch Whopper Dong.

"Good choice."

I rang up Miss Waffler's purchase and she happily went off to take care of business.

And there he was. Mr. Fireman. And me. And dildo display made three. Fortunately, he stood in front of the counter and I wasn't able to look down and see if his Whopper Dong fit inside his uniform pants. Oh god, I was going straight to hell. He saved people's lives and I was thinking about his—

"Um...thanks for waiting." I tucked my curly hair behind an ear.

"Sure. You learn something new every day." He smiled. Not just with his mouth, but with his eyes. Very blue eyes. I saw interest there. Heat, too.

Right there, in the middle of my mother-in-law's sex store, dildos and all, was the spring thaw in my libido. It had long since gone as cold as Montana in January. Who could have blamed it with all of my dead husband's shenanigans? But right then, I felt my heart rate go up, and my palms sweating from nerves. The fireman didn't seem the least bit fazed by my little sex toy talk. I, on the other hand, was having a hot flash like a menopausal woman just looking at him. I needed to be hosed down. Speaking of hoses—

"I'm Jane. What can I help you with today?" *Hi, I'm Jane. I'm thirty-three. I like hiking in the mountains, cross-country skiing, I'm a Scorpio, and I want to rip that uniform off your hot body and slide down your pole.* I wiped my sweaty palms on my shorts.

He laughed and held out his hand. His grip was firm, his skin warm and a little rough. "Ty. Thanks, but no toys for me." A pager beeped. He looked at it on his belt briefly and ignored it.

"Don't you need to answer that? A fire or something?" I asked, pointing to his waist.

"Cat up a tree," he joked, the corner of his full lips tipping up.

I laughed, and heard my nerves in it. I took a deep breath to try and calm my racing heart. It didn't work. All it did was make me discover how good he smelled. It wasn't heavy cologne. Soap maybe. I didn't really care if it was deodorant. He smelled fabulous.

"Actually, it was for Station Two. I'm here for your fire safety inspection." He placed papers on the counter. Had he been holding them all this time? I hadn't noticed.

"Oh, um...inspect away."

*Inspect away?*

He grinned at me as I blushed, ready to slink behind the counter and die of embarrassment. Fortunately, he switched topics. For the next fifteen minutes, we went over fire inspection paperwork with the attraction I felt for him an elephant in the room the shape of a dildo.

---

THE NEXT MORNING, I was out bright and early. If you lived in Montana, you got out and enjoyed good weather while the getting was good. Even in July. Especially in July. The days were long, the sky was big and there was a lot to do before it got cold. I didn't mean November like the real world. This was Bozeman. Summer was over the day after Labor Day. It had even been known to snow in July. With that small window for wearing shorts and flip-flops and the threat of white flakes at any time, I was out and about by seven on a Saturday. I got more done before nine in the morning than the military. Not because I really wanted to, but because I had kids.

My boys, Zach and Bobby, were raring to go. Since it was Saturday morning, that meant garage sales. To kids, garage sales were serious business. Toys to be had, books to find. Even free stuff to rake in. As a grown up, I loved buying things I didn't know I needed. Last week, I bought a shoe rack for my closet and a toaster for the pop-up camper. For two dollars, I could have some toast while camping in the wilderness.

We were in the car, Kids Bop bounced out from the CD player. I had the hot garage sales circled in the classifieds, the *Bozeman Chronicle* open on the passenger seat next to me, ready to guide us to our treasures. The morning's first stop was a volunteer fire department's pancake breakfast. Bargain shopping could wait. With a pancake breakfast, I didn't have to cook—at seven in the morning, who wanted to?—the kids could stuff their faces, and I could get coffee. *Coffee.*

I realized the boys were yakking at me, so I turned down a sugary version of *Dynamite* to listen.

"He's so cool, Mom. He's a fireman and he was a soldier and he said we could play in his yard. He's at least seven feet tall. His snow blower is bigger than ours. His truck is silver and it has four doors," Zach said from his booster in the back.

"He gave me a high five after I ridden my bike down the sidewalk. His name is Mr. Strickland," Bobby added. I peeked in the rearview mirror and saw him nod his head, super serious.

The man I'd heard about ever since the boys woke me up was Mr. Strickland, the new neighbor. Mr. Strickland did this, Mr. Strickland did that. The boys' new super hero had bought the house two doors down and just moved in. I hadn't met him yet, but the kids obviously had. In my coffee deprived mind, I pictured a fifty-something man with half a head of graying hair, a slight paunch—he was a fireman, so it couldn't be too big—and by Zach's description, taller than a basketball player. Great. He'd come in real handy when another ball got stuck up in the gutter.

"The Colonel likes him a lot," Zach said.

Well, that settled it. If the Colonel gave his approval, the man had to be all right, regardless of gargantuan size. The Colonel's real name is William Reinhoff, but everyone who knew him, which was the entire town, called him Colonel. He'd earned the title while fighting in Vietnam and it stuck. Gruff and ornery on the outside with a campfire toasted marshmallow center, he was one of my favorite people. The Colonel's house was wedged between Mr. Strickland's and mine. He was next-door neighbor, pseudo father, close friend, occasional babysitter, and my mother's long-distance boyfriend. The kids had obviously met Mr. Strickland with the Colonel while I was at work yesterday and the man had made a serious impression. No way would the Colonel let the kids call the man by his first name. He was entirely too old school for that.

I pulled into the packed dirt parking lot of the fire department, parked, and turned to the kids. They sat in their boosters with the dollar bills I'd given each of them to spend on garage sale paraphernalia clenched in their fists. At seven, Zach was string bean skinny with knobby knees and dimples. Blond hair and light eyes had him looking like me. No one was sure where Bobby got his black hair and dark eyes as they surely hadn't come from either me or his father. Some people said he might be the Fed Ex man's kid, but I didn't see much humor in that. My husband had been the cheater, not me.

"Take only what you can eat, good manners, and put your dollar bill in your pocket so you don't lose it," I reminded them.

The kids nodded their heads with excitement. Garage sales and pancakes. Could life get any better?

The sun felt warm on my face. It had just popped up over

the mountains, even though it had been light for almost two hours. "Leave your sweatshirts in the car. It'll be warm when we come out." I stripped off my fleece jacket and tossed it onto the front seat. It might have been summer, but it still dropped into the forties overnight.

The breakfast was in the fire department's bay. One big space, concrete floor and walls made of gray sheet metal siding. Two fire trucks were parked out in front with volunteer firemen watching kids swarm over the equipment. My two looked longingly at the apparatus but knew they could explore only once they'd eaten. Inside, it smelled like bacon and coffee. Two of my favorite things. I collected paper plates and plastic utensils and got in the buffet line for food.

"There's Jack from school," Zach said as he tugged on my arm and pointed. I waved to Jack and his parents who were already digging into their pancakes at one of the long tables. Everywhere you went in Bozeman, you ran into someone you knew. It was impossible to avoid it. Even a seven-year-old like Zach felt popular. It was nice sometimes, the sense of community, but once I'd ducked around an aisle at the grocery store to avoid someone so I didn't have to talk to them. Who hasn't? That time it had been my dental hygienist, and I hadn't been overly interested in being interrogated about my flossing practice.

Since I ran Goldilocks, the only adult store nearby—you had to go all the way to Billings otherwise—I had a lot of customers. Local customers. It was hard sometimes to make small talk with someone at the deli counter when you really only knew them from the time they came to the store to purchase nipple clamps for the little wife. Thus, the ducking around in stores. I held a lot of confidences, kept a lot of secrets, and over the years, the general population trusted me with them.

We approached the first breakfast offering. At the word 'eggs', the boys stuck out their plates. I watched them load up and move on to hash browns, which they skipped over with a polite, "No, thank you." I gave myself an imaginary pat on the back for their good manners. They could squawk like roosters at each other but were almost always polite to strangers who offered food.

"Mom! There's Mr. Strickland!" Zach practically yelled.

"Hi, Mr. Strickland!" Bobby chimed.

I searched for Mr. Strickland over the crowd of tables, down the length of the food, looking for the Mr. Strickland of my imagination. Where was the fifty-something man? The paunch? Zach held out his plate for pancakes.

"Hey, Champ!" the pancake man said to Zach.

My heart jumped into my throat and I broke out in an adrenaline-induced sweat.

"Holy crap," I said.

Pancake man was not fifty. Not even forty. He most definitely didn't have a pot belly. Only an incredibly flat one under a navy fire department T-shirt. Solid. Hot. Zach had certainly exaggerated Mr. Strickland's height. He was tall. I had to tilt my head up a bit to look him in the eye, which I found A-OK. Being five-eight, I liked a man with altitude.

The fireman was certainly lighting my fire.

"Holy crap?" Pancake man, also known as Mr. Strickland, replied.

Flustered, I tried to smile, but I was mortified. Not because I'd said holy crap. That had just slipped out. I could have probably come up with something better, but holy crap, he was the fireman who'd come into the store for the fire inspection. The one with the Whopper Dong. The one who—

"I know you," Ty said, smiling. Damn. His teeth were straight and perfect. I could feel my blood pressure going through the roof. No bacon for breakfast for me or I might have an embolism on the spot. "You're Jane from Goldilocks."

His smile widened into a full-on grin. Yeah, he remembered me and the array of dildos.

"You know Mom from work?" asked Bobby, eyeing both of us curiously. His plate was filled with food and he needed two hands to carry it. "Mom says her work is for grown-ups."

Ty nodded his head and looked Bobby in the eye. "I had to inspect the sprinkler system and make sure there are fire extinguishers in the store. I was working, too."

"Boys, take your plates and find a place to sit." I angled my head toward the tables. "I'll be right there."

"Will you sit with us, Mr. Strickland?" Zach asked, full of hope.

"Why don't you two call me Ty, all right?"

The boys nodded their heads.

"Give me a few minutes to finish here and I'll join you," Ty replied, holding up his metal tongs to prove he had serious work to do. The kids scurried off to scarf down their meals. Ty watched the boys go then turned his gaze to me. Grinned some more.

"I learned a lot from you at the store yesterday," Ty said. He appeared to be enjoying himself immensely. Me, not so much. Mr. Tall, Light and Handsome was...was flirting with me.

Standing in the pancake line, I did a quick mental inventory. It wasn't quite eight in the morning so I wasn't at my best. On a good day, or at least later in the morning, I liked to think of myself as better than average looking. I'm above average in height, longer than average in curly, dark blond hair, larger than average in breast size, and lighter than average in weight. The weight part I could thank my mom. Like her, I can eat whatever I wanted and not gain an ounce. My best friend Kelly hated me for that, but what could I do? She should hate my mother instead.

The downside to being skinny was that I had no calves. None. It was a straight shot down from knobby knees to feet. I could run until the cows came home and I wouldn't develop calves. At least Kelly had calves. The rest, including the calves, was just weird genetics.

Of course, this morning I hadn't pulled myself together as I should, or how Kelly said I should. I was what was called a low maintenance woman. I didn't even think I had a can of hairspray in my house.

I went over the crucial things in my mind. Hair, breath, bra, zipper. At least I'd brushed my teeth, but my hair was pulled up into a ratty ponytail, probably curls sticking out every which way. I wore shorts—the zipper was up, an old Sweet Pea Festival T-shirt and flip-flops. No make-up. It couldn't have gotten much worse unless I had decided to skip a bra. Which, being a 34D, would have been *really* bad.

I was a mess! Kelly would disavow any knowledge of me if she came through the door.

Then I remembered Ty was my new neighbor. No matter how much I felt like it at the moment, I couldn't hide from him forever.

What could this guy see in me besides a complete slob who was an expert in dildos? What had I worn yesterday? It didn't matter. He'd probably been too blinded by all the sex toys to have noticed my clothing. I felt like a total freak. And yet he was flirting.

"This is one of those embarrassing moments in life." I pointed my finger at him. Hot or not, I felt very cranky. How dare he flirt with me when I was unprepared! "You need to tell me a secret about you so it balances out."

A corner of his mouth tipped up into a grin. "Fair enough." He leaned toward me over the platter of pancakes, looked to the left and right and whispered so only I could hear. "I can see the perks of the silicone dildo you talked about yesterday, even the one with the top that rotates." He twirled his finger in the air to demonstrate, then looked me straight in the eye. "But I like a woman who goes for the real thing."

Was that steam coming up off the platter of pancakes I was leaning over, or did I just break out in sweat?

---

IT TOOK Ty five minutes to separate himself from the pancakes and tongs and sit across the table from me and Zach, with Bobby on his right. He hadn't left his grin behind.

"When we're done here, we're going to garage sales," Bobby told Ty around a mouthful of egg.

"Yeah, we each have a whole dollar to spend," Zach added. A piece of pancake fell out of his mouth and landed with a plop back in the syrup on his plate.

"No talking with your mouth full," I murmured.

"Sounds like fun. Make sure you show me all your loot later," Ty told them both.

The boys nodded to Ty in answer, their lips tightly sealed as they chewed.

"Aren't you eating?" he asked me.

I took a sip of the heavenly coffee. "I will."

He lifted an eyebrow, but made no comment.

Small talk. I needed to make small talk. The kids could do it. Forget the past. The dildos. Bad hair. It was all about the future. He was my neighbor and I had to stop feeling embarrassed someday. "I...I didn't know you were a volunteer fireman."

Ty shook his head. "I'm not. I work in town for Bozeman Fire. Station One on Rouse. Here, this area south of town, is volunteer. I have friends on the department and offered to help with the breakfast this morning."

So, it was small town coincidence I bumped into him. First thing in the morning looking a total mess. It would have worked better if I'd primped a bit and taken brownies to him at his house, welcoming him to the neighborhood. The only perk of running into him this way was I didn't have to bake.

"What about you? Is Goldilocks your shop?"

"You must be new to town." I reached out and grabbed Bobby's OJ cup before it tipped over, moved it out of the way.

"Yeah, Montana raised, but new to Bozeman. I've been in the military for years and decided to settle down close to home. Bought the house down the street from you."

"Goldilocks belongs to Goldie, my mother-in-law. It's her store. *Everyone* knows Goldie. She's famous around here. You'll know what I mean when you meet her. She's a pistol. I just work there to help her out since my husband died."

Ty had a look on his face I couldn't read. Pity, sadness, heartburn. It could have been any of them.

"My dad died in a hamburger," Bobby told Ty.

Now Ty just looked confused. He was frowning and eyeing me as if we were all crazy.

"All done?" I asked the boys, grinning, glad to see the man at a loss. "You can go check out the fire trucks if you want."

They didn't need to be told twice. They were out of their chairs faster than a hunter at the start of elk season. I slid Bobby's plate in front of me and I dug into the pancakes and eggs left on the plate.

Ty cleared his throat. "Your husband died in a..."

"Hamburg," I said, and then laughed. "As in Germany. Blood clot that traveled to his lung, supposedly from flying."

This was where I usually stopped when I talked about Nate's death. Juicy gossip wasn't something I wanted to deal with. But as I looked at Ty, I decided to share the rest. What the hell. What could it hurt? The man thought I was a Looney Tune already. For some reason, I wanted him to know the truth. The details. "He was there on business—and pleasure. He died in bed with another woman." I took a deep breath. "And another man."

"Holy crap," he murmured, his mouth hanging open just a touch. I could see his straight white teeth.

I got lots of pity parties and uncomfortable sympathy when people heard Nate had died, especially since I wasn't that old. Only a select few knew about his extracurricular activities, that he'd cheated on me. Not only was I a widow, but my husband had cheated on me before he decided to up and die.

I was long over it—and him—when I'd gotten the call. I'd wanted to kill him myself a time or two for being a two-timer, so I found it ironic he'd died going at it. But I was still working on my self-esteem because of him, even years later.

Ty leaned forward, rested his elbows on the table. When they came away sticky with syrup, he grabbed a napkin and scrubbed at his arm. Someone messy must've eaten at the table before us. "Did you know about her—them, his...Jesus...you know, before?"

The fire truck horn, which was probably one of the loudest things in the entire county, blared. Everyone within a mile must have heard it. Those in the bay were lucky if they hadn't dumped their coffee in their lap. And gone deaf. Babies cried, old people placed hands on their chests contemplating a coronary. I saw Zach wave to me from the driver's seat of the fire truck with a guilty look on his face. I waved back. "Long story. Gotta run before they arrest him. Welcome to the neighborhood."

# 2

At seven, the sun was still high in the sky, but I sank lower in my chair, sheltered by the patio umbrella. The remnants of dinner were spread out before me on the teak table. Plates, napkins and silverware were strewn about, cobs were corn free, grilled chicken a memory. The aroma of burning charcoal still lingered in the air. I slumped down, comfortable with my head resting against the high wooden back. Relaxed with a full stomach. Wiped out. The tip of my nose was hot and stung a little, probably sunburn.

It had been a long day. After the breakfast fiasco at the fire station, we'd hit six garage sales then hiked up Pete's Hill and had a picnic lunch. PB&J with a view. I loved that trail as it was right downtown but up on a ridge that offered expansive views, especially at sunset. Bozeman was in a valley bordered on three sides by mountains. The Gallatins, Spanish Peaks and Tobacco Roots. Big Sky vistas in every direction. The kids liked it because we could see the roof of our house from our favorite bench.

While I watched from the patio, the boys played in the backyard wearing their Halloween costumes from the previous year. Zach, dressed as a Stormtrooper, was on the rope swing pretending to be either a futuristic Tarzan or a pirate. Bobby wore his Spiderman suit with Zach's Stormtrooper mask. They had to be hot and sweaty in their polyester wardrobe.

Bobby dug in the sandbox with a garden trowel, pretending he was Indiana Jones looking for lost treasure, although how he could see through the little eye holes was beyond me. My kids weren't obsessed with one favorite children's character splattered across bed sheets, beach towels and lunch boxes. They liked all kinds. They didn't discriminate.

Next to Bobby, tilted at a cockeyed angle, was the ceramic garden gnome he'd bought with his dollar at the second garage sale. It had a little blue coat, red pointy hat, and white beard. A foot tall. It smiled that creepy closed lipped smile. Zach got a gnome, too. His was different, red coat and blue hat. Same white beard. His sat on its own patio chair at the table with me. Zach had insisted it join us for the meal. If I leaned back in my chair, its beady eyes weren't trained on me. Fortunately, there had been two gnomes at the sale because only one would have caused global nuclear meltdown. I couldn't split a ceramic garden figurine down the middle to share like a brownie or cookie. At a dollar apiece, the kids were happy, which made me happy. Life was good.

"Arr, put your blasters down!" shouted Zach as he whizzed through the air. The swing hung from the ash tree that shaded the yard. The fence between the Colonel's house and mine was waist high, so Zach climbed it and launched himself from there. Even though the houses weren't shoehorned into small lots—mine was over a quarter acre—from my position on the patio I could see inside the Colonel's family room at night. He too, could see into my house, although his view was the bank of windows into my kitchen. Maybe that was why he came for dinner so often. He could see what I cooked.

We live on Bozeman's Southside, ten blocks off Main. Each house was different, some original mining shacks from the town's start to sixties ranchers. Mine fell toward the latter. It was a mid-century modern one story with a flat roof and tons of character. Typical dingy basement. Redwood siding painted a dark gray-green with black trim. Deep set eaves gave the house a Frank Lloyd Wright feel. What made it special was the floor to ceiling, wall-to-wall windows. The family room, kitchen, dining room and master all had walls of glass that let the outdoors be a part of the house. Unfortunately, the huge windows let anyone see in. Neighbors, Peeping Toms. They didn't discriminate either.

I loved my house. It had been Nate's before we married, his parents' house before that, and Goldie's parents' house before that. Nate's grandfather bought it brand new in '59, gave it to Goldie and Paul, her husband, as a wedding present in the late sixties. They lived there until Nate and I married and gave it to us as a wedding present. I would have been perfectly content with china or a fondue set for a present. But giving the house to the next generation had turned into a tradition. Nate, being the selfish bastard he was, hadn't turned down a free lunch. Or a free house.

When Nate died, I'd expected to give the house back to Goldie and Paul and move out. Find something smaller for just me and the boys. They'd been practically babies then. Bobby actually had been. But Goldie had insisted the house was mine. I'd more than earned it, she'd said. She'd loved her son and still missed him, but she knew all that Nate had put me through. Besides, she'd said the house was too big for just her and Paul.

And so I stayed and the house was mine. But three generations of Wests had put their stamp on the home. I'd always been a little nervous to mess with that, but I had to admit I was getting sick of Nate's eclectic hand-me-down furniture. He'd died years ago so maybe it was time to pass on his furniture, too. This winter, I promised myself.

But with a great house with great windows came a whopping heating bill. Those windows were single pane, original glass which weren't the best choice for Montana winters. Or little boys with aspirations of making it in the major league.

The Colonel's house didn't have quite as much vintage as mine. It, too, was a ranch, but all similarities ended there. It was wide and squat, had a shallow peaked roof, white siding with brick accents and was as vanilla as they came. He did have a pristine yard with the most amazing flowerbeds to add spice the house lacked.

Ty's house had been built at the same time as the Colonel's, but had wood siding painted a mud brown with a bright orange front door. He'd bought the house from the estate of Mr. Kowalchek who had been ninety-seven when he'd died. The dearly departed had been the original owner and the man hadn't done a thing since the day he moved in. The bathroom was probably avocado green. I could see Ty filling his days with updates and renovations that could last as long as his mortgage.

"What's Mom up to today?" I asked the Colonel. He ate dinner with us often and tonight, brought a Jell-O mold for dessert. It was his specialty. I personally loved a good Jell-O mold as long as there were no weird vegetables or nuts in it that would ruin it. Today, it was in a Bundt shape tiered with four different colors. Very impressive.

"Golf," the Colonel muttered. "Damned if I know how that woman can play in that heat. It's like a furnace down there. Chasing a little ball around for hours on end. Always sounded stupid to me."

One thing about the Colonel was he didn't mince words. You knew where you stood with him. At sixty-five, he had a full head of gray hair. Helmet head. His hair was too scared of the man to fall out. He wore crisp khakis and a white button-down shirt, his standard uniform. Sometimes he wore shorts, but they were his old khakis sheared into cut-offs.

"It's not a furnace to her. She says Savannah is 'like a soft baby blanket' in July." I thought Savannah, Georgia, in July was a furnace. With the heat turned on full blast, windows closed and an electric blanket on top of you. Plus, a steam sauna. Couldn't forget the humidity. "She thinks golf is calming."

The Colonel harrumphed. "If that woman gets any calmer she'll be dead."

"Mommy, I found a prehistoric car that used to chase the dinosaurs!" Bobby shouted from his sandy seat, his mask propped up on top of his dark hair. He held up a Matchbox car he'd gotten from a birthday party favor bag earlier in the summer. I raised my eyebrows and feigned interest. Satisfied with my attention, he shoved the mask back down and went back to his dig.

"When's she coming next?" It might have seemed strange I asked the Colonel about my own mother's comings and goings, but she talked to the Colonel ten times more often than she talked to me. Not that she didn't love me. But she *loved* the Colonel. And being two thousand miles apart made that love all the stronger.

"End of August when school starts. She wants to be here for the first week."

Worked for me. I liked my mother. We got along well and when she came to town, it was great. She took care of the little details of raising kids. Baths, story time, lunch boxes. It was nice to be taken care of for a change. A mother hen clucking at her chicks. She didn't do laundry, but that I could handle.

Zach ran over and grabbed his gnome. "Can I go show Ty my George? He said this morning he wanted to see our booty."

My mouth dropped open but I shut it before I could laugh. Actually, I wasn't sure what I should laugh at first: his costume, his gnome or his pirate jargon. "George? You named your gnome?"

Zach nodded his head. "Sure, everyone needs a name."

I wasn't aware everyone included a ceramic garden statue, but I wasn't going to ruin Zach's fun. "Sure. Don't go out front by the road, cut through the Colonel's backyard to get to Ty's."

Zach was off like a flash. Bobby, realizing where his brother was headed, hurried after him, his gnome—whatever its name was—in hand.

"So, tell me about our new neighbor." I was desperately curious about Ty. As the first man to make my pulse rise in forever, I wanted to know more. Even if I was too chicken to act on it. I could have sexy thoughts about him though. Those didn't harm anyone and I'd be having those sexy thoughts as I pulled out my own vibrator in bed later tonight.

"He's from over by Pony. Parents have a ranch there. Cows. Lots of cows." Pony was a tiny speck of a town west of Bozeman, right smack dab in the middle of nowhere. Beautiful country, but isolated. Even more so than Bozeman. Heck, with forty-some thousand people, Bozeman was like New York City by comparison. The Colonel shook his head. "I don't mind eating 'em, but I don't need several thousand as pets."

I rolled my eyes. There really was nothing to say to that.

"Went into the army right out of high school," he continued. "Did two tours in the Middle East. Serious stuff. Came back with all his parts and now he's a firefighter."

The man's entire life story in four sentences. I should have asked a girl to get the juicy details. I inhaled sharply—in the way a person would if they found a bee on their nose—when I realized I didn't even know if Ty was married. It was impossible to remember if he had a ring on his finger. I'd been too blinded by his wide shoulders and blue eyes. I needed to get a woman's inside scoop. First off, wedding ring. Then current girlfriend, bad relationships, what side of the bed he slept on. The important stuff. Kelly. I'd have to call her later. My best friend had the fast track on information I couldn't get. With seven kids involved in school, swim lessons, soccer practice, orthodontist appointments and whatever else, she ran into every person in town I didn't.

Or I could go right to the source. Which, based on the hooting and hollering getting louder and louder, was coming my way. Through the backyard tromped Fireman, Spiderman and Star Wars-man. I felt protected from flames, bugs and aliens. Two, though, were carrying garden gnomes so the image was slightly tarnished.

Ty had changed out of his volunteer fire department T-shirt and wore a pair of jeans, white T-shirt and flip flops. Oh my. He did casual *really* well. And those jeans, they were well worn and *very well* molded. I blinked, realizing I was staring at his crotch. Why did he make me so nervous? He exuded manliness, that easy way he moved, with a confidence in himself. Montana sure knew how to make a man. Testosterone seeped from his pores and I just sucked it right in. That was what I found so attractive about him. His appeal went beyond his good looks. I had been married to a good looker and he hadn't exuded anything. Maybe ego. Not much had come out of Nate's pores except bad-karma goo as he'd been so slimy.

Ty shook hands with the Colonel, smiled at me. Our eyes met, held. And held. His were so blue, intensely focused on mine, then lower, to my mouth. I melted inside. Other places, too. I smiled back. The boys yanked on Ty's arms, breaking the spell between the two of us.

Ty cleared his throat. "Looks like you did well at the garage sales," he said, enjoying the kids' gnome enthusiasm.

"Yeah, George is great!" Zach exclaimed, placing his ceramic friend on the table next to the chicken platter.

"Glad the fire department put Zach on the 'No-Fly List' instead of arresting him outright," Ty said as he sat down. Bobby, still hugging his gnome, climbed up in his lap.

In his lap, completely comfortable and at ease with the man. My heart flip-flopped and I felt like I was fifteen again. Just looking at him gave me butterflies in my stomach, made my palms sweat. I was afraid I might start to ramble and giggle. I laughed instead. I couldn't help it. Nice to see someone poke fun at life's little foibles.

---

AN HOUR LATER, so I could go to work, I left the boys with the Colonel. They were camping out in his backyard for the evening, the tent going up as I left. The sun was setting, pink and purple streaked the sky. The air had finally started to cool. I zipped up my hoodie sweatshirt.

"Camping will put hair on their chests," he said.

Zach and Bobby glanced at him and didn't look particularly excited about that concept.

"You get to pee outside," he added, and the boys jumped up and down for joy.

I gave the boys quick hugs and kisses before they dashed over to the nearest pine tree to pull down their pants and water it.

"Don't worry about anything," the Colonel told me. "I'm more comfortable in a tent than inside anyway."

Probably true after all the years in the military.

"I'll wake you when I get home and lug them into the house," I said, then dashed off.

---

I OPENED a shipment of peek-a-boo lingerie. It was pink, it was stretchy and it was all see-through. It left nothing to the imagination and gave a ton of access to all the important places.

The store smelled like piña colada as a customer had dropped a canister of tropical scented dusting powder on the floor. It had taken me fifteen minutes to vacuum up what looked like flour, but its use was less culinary and more sexual, although there was some licking involved. The scent lingered. I probably smelled like it, too.

The phone rang.

"Goldilocks." Goldie listened, and then answered, "You got

it stuck where?" She listened some more. "Uh huh." And then some more. "We don't give advice on medical conditions, but if it's stuck where you say and you can't reach it, then you need to go to the ER to get it out. Come in next week when you're feeling better and I'll give you a replacement, on the house." Goldie hung up.

Nothing like customer service!

"So, I heard about the incident at the fire station this morning," Goldie commented, gum popping between her capped teeth. My mother-in-law was seventy, five feet nothing, lots of dyed blonde hair piled high on her head. She wore a black V-neck stretchy top, which showed off ample cleavage. Trim jeans and a pair of clogs. She aimed for under forty above the ankles, and went for comfort when it came to her feet.

Her husband, Paul, was her antithesis. Calm, quiet, reserved. He chose his words wisely. When he spoke, I listened, as it was always something good. I had no idea how they'd stayed married for almost forty years but, whatever it was, it was working.

Paul was an obstetrician who'd delivered more than half the babies in town. Now he delivered those babies' babies. He'd been on call when I went into labor with Zach, but I drew the line—even at nine centimeters dilated—at my father-in-law seeing my hoo-hah, so they'd called in an alternate. It was no small stretch that as a couple, my in-laws knew more about a woman's hoo-hah than anyone else in town. She was the expert on fun, he the consequences.

"John Poleski was at the breakfast with his wife and grandson. Fortunately, he had that pacemaker put in last year."

John Poleski was eighty if he was a day, shaped like a tall Humpty Dumpty and bald. He'd worked for the railroad on the highline near Malta, a small town near the Canadian border, for decades. I'd never seen him in anything but overalls.

I rolled my eyes at her as I rung up a sale for strawberry-flavored body lotion and a DVD rental of *Hit Me With Your Black Cock.*

"Wish I'd been there." She chuckled. "I've got to kiss my grandson for stirring things up." Goldie was all for stirring things up. She was Bozeman's Stir-Things-Up Queen. She liked to stick her nose in everyone's business, which was easy to do around here. "John also said you met Ty Strickland. He's a *real* man. I bet he's good with his hands." She waggled her eyebrows at me.

I dreaded where this was going. I decided to take the high road because I was *not* talking with her about my dirty thoughts involving my new neighbor. "I'll definitely remember him when my snow blower stops working."

She clicked her manicured nails on the glass-topped display case full of the higher end toys. "Snow blower, my ass. He can take care of other things you need worked on, Jane." She looked at me, her head tilted down to give me a beady-eyed gaze. "You need sex and that man can give it to you."

"I'll keep that in mind," I grumbled, walking over to the hanging racks with the lingerie. I had no doubt Ty Strickland could *give it to me.* I also had no doubt he'd be really good at it. *Really, really* good.

"It's been three years since Nate's been gone," she replied, breaking me from my thoughts of having sex with Ty. "How long before that?"

This was a typical conversation I had with my mother-in-law. She'd talk sex with the pope. Although I thought the pope would be more comfortable than I was at the moment. This was her son—her dead son—she was talking about. But she was the first to admit his elevator hadn't gone all the way up and it had skipped the morals department altogether.

"Obviously, you did it to have Bobby and that's been, what, five years or so?" She looked up in the air at her imaginary calculator.

"Holy crap," I whispered. I'd have sex with the first guy who came through the door if Goldie would just shut up.

"Honey, I've known you since you were a little baby freshman at MSU."

MSU, or Montana State University, was practically downtown, in fact, only a few blocks from my house. "Coming from a state like Maryland, I swear you didn't know one end of a cow from another."

It was true. I hadn't.

"Didn't know one end of a man from the other, either." She chuckled. "You met Nate right away. I bet he was your first too, hmm?" She winked at me.

No way was I answering that one. She knew the answer. Making me say it out loud was cruel and unusual punishment.

"Then you up and married him. Your first. Your *only*." She casually rearranged the basket of foiled condoms we offered like mints to customers. "Your mama has always entrusted me to be there for you. I swear Savannah's gotta be on the other side of the world and you needed all the help you could get. Still do, for that matter."

Goldie had been a fixture in my life from the very beginning of my fateful relationship with her son. Sweet and kind, yet over the top crazy, I'd fallen in love with her almost as fast as I had Nate. Since I'd grown up in Maryland, Bozeman was as far from home geographically as possible, barring moving to Alaska. Lifestyle-wise, it would have been more familiar to me if I'd been launched into space.

At the time, I'd wanted something different, something far away. My dad had walked out and my mom divorced his sorry ass lickety-split. I'd figured I'd *find* myself in Montana. I was still working on that one. During my college years, my mom had moved south to Savannah to find herself, and Goldie became a substitute mom as I settled into Bozeman. My real mom, more apt to wear Lily Pulitzer than Levi's, had forged an unusual bond with Goldie and was comfortable with her acting as mom-by-proxy.

"The way I see it, you're due."

I groaned and shook my head. Not because she annoyed me, which she did, but because she was right. I was due. Overdue, like a carton of milk.

The night Bobby was conceived was the last time Nate and I had had sex. The last time I'd had sex *period*. I'd discovered I was pregnant the same day I'd discovered Nate with another woman in Goldilocks' storage room. Pants around ankles, Nate's white butt thrusting Bimbo into the shelves of porn. I'd had his clothes tossed out across the front yard an hour later.

"Ty seems nice," I replied as neutrally as possible. "I don't even know if he's got a girlfriend. Besides, I've only talked to him for about five minutes. Total. I think I need a little more foreplay than that."

She winked at me again. "Don't worry, sweetie. I'll help."

Oh god. Goldie help? This was so not good.

---

FOUR HOURS LATER, I unzipped the tent to haul my kids back to their rooms. They weren't up for an all-nighter yet. I whispered goodnight to the Colonel as he climbed out and went into his house.

It was really dark. No street lights shined, the Milky Way easily seen stretching across the sky. All was quiet. Even though we lived only a few blocks from MSU, and on the south side of town near Main, not much happened this late at night in the summer. Except snoring. Or sex.

The college students were off partying in their hometowns. The locals had church in the morning. I was inside the tent lifting Bobby into my arms when I heard the ruckus. It sounded like a large animal foraging through my yard. Plodding footsteps, leaves rustling. Had a dog gotten loose?

Was a deer eating my tomato plants? I froze in place, Bobby's heavy head cozy on my shoulder. Neither he—nor Zach—would have woken up for a parade coming through the Colonel's backyard. They were no help.

Wild animals didn't scare me. Bears hadn't been seen in town since spring when they'd woken up from their long winter's nap. All other creatures of the night were more afraid of me than I of them. Except snakes. I was definitely more afraid of them. But snakes didn't have feet, or hooves, so I ruled them out. I figured all the noise I'd make to get Bobby—and myself—out of the tent, across the Colonel's yard, through the gate and into mine would scare away any animal. By the time I got to the fence, I heard its retreat across the grass and past the lilac bush separating my yard from Mr. Blumenthal's behind us.

The next morning, bright and early, my right eyelid was pried open by little fingers. "Mom! There are footprints in the backyard!" Bobby exclaimed. "I think Santa was here."

My brain was slow and foggy. I blinked several times and peered at the clock on the nightstand. Eight. Not too shabby for a Sunday. I wouldn't have minded ten, but beggars couldn't be choosers with kids around.

"Mooom!"

"Shh! Zach's still asleep." Footprints, right. "It's July. No Santa. But I think Shrek or Donkey was out there rustling around when I came home last night."

The previous winter, we had a family of deer visit the crab apple tree in the side yard, rooting around in the snow searching for fallen fruit. The family of four had made a path through the snow in a circuit around the neighborhood. They'd known where to forage for food in the lean months. Stopping to paw at the crusty snow and frozen ground, they'd eaten up the rotten fruit. The cold winter morning we'd first seen them the boys were watching Shrek II. Thus Shrek, Donkey, Dragon and Fiona joined the family, if only extraneously. Once spring came, they'd moved to greener pastures. Literally.

Bobby shook his head, kneeling next to me. "No, Mommy, people footprints."

That woke me up faster than a cup of coffee. "What? People footprints?"

Bobby nodded.

"Wait, what were you doing outside by yourself while I slept?"

"You didn't bring in the gnomes from the tent last night. They were out there all alone. 'Sides, the Kernel is out having his coffee so I wasn't by myself."

The gnomes. Couldn't leave the gnomes alone outside.

"Okay." I sighed as I hoisted myself out of bed. I wore pink and white striped cotton drawstring jammie pants and white tank top. Following Bobby out the back door, I crossed my arms over my chest in deference to the coolness of the morning and my lack of bra.

Bobby ran to the lilac bush. "See!" He pointed to the ground and walked all around the yard. I decided to follow him, careful not to step in deer poop with my bare feet. Where there were deer, there was always poop. Shrek and family were nice leaving little presents like that. But instead of deer poop, there were footprints. Bobby was right. The ground was soft from the sprinkler and slip-and-slide and it was easy to see indentations of footprints all around the yard. My arms fell to my sides as I took in the big man prints shaped like work boots. It looked like someone had been blindfolded for Pin the Tail on the Donkey and hadn't found the donkey.

Who was in the yard last night and why?

Crazy things happened when you lived near the University. One summer night, a car had driven up on the front yard, realized there was a house in the way, did a three-point turn and kept going. I hadn't seen—or heard—it happen as my bedroom was at the back of the house, but the tire marks gouging the front grass was proof enough. Having someone in the backyard though was way too creepy. A little too close to home.

As I looked around assessing the nocturnal activity, I saw the Colonel, coffee cup in hand, head into his house. He hadn't seen me before he went inside. Left standing at their shared fence was Ty. He too, held a mug. It must have been the morning coffee klatch. His gaze was intense, his look serious as he stared at me. No smile. I gave a small wave and noticed Ty wasn't looking at my face, but a foot lower. I felt heat rush to my cheeks as I remembered.

White tank top. No bra. Two mornings in a row of looking bad.

I crossed my arms over my chest for modesty's sake, although I was already past embarrassed. Even with the Colonel's yard between us, I could see Ty's mouth drop open. His gaze was aimed on my chest like a heat-seeking missile on a target. I dared a glance down at myself.

Instead of covering myself, I had all but hoisted the girls up so that inches of cleavage showed. One nipple had popped out the scooped neckline and was pointed right at Ty. Holy crap! I tugged the tank back up and back into place, then dashed into the house to get dressed before anything more mortifying, if that were even possible, could happen. I'd given a talk on dildos and flashed him all within two days. Just great.

## 3

Ty and the Colonel couldn't make heads or tails of the footprints and were not happy, to say the least, about someone traipsing through my backyard. We sat on my patio having second and third cups of coffee. I pretended I wasn't absurdly embarrassed about the whole nipple incident. The Colonel was oblivious to the whole thing and Ty was a gentleman and didn't bring it up. But his lips quirked up frequently as the three of us talked and I caught him glancing at my very covered chest. Nothing was falling out now that I wore a big, baggy sweatshirt. It didn't stop him from looking though, nor from my nipples getting hard wondering exactly what he was thinking.

We chocked the footprints up to some college kid, drunk and lost. Happened often enough to be plausible. We debated what to do about preventing another late-night visitor. Options ranged from Zach's idea of setting booby traps to the Colonel's thoughts about adding motion sensors to my exterior lights. The motion sensors won.

Zach and Bobby weren't completely convinced, so they strung some red velvet holiday ribbon with little sleigh bells attached—dug from our Christmas box in the garage—over the fence gate. Just in case. They believed this might notify us of intruders or bad guys. Worked for me.

Two days later, the hubbub had died down completely. No nighttime motion had been sensed. Thunderstorms had passed through which made the ground even softer and the grass taller. The footprints all but disappeared. The boys moved on to the excitement of the upcoming camping trip with the Colonel. Every summer we ventured up to Hyalite, settled into our usual spot at the base of the reservoir with a view of the peak for two nights of wilderness splendor. Even though it was still three days away, they were super excited.

So far, we'd ridden our bikes to morning swim lessons at Bogert Pool, peddled home and eaten lunch on the patio. Sounded simple, but getting two kids to ride a mile down a straight, flat bike path—two ways—was super hard. Someone complained about something. Tired legs, thirst, heat. A chain usually came off or something was dropped more times than humanly possible. To me, it was almost worth depleting the ozone by driving to prevent me from strangling my children. But they had endless reserves of energy that needed draining and bike riding wore them out. Besides, when the first snowstorm hit—most likely mid-September, only a short six weeks away—I would think longingly of the leisurely summer days cruising around on our bikes.

I was folding clothes in the laundry room when I heard Zach call for me, launching himself down the basement steps like a crazy man. He had that Holy Crap look on his face. "Mom, come quick. Bobby's stuck."

"Stuck? Stuck where?" I had a beach towel half folded but dropped it and ran up the steps like the house was on fire. "Bobby!" I called, panicked.

"On the patio," Zach said.

I skidded to a stop, did a U-turn in the family room and headed outside. There, I found Bobby standing next to the patio umbrella stand, bent at the waist, his left arm inside the PVC pipe. Stuck. "Hi, Mommy," he said calmly.

I grabbed gently at his upper arm and tugged. Definitely stuck. "How on earth did you do this?" There was no blood, his arm was still attached, and Bobby wasn't freaking out, so I didn't freak either.

"Zach put candy down the pipe and dared me to get it."

I gave Zach the evil eye and he had the smarts to look contrite. The situation was actually really funny and I tried not to laugh. First, I had to get Bobby's arm out, then I could go laugh in private while the boys contemplated life in their rooms for an hour or two of time-out.

The umbrella stand was of the homemade variety. Wind in Bozeman could gain hurricane strength without trying too hard. A thunderstorm or just the summer version of Chinook winds could take down trees, whisk kiddie pools away to another county and blow down patio umbrellas. To combat having to replace a broken umbrella every thunderstorm, the Colonel and I made our own sturdy variety, sure to keep the strongest winds from blowing over and damaging the weakest of umbrellas. Even though I had a covered patio, the umbrella shaded various spots in the yard, like the sandbox, on the hotter days.

We'd taken a five-gallon paint bucket, dropped a three-inch PVC pipe in the middle and filled the bucket around it with quick dry cement. The PVC pipe stuck out the top about a foot and the patio umbrella pole slid right in. Nothing tipped that much concrete since it was so heavy. Unless it was a tornado—but living in a valley between three mountain ranges—made that impossible.

"Are you hurt at all?" I knelt down and talked to Bobby at his level.

He shook his head, although his dark eyes looked a little wary. I was sure mine did, too.

"Okay, let's think about this." I took in his arm, the PVC

pipe and contemplated. I could cut the pipe above the concrete, but I'd have to measure Bobby's other arm to see how far down his fingers went. Didn't want to lop off any necessary appendages. But I didn't have the tools to cut through PVC. Screwdrivers, a hammer and a couple of wrenches. No major power tools or saws. There wasn't much choice but to call in reinforcements.

"I'll be right back," I told Bobby calmly. I dashed into the kitchen and got my cell. I found the non-emergency number for the fire department on the side of the fridge and dialed.

"Is Ty Strickland there, please?" I crossed my fingers he wasn't out on a call. Was it his day on shift or had I forgotten? What had he said the other night? I walked back out to the patio to sit with Bobby. After a minute, Ty came on the phone.

"This is Jane West. I'm sorry to call you at work, but I've got a problem. No one's hurt, but Bobby's arm is stuck in our patio umbrella stand."

He was quiet for a moment, probably processing this and trying to formulate a mental picture. I heard him chuckle. "We'll be right there. Tell Bobby to hang tough."

Ten minutes later, a fire truck worth of firemen traipsed through the kitchen to tend to Bobby's arm.

"We've taken bets on how this happened," Ty told me, his eyes bright with humor. They briefly dropped to my mouth, and then lower still to my breasts.

Why did my nipples get hard whenever he was around? One glance from him was all it took. My eyes darted to the other firefighters to see if they'd noticed. They hadn't, too busy putting Bobby at ease. But the way Ty's mouth ticked up at the corner led me to believe he had and the way his eyes heated, he liked what he saw.

"You have a one-track mind!" I hissed.

Ty laughed, then leaned in close. Real close "With you and that pretty pink nipple? Absolutely."

My mouth fell open and my cheeks flushed. "I have two of them," I countered, stunning myself at the witty response.

I couldn't help but laugh, because it was his turn to blush. It felt good to banter with a man. Special, like there was some secret between the two of us, especially with a bunch of firefighters a few feet away.

Yeah, I'd just flirted about my nipples. Kelly would have rolled her eyes at how I'd gone about luring Ty in, but it seemed to have worked. He was interested based on the way his eyes got dark and his jaw clenched

"Hey, Ty! Look at me. I'm stuck!" Bobby said, his free arm waving around and tearing Ty's eyes from mine.

Once he turned his attention to Bobby, I took a deep breath to calm my nerves. Sure, they were frazzled because I was worried about my child. It had nothing to do with Ty's heated glances, his obsession with a certain part of my anatomy. Yeah, right.

With everyone focused on Bobby, I got to check out Ty in his firefighter uniform. Blue dress shirt with a shiny silver badge on his chest, navy pants that made his butt look amazing. If he was going to look at my chest, then I had free rein to look at his ass, and the rest of him. He had on heavy black work boots, a walkie-talkie and other various electronic do-hickeys clipped to his belt. The few times I'd seen him, he always looked crisp and precise. Not a hair out of place. Although a military buzz cut made that part fairly easy. I had my suspicions he was a neat-nick, just like the Colonel. Probably a lengthy stay in the military did that to you.

I had to admit, Goldie had been right. He was a *real* man. A real man who looked at my mouth as if he wanted to kiss it! At my breasts as if he wanted to kiss them, too. I stole a quick glance at his hands. Big. Rugged. Yup, he could probably do a lot with those hands. And I wasn't thinking about a snow blower either.

No one rushed to get a gurney or call in an ambulance for

Bobby. I made Zach tell them what had happened. I figured it was punishment enough.

"I guess this is the kind of call you like. No one's hurt, no fire to put out," I said as I snapped a quick photo with my phone of Bobby with his arm stuck, grinning. I had to email the photo to my mom and Goldie and everyone else who wouldn't want to miss seeing it. Besides, I needed a picture to show Bobby's girlfriend in twenty years to embarrass him. I stayed out of the way as Ty knelt next to him.

"Okay, champ. No big deal here. I'm going to use this hacksaw and cut the pipe." Ty ran a reassuring hand over Bobby's dark hair. "When you go to preschool next month you're going to have a great story to tell!"

Bobby nodded his head happily, probably excited about sharing this experience with his fellow four-year olds. He seemed to trust Ty and didn't panic as the blade went back and forth. I realized I was holding my breath and let it out. I had faith in Ty, too, but I wanted Bobby to keep all of his fingers.

Within a few minutes, the PVC pipe that stuck out of the cement was sawed off. The firemen cheered and made a big deal out of it for Bobby, arm still trapped in plastic tubing up to his armpit. He smiled and loved all the attention. Zach did not. Served the little bugger right.

"Cheese, Mommy!" Bobby held his arm straight from his body and hammed it up for the camera some more.

I fumbled for a moment, but got the shot. I shook my head and laughed as a few firemen tended to him.

Ty stood up and came over to me. "Doing okay?"

"I could have used a little reassurance my baby wasn't going to get his arm sawed off," I grumbled.

He moved in close, his hip brushing against my waist. "You kept a brave face," he whispered in my ear, placing a comforting hand on my shoulder. His warmth seeped into me through the thin cotton of my shirt. "Show me the picture," he added, probably trying to distract me. I didn't need to show him my phone to do that. Just his scent and closeness distracted the heck out of me.

Since I couldn't tug him into my bedroom for a little grown-up time out, I held my cell up for him to see the screen. I tried to click the buttons for the photo to come up, but his warm breath fanning my neck made such a simple task extremely difficult. Ty was very good at distraction.

"This week we've been on three meth ODs. That's not what I call fun." He didn't sound happy about it. "We sure do like a good fire, but this," —he pointed to Bobby's image when I finally pulled it up and chuckled— "we'll talk about at the Christmas party."

He winked at me.

I licked my lips and his eyes watched the motion. "I'll... um...make sure to email you a copy."

One of the firemen asked for some dish soap and I went to get it. They used it to lube Bobby's arm and he quickly wriggled free. First thing, he launched himself at Ty and hugged him around the legs, soap and all. Ty knelt down and hugged him back. Pagers and walkie-talkie's squawked, signaling another call. Before the men dashed off, they quickly gave both boys Junior Fireman badges, Bobby for bravery, Zach for creativity.

---

I CALLED Goldie and told her about the boys and the patio umbrella stand before she heard it somewhere else first.

"They're boys," she replied. "This is only the start of the shenanigans they're going to pull."

Great.

"Oh! I forgot to tell you. I heard from Mary Trapp's sister who is the hair dresser for Carl Winkler's first wife. She's the Fire Marshall's godmother. They were at church together on Sunday and she found out—"

Huh? "What are you trying to tell me?"

"I'm getting to it," she scolded.

"Well?"

"Ty doesn't have a girlfriend."

The Bozeman grapevine at its finest.

No girlfriend, significant other, attachments. I felt elated and petrified all at once. Just one look or a casual touch of Ty's hand sent me into heart palpitations. What would it be like to actually kiss him? And if he got his hands—or mouth—on those nipples he seemed so eager about, I would probably come.

---

By eight, the kids were conked out. The full day had finished them off. After their baths, they'd insisted their plastic badges be clipped to the collars of their jammies. Deciding on a sleepover, Bobby was on the bottom of Zach's bunk bed, Zach on top.

They'd thought instead of having the gnomes in bed with them, they'd put them out on the front stoop to watch for the newspaper man. They believed the newspaper appeared on the doorstep by magic. I kept trying to explain about the newspaper man delivering the papers early in the morning, but they didn't buy that logic, especially since they thought everyone else was asleep when they were. It was magic something akin to the tooth fairy. So, they left the gnomes out front to watch and see what really happened.

The windows were open, which brought in cooler air and the smell of cut grass. Fresh Montana air. None of the polluted big city stuff.

The phone rang. Caller ID said Olivia Reed.

"Hi, Mom."

"I love the picture you emailed. It was impossible not to laugh when I saw it. Are you sure Bobby's all right?"

I knew she'd be worried if she heard about it from the

Colonel or Goldie. Fortunately, the photo downplayed anything they might have told her.

"He's fine. You should be more worried about Zach. The little bugger."

My mom couldn't help but chuckle at that. "Tell Bobby I said he was very brave and I'll see them soon. I have my ticket for the fifteenth."

"Can't wait to see you."

It was two hours later in Savannah so my mom didn't linger on the phone. She was the early-to-bed, early-to-rise type. Ten at night was pretty late for her. I loved it when she visited since she woke up before the kids. Meaning, I could sleep in.

I plugged my cell into the charger and started cleaning up the dinner dishes. For a fifties house, the kitchen reeked of early eighties. It had dark wood cabinets with forest green laminate counters. The floor was a light pine, which matched nothing. The only updates in the past twenty-five years had been recessed light fixtures, a new fridge and stove top.

I wasn't in a rush to update. The garage was off the kitchen and the room became a catch-all for coats, boots, school projects and all and sundry that came into the house. It didn't make sense to modernize if it was a mess all the time.

The fabulous feature of the room was wall-to-wall windows in front of the kitchen table that looked out on the back yard. It made the outdoors a part of the room. I was closing the dishwasher when there was a knock at the door. Ty.

"Hi. I wanted to see how Bobby was doing," Ty said, a small shipping box under one arm.

He wore his work uniform and looked perfect. Hot. Jumpable.

I wore "The Usual". Shorts and a T-shirt. Barefooted. My hair in a ponytail. I'd looked better, but I was learning this man seemed to only see me at my less than fashionably-perfect moments. Maybe I had less of them than I'd previously thought. Pushing him out the door and getting pulled together was a stupid idea. Having a door slammed in his face for ten minutes—how long did it take to shower, blow dry long hair and apply makeup?—would be a sure sign I was trying too hard.

I stood back and let him in. "He's fine. They're asleep already. I really appreciate your help today."

"All in a day's work." Ty placed the box on the counter, and then shoved his hands into his pants' pockets.

"I just finished doing the dishes. Want a beer?" I walked over to the fridge and pulled out two. I wasn't curious about the box at all. Nope.

"Sure." Ty leaned a hip against the counter, took the beer I handed him and twisted off the top. "Can I ask you something?"

He took a swig.

I wasn't sure what he would say. He could ask anything from borrowing a cup of sugar to what color underwear I wore, so I just nodded my head.

"Should I be making a move on you or something?" Ty's mouth tipped up in a sly smile.

*Yes! Make a move!* I got that nervous feeling in my stomach, the one where the butterflies tried to escape, and took a glug of my beer to stall. And hopefully drown the butterflies. I definitely fantasized about kissing him a whole heck of a lot. More than kissing. Kissing was so seventh grade. I wanted him naked and deep inside me. Maybe his head between my thighs. I cleared my throat realizing he was waiting for some kind of response. "Why...why do you ask?"

"When I got home from work tonight,"—he pointed to the box—"this was on my doorstep."

I frowned at it. "Order something?"

Shaking his head, he said, "Not quite. Inside there's a super-sized box of condoms, ribbed variety." He used his fingers to help him count off the items. "One of those fingertip vibrators, a big bottle of lube, a pair of pouchless briefs and some anal beads. Are the beads meant for you or for me?"

"Holy crap." I was so mortified I might throw up. I put my beer on the counter with a loud thud and held onto the surface for support. I tilted my head and looked up at Ty. He seemed relaxed and unruffled, once more enjoying my embarrassment. Saying the words 'pouchless briefs' didn't seem to bother him at all. In fact, he was smiling.

I pulled the box toward me and pried back a cardboard flap with a finger. Yup, there was the great big box of condoms. Then I realized he thought I was the culprit.

"You think I did this?" I sputtered. "This isn't really my style. I usually take a plate of brownies to new neighbors."

"Maybe you're the aggressive type. Likes to show a man what she wants. Or certain parts of her," he replied, smiling. His eyes moved blatantly to my breasts. "I like that in a woman."

It was so absurd, I laughed. There was casual flirting and then there was this. Goldie's box.

"Me? You think I'd pick out pouchless briefs for a guy?" If he only knew. I was so un-aggressive. I wanted desperately to tug him down the hall to my bedroom, maybe to begin with just to kiss him, but I couldn't even do that. My nerves would make me start to giggle. I was such a mess! If I couldn't even make the first move, how could I push pornographic underwear on him? Or anal beads!

"Just because I work in a sex store doesn't mean I go for,"—I held up the black mesh pseudo-briefs with one finger—"this!" I slingshot them across the room. They landed on top of the toaster oven. I shivered. "I'm not getting a good mental image right now."

Ty or any man, no matter how hot they were, would look ridiculous in a pair of underwear that left his bits and pieces hanging out. It was like the crotchless panty for men. And in black mesh. Again, whatever floated a person's boat, but it didn't do a thing for mine.

"I'm more a boxers kind of girl." I darted a quick glance at Ty's lower region wondering what he had on.

He noticed and waggled his eyebrows. "Wanna see if I'm a boxers kind of guy?"

*Yes.* "Um..." I felt like a fifteen-year-old girl with brand new, raging hormones mucking up all modest thoughts. I tapped the box. "This is *all* Goldie. My mother-in-law. She thinks I need... sex. She thinks I need sex with *you.*"

I ran my hand over my face, hoping to wipe off some of the scorching heat I felt there. I was more than competent to embarrass myself without any help from Goldie. Especially since I'd been caught checking out his package. I considered how I was going to murder her. Strangulation was good. I could strangle her with the pouchless briefs.

"Your mother-in-law...your MOTHER-IN-LAW thinks we should have sex?" Ty's eyes bugged out, his mouth open, looking stunned. He took a big glug of beer. "Jesus. Your mother-in-law thinks we should have anal sex."

"Can you please stop saying anal?" I asked, dying a slow death.

"I'm not sure if I should be thankful or hurt. Does she think I need that much help with a woman?" He pointed at the box.

I groaned. I had no doubt Ty knew *exactly* what to do with a woman.

"Let's take Goldie out of this for a minute because she'll be dead by morning. You haven't thought about having sex with me?" Might as well put him on the spot.

"Well...yeah," he replied. He grinned, looking a mixture of sheepish and eager. "Definitely. Very thoroughly and in about twenty different ways."

Twenty? My panties were now officially ruined.

"Especially the other morning when you weren't wearing a

bra and your nipple... And that other time when your nipples—"

I held up my hand to stop him. Obviously, the man wasn't a monk and had a breast obsession. "I get the picture." I did. I had the image in my head of his mouth on my breast, sucking and licking, tugging on the tip, maybe even using a little bit of his teeth, my fingers tangled in his hair. Yeah, that was a really good picture.

"I really like your nipples." One side of his mouth tipped up in one of those wicked male grins. It was the grin of a man with sex on the brain. "And they really seem to like me."

They did. They certainly did.

I felt heat shoot to the roots of my hair as my very desired nipples got hard beneath my thin bra. Time to change the subject.

I cleared my throat. "Goldie doesn't think *you* need help, she thinks *I* do."

He raised one eyebrow, then looked me up and down. The gaze was heated and intense. He took his time doing it, too. Especially in the nipple region. "If you keep going the braless route, you'll have guys lined up around the block."

Thank goodness I was wearing one right now, although it wasn't doing much to hide my...interest in him. "I'll...um, keep that in mind."

Ty took another swig of beer. "You have an...interesting family. Never a dull moment around here."

"Excitement's not so bad," I said. My life had been ho-hum for so long, I had to admit the past few days had been...action packed. Exciting. Thrilling.

Ty shook his head. "I'm done with excitement. Two tours in the Middle East and I'm full up on excitement. I'm trying for the quiet life." He grabbed the box of condoms, left the rest. "I've got to go."

I frowned. "Hey, I thought you didn't need Goldie's help."

His grin was back when he turned to me. "Goldie helped by

saving me a trip to the store." He held up the box of condoms. "Tell her thanks for me."

He walked toward the door but stopped and came back, stood right in front of me. Close enough I could see the blond stubble on his jaw, smell his fabulous scent, whatever it was. "Look, I'm more than okay with sex. That's adventure, not excitement. A relationship, not happening. That's more than I can handle right now."

"What are the condoms for then?" I wondered.

He lifted the box. "Condoms are for sex. A relationship is when you don't use them."

Made sense to me in a single, commitment-phobic male sort of way. Goldie had said that I needed sex, not a relationship. She obviously thought an orgasm or two would help. In theory, I couldn't argue with that. An orgasm would be darn good, but in reality, unless I pulled out that fingertip vibrator from the box, I'd have to get up enough nerve to be with a man. And with Ty, it was obviously no-strings-attached. While I wanted to jump him right now, it was something to think about

Ty brushed the knuckles of his hand holding the condom box ever so gently over my left breast. I felt my nipple harden from the contact and I watched as his pupils dilated at the sight. "Let me know."

My mouth dropped open, my eyes briefly closed at the scorching, and surprising touch. It had been years since I'd had male contact like that.

Before I had time to react, Ty opened the door to leave and ran square into a man who had George the Gnome hugged against his chest. He was about five-ten, white, scraggly brown hair with an attempt at a mustache above his lip. He had a startled look of a deer about to be run over by a semi.

"What the...?" Ty said, surprised.

The man turned and bolted, Ty making chase after a moment to process. I dashed after them once I'd gathered my wits about me. I had a slower pace as my legs weren't nearly as long as Ty's and I didn't have the same adrenaline rush as Gnome Stealer. Ty grabbed the guy's arm but he wriggled free, stripping off his shirt in the process. He kept going as if the hounds of Hell were on his heels.

The gnome slipped out from under his arm and fell onto the street, breaking into pieces. Ty skidded to a stop, breathing deeply, the man's flannel shirt dangling in one hand, box of condoms in the other. We watched the man take off around the corner onto Lincoln. He wasn't coming back anytime soon. He was halfway to North Dakota.

After a moment of stunned silence, we looked down at George. He was broken into four large pieces of ceramic. I wasn't sure how I would explain this to Zach. I couldn't even explain it to myself. Hopefully, it could be put back together with the glue gun.

"What the hell?"

Ty knelt down next to the pieces and picked up a small bundle that had been hidden inside the gnome. Clear bubble wrap protected something that wasn't gnome gizzards. It fit easily in Ty's palm. I heard a car approach, so I quickly scooped up gnome parts and we walked together back to the house. I placed the pieces on the kitchen counter and watched as Ty unwrapped the packaging. Inside were an empty plastic bag and a glass vial with a black plastic screw top, the kind scientists used to create secret potions. It was filled with some kind of white goo.

"What is that?" I peered closely at it, squinting. "Glue? Dish soap?" This was super weird. Why was glue inside a gnome?

Ty lifted it up to the light, turned it around. Eyed it funny. "Looks like bull semen to me."

That was the last thing I thought he'd ever say. *Bull semen?* I tried not to think about how one got sperm from a bull and into the vial. Yuck. Double yuck.

"I need to wash my hands."

# 4

"Can you please explain to me how you know that's cow sperm?" I pointed at the vial and cringed before I went to the sink to pump and pump soap onto my hands.

I knew a little about sperm. My eggs had met some sperm and made two babies. I worked in a store that sold products to keep sperm away from eggs. But that was it. None of this vial stuff.

"My parents run a cattle ranch," he replied, still eyeing the stuff. "The term is bull semen. Cows are female. They can't have sperm. Bull semen."

Right. I forgot about that one. "Then how did it get into Zach's gnome? And why?"

Ty didn't look any happier about this than I did. "I have no idea. I'll call my parents to help figure this out."

He pulled out his cell. I was glad there was an expert for everything. As he waited for someone to pick up he told me, "This isn't some kid's prank. I guess we just figured out it wasn't a damn deer in the yard the other night."

That was a scary thought.

He held up a finger signaling me to wait. "Hey, Mom—"

I pulled the glue gun from the craft bucket, plugged it in and waited for it to heat up while Ty talked with his mother. Unnerved, I went in and checked on the boys. They were conked out, Bobby on his back with his arms flung over his head, Zach on the top bunk completely buried in the blanket except for one exposed foot.

When I returned, Ty was off the phone and downing the rest of his beer. "My mom can't say for certain it comes from a bull. There's really no way of knowing by looking at it. She said it also might be from a horse. Or, it might not be semen at all."

Ick. I wrinkled my nose. "Could it be from a...person?"

Ty pondered my question for a moment. "It's possible, but there's no real black market for it. There are sperm banks and more than enough willing guys to make donations. This baggie was wrapped in with the vial." He held up the plastic bag. "I think dry ice was in there to keep the semen fresh."

Again, ick.

"If someone was selling it to make money, it would only be worthwhile if the semen was viable. My mom said it has to be kept below thirty-eight degrees to be worth anything. Frozen even, to last as long as possible."

"I'm impressed you recognized what it is. If I'd found it on my own I probably would have opened it and used it as glue for a kid project." I was making myself nauseated. "That's so gross."

He offered a small smile. "I grew up on a cattle ranch, so this isn't all that gross for me. My parents still run it with my two brothers. Cows, chickens, pigs. The works. What freaks me out is the fact that it was in a garden gnome and that some crazy son-of-a-bitch has come back here twice to steal it. He could come back again."

"So you've had tons of experience with horny bulls?" I kidded, trying not to think about the man returning, a possible danger to the boys, cow sperm, no, make that bull semen. All of it.

He chuckled and scratched the back of his neck. Obviously,

he didn't know how to respond to that. I guess I wouldn't know what to say to that if I was asked, either. Nice. I'd done it again. Nerves made me say stupid things.

"Bulls, no." He lifted a brow and said with a sly grin, "Horny, definitely."

I rolled my eyes, realizing I'd set myself up for that one. I wanted some sexy times with him, but with bull semen on my kitchen counter between us, I'd lost some of my eagerness.

"Now what?" I asked, changing the subject.

"I suggest we look in the other gnome, see what's inside that one. Then we throw out whatever we find," he said as he tossed the plastic bag into the trash.

My roiling stomach gave way to anger. How dare someone steal from my kids! The man had taken the gnome right off my front stoop and the other night traipsed through the back yard. And Ty wanted to forget about it? "I'm going back to the garage sale where we bought the gnomes."

His head whipped up to look at me, his blue eyes blazing, and not with heat, but with anger of his own. "No way. It might be dangerous."

"A dangerous garage sale?"

A muscle in his neck grew taut as he was most likely grinding his teeth. "You have no idea why that vial was in the gnome or what kind of people we're dealing with here. This guy,"—he pointed his thumb toward the front yard—"can't be a big player in this. He's pretty stupid to try and steal back his vial while it's still light. He could have waited two hours when it was dark and you were asleep. He's either desperate or an idiot."

I stood facing him, arms folded over my chest. "That's why I need to go back there. To find out why and who and what. I definitely want to know what."

"Someone wanted this stuff enough to snoop around your backyard at night. He even came right up to your kitchen door.

Which was unlocked!" He was breathing hard, his hands on his hips.

"That's because I let you in!" I poked my finger at his chest with each word. He might be stubborn, but I could do stubborn really well. I could be more stubborn than a pack mule in the summer.

He took hold of my hand, held it over his heart. I felt it thump-thumping, its cadence strong and reassuring. "Why do you want to look into this? Let it go. It could be dangerous."

I shook my head, pulled my hand free, although he'd felt pretty darn good "I don't want the boys to get hurt." Duh. "That crazy man could come back. So, I need to know what's going on, to know that lunatic isn't going to show up again on my doorstep. The next time he does, the kids might be awake. Or out front playing."

Ty went to my fridge and helped himself to another beer. He downed half of it before he spoke. I watched his throat muscles work before he wiped his mouth with the back of his hand. "Fine. When do we go?"

---

By six thirty the next morning, I was out the door with the kids in the car. I had successfully glued George the Gnome back together before I went to bed, although he did look a little rough. Zack had minded a lot less than I expected and decided it needed a Band-Aid on one of the glued cracks. After close inspection, Bobby's gnome had no signs of tampering. No vials. No semen.

I called Kelly, my freshman roommate at MSU and best friend, and dropped the boys and the gnomes—couldn't leave them behind—off at her house so I could track down the Gnome Stealer.

Kelly lived west of town about ten miles, south of Four Corners in a neighborhood called Elk Grove. It was a subdivision about fifteen years old built on a swath of farmland. Surrounding it was more farmland. No trees. The Spanish Peaks were front and center and that meant Big Sky, the ski resort was nearby, and further on, Yellowstone. The Gallatin River flowed just across the road, home to some of the best rainbow trout anywhere. The houses were all different, the fences the same and the neighbors were friendly. You had to drive slowly or you'd run over a kid or two. They were everywhere. Kelly's house looked like a red barn. You couldn't miss it as it was the only one in that unusual style. With seven kids, they were piled in, but she was happy and that was what counted.

She'd married her college sweetheart, Tom, at twenty-one and pushed out her first kid a year later. Every two years after that another one came. She had a brood ranging in age from fourteen to two and she'd wanted each and every one. They were all planned, although she seemed to get pregnant by just being in the same room with Tom. They didn't need any help from Goldilocks.

If Kelly was über-mom, I was average mom. She home schooled. I'd rather stick a fork in my eye than do it. Her kids were well mannered and they all got along really well. No bickering or fighting. Or at least not much. I was so impressed by her ability to juggle everything life had to offer. But she'd known what she wanted way back in college. A big, crazy family. I, on the other hand, was still trying to figure out what I wanted to be when I grew up.

Zach and Bobby ran to the jungle gym in the backyard to play with Kelly's kids before I could get out of the car. I saw at least five or six heads jumping and swinging and heard a whole lot of screaming and yelling—even at seven in the morning. No hugs and kisses for me. Oh well.

Kelly waved to me from the front door. She wore shorts, a pink tank top and flip flops. At five-one, she was what you'd call petite. After seven kids, she was round in all the right places but seemed to melt off the baby fat like Crisco in a hot pan after every birth. Keeping up with them could do that. Her hair was blond and cut short into a chic style. A cross between Meg Ryan and Tinkerbell. I wasn't not sure how she did it, but it always looked good. Brushed, never a hair out place. Maybe she used tons and tons of hairspray. I never asked. I didn't want to seem petty and jealous of her gorgeous hair. My curly, dirty-blonde mess always looked like I kept my head out the window of a car like a dog. And that was after attempts at styling. It was impossible to tame wayward curls. Usually, my hair went into a ponytail and stayed there.

Kelly was jealous of me being skinny, I was jealous of her hair. Go figure.

Cute or not, jealous or not, I did not want seven kids. Having only two was worth a perpetual bad hair day.

I stepped out of the car and leaned an arm on the top of the door. "They're in the backyard," I told her.

She laughed from the porch. "Seven kids, nine kids, what's the difference?"

To me, a lot. To her, not much.

I promised her an update when I came back later and was off.

I cruised back into town to get Ty, my older-model Jeep Cherokee chugging along. It was black and I'd had it longer than I've had the boys. It wasn't that pretty anymore. It only got an occasional summer wash so the shine was gone. A few door dings, kid stains and hail damage from the storm last summer. But it got me where I wanted to go, especially in the snow and cold. There was no point in wasting money on a flashy car when I didn't go far and had messy kids, so it would have to catch fire before I replaced it.

Ten minutes later, I pulled in front of Ty's house and knocked on his door.

He was holding a cup of coffee when he let me in. He looked me up and down.

I wore a pair of olive capri cargo pants, a white V-neck T shirt and a pair of Keds sneakers. My hair was down as I'd showered and let it wind dry in the car on the way to Kelly's. It now spilled around my shoulders in a windblown casual look. Or at least that was what I was going for.

If you had to dress up in Bozeman, you wore a clean pair of jeans and your best boots. My wardrobe screamed casual. Why dress fancy when I usually collected dirt, grease—from food and bike chains—grass stains and other mystery spots over the course of a day? At least I had mascara, sunscreen moisturizer and lip gloss on, and that was pretty darn fancy. Oh, and a bra which if Ty were asked, he'd have said was optional.

I felt as if he was looking through my clothes and picturing me naked. Which he already had, at least one part of me. Yeah, optional.

"I'll drive," he said. "Be right back."

"Um, sure." As I slipped on my sunglasses, I made a mental note to wear nicer underwear tomorrow. If he were going to undress me with his eyes, I might as well be dressed to impress.

"Sure you don't want me to drive?" I asked after he locked his front door.

He lifted one eyebrow in a look that screamed I was nuts to even consider it. "If I'm going with you, I'm driving."

"Control freak?" I asked.

"Definitely." He beeped his truck open with the lock remote. It was a very nice and new four door pickup truck that could haul anything and everything. Silver. Typical rugged, outdoors guy car. Immaculately clean as if he spent hours washing and buffing it. Even smelled brand new. If I locked him in my house for a couple hours, I'd bet it would be super clean, too. Something to remember.

Ty wore navy shorts that came to just above his knee, a BAHA T-shirt and running shoes. BAHA was Bozeman's amateur hockey league. I warmed in all the right places thinking about how hot that was. A hockey player *and* a fireman. My kind of guy. Ty opened the passenger door for me. Holy chivalry! I hadn't seen that one in a while. Or ever. Nate had been obnoxious, not chivalrous.

We took Kagy to 19th and headed south. The windows were open and sunshine was on my face. We skipped small talk for the drive, which suited me fine. I enjoyed the peace and quiet with no kids yakking away from the back seat. But with Ty, the silence was a little unnerving because I knew he wasn't super excited about this outing. I felt a little bad. Not enough to change my mind though. My mission was to find Gnome Stealer and kick his ass. Reality would be different, as I had no expertise in ass kicking, but I could dream. Ty's mission was to keep me safe. Or at least that's what he'd alluded to the night before. A knight in shining armor under duress.

Minutes later, I directed him to a seventies era subdivision. Houses had been built on two roads running perpendicular to 19th. They had big lots, close to an acre, with established landscaping. A few trees dotted the lawns here and there, but none were taller than fifteen feet. The winds and snow hammered down all winter long and they were afraid to get any taller. Most of the homes were vintage, no remodels or exterior updates to the split-level style. Without any type of zoning or HOA, the homes were painted an eclectic mix ranging from light tan to a bright turquoise. Full sized RVs were in driveways and stuck out above backyard fences.

The garage sale house was half brick, half wood siding painted dark green. An attached two car garage jutted off the left side. Black shutters graced the average looking windows. Junipers grew large and scraggly around the foundation. Enormous lilac bushes bordered the neighbors on both sides.

Ty pulled the car into the driveway and turned off the engine. "This is it? Looks like they're on vacation."

No signs of life were apparent. Windows were closed on a hot summer day. No trash cans at the curb like the neighbors.

Must be trash day. Several newspapers rested on the mat by the front door and the grass could have used a mow.

I took off my seatbelt and climbed from the car. Away from town the wind was stronger. It blew my hair into my eyes and I swiped it behind an ear. Ty stood behind me when I knocked on the door. Nothing. I knocked again. Still nothing. I looked around as I waited.

"They must have put all the stuff that didn't sell in the garage," I guessed.

Ty walked up to the garage door and peeked in the dirty windows. He tilted his sunglasses up to get a better look. "No car. A workbench, an old fridge. You're right. There's a pile of junk in the middle of the floor."

By then I'd joined him. I wasn't as tall and didn't get the same view, but I got the gist. Nothing interesting. "Now what?" I asked, disappointed. Frustrated.

"Let's look around back." Ty slipped his sunglasses back on.

Montanans were very particular about their personal liberties, especially gun rights. Everyone had a gun and they knew how to use them. Mostly for hunting and a lot because they were constitutionally able. When it came to personal protection, in other states people shot first and asked questions later. In Montana, people were so friendly to a stranger they'd give them a cup of coffee before they shot them. So I wasn't too concerned about being shot while exploring around a stranger's house. But I let Ty go first.

Ty's long legs ate up the distance around the garage and beat me to the concrete patio out back. He wasn't in a rush, but he wasn't one for dilly-dallying either. He peered in the glass of the back door then shook his head. I was walking up to join him when the wind kicked up again and I smelled eggs. Rotten eggs, and lots of them. It was overwhelming. I froze in my tracks. My heart stopped. Uh-oh.

"Ty," I said. He must have heard something in my tone

because he turned to look at me from the patio without hesitation. "I smell—"

I saw his eyes change with awareness to an 'oh shit' look.

"Gas!" Ty grabbed my arm in a heartbeat and we bolted around the house away from the garage, opposite of the way we'd come. "Propane tank," he said, breathing heavily as we jumped over an old lawnmower. "On the back side of the garage. We walked right past it. Not always dangerous, but we're not sticking around to find out."

I practically sprinted to keep up with him, my arm still in his grip. We'd turned the corner and were back in front of the house when I heard a *whoomph*. Not overly loud, but a weird sound as if a balloon had imploded. Ty practically yanked my arm from the socket as we sprinted to the drainage ditch by the road. Obviously, he knew what *whoomph* meant and it wasn't good. One second I was vertical, the next I was face down in weeds and dirt with all of Ty's weight crushing me. I contemplated how his heavy breathing tickled my ear when...KABOOM.

It was a Batman comic KABOOM with the big word bubble and big capital letters—make that HUGE. Debris rained down on us for a full ten seconds. Ty slowly extricated himself from me and raised up onto one knee, brushing small bits of drywall and pink insulation from his back. I pushed myself up on my hands to see what had happened even though I had a pretty good idea.

"Not dangerous?" I questioned.

The left side of the house was no more. The garage had been blown to kingdom come. Only stumps of the lower walls remained attached to the foundation. The main part of the house was mostly intact, but the side closest to the garage was now nothing but a bunch of pieces all over the yard, the driveway and out into the street. Only the far right side remained intact, although most of the windows were blown out. Furniture and other household items littered the yard. A blender was three feet in front of us on the grass.

"Your truck," I said, pointing to what was left of it. Somehow, the old fridge we'd seen in the garage had been hurled through the air in the explosion. And landed dead center on top of Ty's truck.

# 5

Ty looked over his shoulder at the new addition to his truck. The avocado green side-by-side fridge was lodged in the front windshield and roof at a forty-five-degree angle. One door was wide open and frozen foods spilled out. He shook his head and swore. I only heard a few cuss words as he'd done it so quietly and the neighbor's car alarm was going off. It could have been the ringing in my ears. It was hard to tell the difference.

A small fire sent black smoke up into the air where the back of the garage had been, but was minor enough not to set the whole house ablaze. The smell of cooked house blew on the breeze. As I couldn't smell gas anymore, I had to assume it was all used up in the explosion when it launched the fridge through the air twenty feet.

Ty's body was rigid, strung tight like a bow, but he didn't shout or rant his anger like I would have if my car had been smooshed. When he turned to face me, he'd bottled it up tightly.

"Are you hurt?" He took my shoulders in his big hands and looked me up and down, probably checking for any broken bones, bowel evisceration or hangnails. Exposed nipples. His voice had a rough edge, his grip strong. I'd never seen such intensity in his eyes before. This must've been the look he had in battle in the Middle East. No doubt he'd seen worse in war.

My sunglasses were no longer on my face. I'd scraped my knees and hands where I'd skidded in the dirt. It stung, but I felt lucky with just that. He pulled a weed from my hair. Dirt covered my shirt and I noticed there was a small rip at the shoulder.

I shook my head. Stunned. "The house just blew up." Duh.

Ty pulled me into his arms in a fierce hug, my face pressed against his chest. His rock-hard chest. He smelled like soap, dirt and fire. I could feel his heartbeat pound against his ribs. At least the explosion affected him on a cardiovascular level.

God, it felt good to be held, to be comforted by a man. A man who was actually worried about me, that the reason for his tight grip was because he was reassuring himself I was whole.

One of the black shutters fell from the second floor and landed in a juniper.

"I know you've seen lots of crazy things with the fire department and stuff I can't even imagine with the army, but in my little world houses don't just blow up," I said into his shirt.

"In everybody's world houses don't just blow up," he said, his lips at my temple. "Not from a propane tank. This house had help."

---

AN HOUR LATER, I sat in a vintage lawn chair—the kind with the colored woven plastic from 1974—supplied by the elderly couple who lived across the street. I positioned myself in their driveway, a mug of coffee in hand—I told you Montanans were friendly—and watched the action across the street. The sun was warm and my shirt stuck to my body, damp with perspiration. The scalding hot coffee wasn't very refreshing, but no one could see my hands still shaking while I held the cup. Mr. and Mrs. Huffman sat on either side of me, running a constant chatter about their suspicions.

"Those propane tanks are such a danger. I lay in bed thinking we'll be blown up any minute," Mrs. Huffman said. She had long white hair pulled up into a bun at the back of her head in a style reminiscent of *Little House on the Prairie*. She had a sweet disposition and was a Nervous Nelly.

Mr. Huffman was the complete opposite. Short and round, he'd be a great Santa Claus at the mall. Except for his carrot red hair and lack of beard. Even somewhere in his seventies, his hair was still red. "For Pete's sake, Helen. You snore through this ridiculous worry of yours every night. Propane tanks don't just blow up. There has to be some kind of ignition, a spark. I think we're safer with our propane tank than on the city's natural gas lines." Mr. Huffman harrumphed and settled into his lawn chair, arms folded across his ample belly.

I actually couldn't blame Mrs. Huffman her worries, or Mr. Huffman his grievance with public works. The whole town had been on edge about gas explosions since 2009 when one morning, a block of Main Street blew up. No warnings, just boom. Sadly, a woman was killed and an entire city block blown to smithereens when, by accounts, she'd done nothing more than flip a light switch. The gas lines that ran to the downtown buildings were ancient, 1930s old and cracked. Gas had seeped into the ground and up into the building. I'd been just down the street at the time when it happened. I had been a bit too close for comfort on Main that morning, and now once again.

I never really thought about how I got my furnace to work before the downtown explosion and realized I took quite a bit for granted. I lived in the city linked up to the public gas lines where, by all accounts, I shouldn't be concerned. As my house was built in the fifties, my gas lines couldn't be more than fifty-some years old. No problems. Or so I made myself believe.

Out here, the garage sale house—the entire neighborhood—used propane. Propane heat, the stove and water heater. There weren't any old underground pipes, just a separate tank behind each house. So, what caused this explosion?

A county sheriff patrol car and one fire truck remained. It, of course, was from the volunteer fire department that had hosted the lovely pancake breakfast the weekend before. Outside of city boundaries, the home was serviced by the volunteers, not the paid city fire department.

Once they remembered me from Zach's horn incident, they quickly looked me over and I was deemed unharmed by the paramedics, then kindly removed to the Huffman's yard across the street. Ample distance away from the fire truck and its horn. Obviously, they didn't want a repeat performance from a member of the West family. As if.

Ty remained with them, recapping what had happened. As he wasn't a member of the department and the city hadn't been called in for support, he only acted as witness to the incident. The sheriff took notes while the firemen poked with their tools through the rubble to make sure there were no hot spots. Often Ty would point to different parts of what remained of the house or his maimed truck. I was either too far away to hear what he said or my ears hadn't recovered full function yet. On occasion, he pointed at me and they all had a good chuckle. Who knew what they were talking about, but I could only guess. They seemed to be enjoying themselves at my expense. I grumbled from my spectator seat as I imagined their words.

"Do you know the people who live in that house?" I asked. Mrs. Huffman took my coffee cup and refilled it from a Thermos.

"Cookie, dear?" she asked, holding out a plate.

Of course, I took one. I never turned down a cookie from an old lady. And I was in shock. Sugar was good for shock. I contemplated adopting her as my grandma as I sipped my coffee.

"The Moores live there. Alma and Ted."

I had a terrible thought and tried to swallow the bit of homemade chocolate chip cookie past the lump in my throat. "You don't think they were home, do you?"

Firefighters had been in and out of the house. If they'd discovered someone—dead or alive—they'd have been brought out by now. Hopefully.

"They moved to Arizona last fall. Had enough of the winters. Ted retired last year from the post office, Alma the year before," Mr. Huffman told me. He too, ate a cookie. A few crumbs landed on his tummy that jiggled like a bowlful of jelly.

"Alma was a school teacher. High school English," added Mrs. Huffman, taking a sip of coffee.

"Then who lives there? I came to a garage sale over the weekend, so someone has to be taking care of the place." Although not that well. Unmowed grass, gas explosions.

"Right, that was a good sale. Got myself one of those new-fangled quesadilla makers," Mrs. Huffman said. She'd murdered the word quesadilla so the end sounded a lot like armadillo. "They have a son who stays there. Morty. Works at the Rocking Double D ranch."

"That boy's always been a little...odd," said Mr. Huffman.

I wasn't sure what odd meant to him. Even at the forty-fifth parallel this was still the Bible belt and so it could mean anything.

"Odd?" I wondered, hoping he'd clarify.

"He's twenty-four and lives in his parents' house. Never had a lot of motivation in life. Even as a little kid. Watched TV. Played those shoot-em-up video games all the time."

Did this Morty Moore have enough motivation as a grown up to steal a vial of semen off my stoop? Was he in over his head with something? Someone? Did he have enough smarts to take the semen from where he worked? If he did, why did he put it in a garden gnome? The gnome part really was odd. Maybe he did do it, after all.

I'd had enough of being pampered by the Huffmans. I thanked them for the refreshments and headed back across the street.

My phone rang from my pocket and I stopped in the middle of the blocked-off road. I read the display.

"Hi, Mom," I said brightly.

"I just came from a sale at the mall. I was fixin' to get some new lipstick at the makeup counter but picked up some jammies for the boys and some sun hats instead." My mom sounded as pleased with a sale at the mall as I did by a good find at a garage sale. I'd learned it from her. Her malls were just better—and cooler. No sense sweating outside at garage sales in the summer in Savannah. No find was worth heat stroke.

I caught Ty's eye and he headed my way.

His shorts had a pocket ripped at the seam. Dirt smeared his T-shirt on one broad shoulder. He still looked pretty grim and yet hot as hell. His biceps bulged, his forearms were corded. His legs were dusted with sandy-colored hair, but I ogled the well-defined calves. He worked out. A lot.

"That's great, Mom!" I replied, all of sudden very dry mouthed. "I...um...can't really talk now. I'll call you later." Before she could get in a goodbye, I ended the call. Didn't want her to learn anything about the little mishap with the house. There was a time and place to tell your mother you were almost exploded and it wasn't now.

"Thankfully no one was inside, no one was hurt." Ty's eyes grazed over every part of me that he could see. New nerves fluttered up and rattled me.

"Sorry about your truck," I said as I watched a small clump of firemen stand around it, probably contemplating how to get the fridge detached. A few bags of frozen vegetables were strewn on the ground by a front tire.

He grimaced, rubbed his thumb over my forehead. I must've had some dirt smeared there. "It's just a truck."

Why was he so nonchalant about it? I'd be super upset if

my car just got leveled by a fridge. It reminded me a little of the Wicked Witch of the West. "I did offer to drive."

Ty glared at me and his jaw clenched tight. I realized I might have just poked a bear with a stick. He looked left and right, grabbed my upper arm, gently this time. "Come with me."

I followed him around to the back side of the fire truck, away from all the action, the people. He leaned in close so his eyes were level with mine.

"It's just a fucking car. I can get another one." His blue eyes dropped to my mouth and back up again. "But you, you're irreplaceable."

Oh. Heat and something else flared to life. Something...good.

"Shit." He shook his head. "I'm having thoughts about kissing you."

My breath lodged in my throat and I felt my blood pressure soar.

"But it's the wrong thing to do," he continued. While he stared at my mouth, he looked as if he had heartburn, that kissing me was what he wanted, but excruciating at the same time. "Hell, I don't kiss women who are demented."

Huh? Now I gave him a funny look. That wasn't what I'd imagined coming next.

"Demented?" I asked. I was stuck on the word *kiss* which made my brain slow.

He ran his hand over the back of his neck, his frustration obvious. "If you'd come out here by yourself like you'd wanted the men would be picking up pieces of you along with the house."

I jabbed my finger into his chest. "If I'd come by myself I would have parked in the street!" What a lame comeback. I wasn't very good at confrontation. I'd hated when Nate had gotten in my face, told me how everything wrong in his life had been my fault. Maybe I *was* demented.

He frowned, blue eyes blazing. "What the hell does that mean?" He had the look of a man who was talking to a woman who really was demented. I couldn't blame him.

I felt tears burn the back of my eyes, knew that while he wanted to kiss me, he didn't want *me*. "I have no idea!" I swallowed the lump of frustration and old fear trying to escape. "Nate used to yell at me and I don't like it."

I looked down at the ground. Anywhere but at Ty.

"I bet he never yelled at you about a house exploding."

I shook my head. "No. Just sex," I replied, nonchalantly. I looked up at him, surprised. Crap, I hadn't meant to let that slip out. Too much information and no one wanted to hear about the guy who came before, even if he was dead.

Ty pulled his head back a bit and looked at me strangely. "Sweetheart, I can guarantee I'll never yell at you about sex." He leaned back in, this time so close he whispered in my ear. I felt his breath hot on my neck and I shivered. His knuckles ran up and down my bare arm, goose bumps rising. My body responded to him so well. *Too* well. "You, however, can yell all you want. Hell, I bet I can make you scream."

He was right. I *was* demented. Demented enough to turn my face into his and kiss him. Not just a little peck on the cheek, but the kind where you grab the hair at the back of his neck and settle in for a while.

After a second of stunned stillness, he took over. Gentleness was now over. His kiss was a little rough, his tongue moved quickly to find mine. Heat flared and I moaned, which only spurred him to take it deeper. His hand cupped my nape and held me in place, tilted me as he wanted.

God, he was a good kisser! Amazing. Deep licks, soft pecks, dominant possessiveness.

I was equally desperate to lose myself in the kiss, holding him close, even hooking my leg around his. I could feel every *hard* inch of him.

What an insane morning! The adrenaline was bleeding into

the kiss, into the need to take him right here on the street. I went hot all over, and weak. I felt alive, and after the death-defying experience, it was wonderful. I was walked backward and my back pressed up against something hard and cold. The fire truck. Ty's chest was equally hard against my breasts and he could no doubt feel my hard nipples. His knee nudged my legs apart and he was even closer, his hard cock settling right at my pussy, our clothes the only barrier. Like a total hussy, I rolled my hips, rubbing against him. We groaned together.

I was so totally lost, so in over my head. So...forgetful. This couldn't go anywhere, not here, not against a fire truck—although I was sure Goldie had an adult film of it in her collection at the store. But the actress wasn't me. *This* wasn't me.

I pulled back as best I could, remembering where we were.

"We...um...need to stop." I breathed as if I'd run a mile.

Ty grinned, his eyes dark with lust. His lips were red and a little shiny. He pressed his cock into me once, then stepped back. "I've got that box of condoms if you want to start back up someplace a little more private."

He kissed the tip of my nose and walked away, leaving me leaning against the fire truck, the only thing keeping me up.

---

AROUND LUNCHTIME, I got a ride home with a sheriff. Ty'd had to stay behind and wait for the insurance adjuster and complete the paperwork about his flattened truck. Kelly had been kind enough to drive Bobby and Zach into town in her epic van that held all her kids, and mine. The decibel level in the back had to be close to rock concert proportions.

I met them at Bogert Pool. Everyone piled out, pool noodles, goggles and towels flying every which way, ready for an afternoon of swimming. Bogert was the city's outdoor pool which had swim lessons in the morning—which Zach and

Bobby went to—and open pool hours all afternoon. It was noisy and chock full of kids, but usually the boys ran into someone they knew and played the afternoon away in the shallow pool. I was content with the sun and cool water.

Kelly and I sat on the edge of the shallow end and watched the younger ones splash and swim. I wore the green bikini I'd gotten two years before from mail order. It wasn't super revealing, although my larger chest size provided ample cleavage no matter what I wore and made me feel a little self-conscious. Kelly wore a typical mom-kini. A brightly patterned, mostly pink tank and swim skirt. It, of course, looked cute on her. If I wore her suit, I'd be spilling out the top and the little ruffles on the skirt would look like bloomers on me.

"I don't know if I should laugh at you or hug you. I'm so glad you're all right, but I can't believe it. The house blew up and Ty's truck...." Kelly shook her head. There really wasn't much else to say. The rest—the why, the who and how—were still mysteries. I had hoped to go to the garage sale house and get answers. Instead, I only had more questions. More problems.

And that was just the gnome mystery. That didn't even include Ty and the mystery of the kiss. The Kiss. It deserved capital letters because it was monumental. Memorable. Unforgettable. At the same time, it really wasn't that complicated. It was just a kiss. An extremely hot, steamy, frantic kiss. My bones had practically melted, my brain had seeped out my ears. My nipples got rock hard just thinking about it. And lower, I was achy and eager for that thick cock I'd felt.

"Explain to me again your problem with Ty?" Kelly asked. "It was a kiss."

When I'd told her about the incident behind the fire truck, and she'd fanned herself with her hand. I felt like I was in high school, talking through a make-out session, analyzing it in minute detail.

Hell, yeah. It was a *Kiss*.

My cell rang from my bag and I dashed over to it, leaving wet footprints behind me. Goldie.

"What the holy hell happened?" She didn't waste time on hello.

I knew what she was asking about and I refused to enlighten her before I yelled at her first. "What the hell is right! Why on earth did you give Ty that box?"

"I didn't think you'd do anything about the lack of sex in your life. Thought I might give him a little push."

"A push?" I turned away from the other pool patrons and covered a hand over the phone. "Anal beads are not a push! Do you have any idea what he thinks of me now? I certainly don't!"

"He'll think you're sexually adventurous and open to trying new things."

"I'm not into trying anal beads on the first date!" I whispered. More kisses would be okay though.

"Fine, fine," she grumbled. "I'll come up with something a little tamer. Just save them for date three." Chuckling came across the line loud and clear.

I tried counting to ten but made it to six. "You will *not* send him another box." My voice was two steps below a shout and one I used for the boys when they stuffed their toys down the toilet. "If you do...I won't tell you about the explosion." A threat was all I had. And it was a weak one as she'd find out all about it from someone else anyway.

"All right. I won't send him another box." She sounded contrite, which meant she had something up her sleeve. Her fingers were probably crossed.

"Good. I'm at the pool so I'll explain it all later. Ten still?" I was supposed to work with her tonight as Veronica, another employee, was on vacation.

"Please."

"How come you never torture Veronica with a box?" I wondered.

"One lonely vagina at a time."

Goldie hung up without a goodbye.

My mouth fell open and I stared at the phone. Had she really just said that? Lonely vagina?

I mindlessly waved to Bobby who cannonballed off the side of the pool. Kelly clapped when he popped above the surface. I put the phone away, still stunned by Goldie's words and rejoined my friend.

"Hello? The kiss?" Kelly prompted.

"Like I said, it wasn't *just* a kiss." I sighed. I couldn't deny it. "It was way more. Whenever I see Ty I have that sick, nervous feeling in my stomach. There are cute guys out there that haven't done a thing for me. Like Luke Newsom's dad from second grade. He's really attractive, but I feel nothing. But then Ty walks in the room and...zing. There's a zing I can't explain." A zing that went straight to my clit.

Kelly waded through the shallow water to pick up Emmaline who was crying because she'd gotten splashed by a big kid. Appeased by her mom's attentions, the four-year-old wriggled down out of Kelly's grasp and went back to her water toys.

"God, I love that zing," Kelly said, looking dreamily up at the sky as if she remembered her own special zing. "So, what's the problem?"

Exactly. What was the problem? I was chicken. Too chicken to be interested in someone again, even with all that heat between us. The chemistry was off the charts. Even Ty couldn't argue with that. But I didn't want him to find me deficient. Unappealing. Like Nate. Life had been plugging along just fine until...zing. Once you get the zing, you can't go back.

"I need to figure out what's going on with this ridiculous vial of semen." I whispered the last as we were in mixed company. Grown-ups and kids.

She frowned. "What does that have to do with the kiss?"

Crap, I hadn't distracted her. "Nothing. Nothing at all. I just know what comes after a kiss and I'm not sure if I'm ready for it."

"The *it* is the best part! I say go for it." Kelly pushed her straw hat down further over her eyes. The glare off the water was intense. She put her hand up by her mouth and whispered, "I'd get some of those condom samples at the store, just in case."

I rolled my eyes. If she only knew about Goldie's package and the huge box that Ty now had. I went to retrieve the sunscreen from my bag and started spraying. I felt extra heat on the back of my neck. Was it from the sun or from talk about sex with Ty?

"Can we talk about something else now?" She and Goldie seemed to love to gab about my non-existent sex life. Way more than I did.

"Fine, fine. What was the name of that ranch again where the guy, the gnome stealer, worked?"

"Um...Rocking Double D."

Kelly's third youngest, Kyle, stopped by for her to adjust his swim goggles, and then was gone. "I've heard of that place. It was in the paper last month."

Montana, the fourth largest state in the US, is huge. With less than a million people living in the entire state, there was a lot of open land. Lots of ranch land. For Montana, I was considered a city dweller and rarely, if ever, became involved with ranch life. The only time I saw ranchers was at the county fair when they brought in their cows, sheep and other animals to promote their ranch, sell or compete for blue ribbons. I didn't know anything at all about growing crops or raising cattle. I got my food at the farmers market, grocery store or butcher shop.

But Kelly had grown up in Bozeman and knew lots of people, and lots of people knew her—way more than I did. Ranchers, townies, whomever. Her parents knew even more. Add Goldie to the mix and I swear they knew everyone between Butte and Billings. But the fact that the Rocking Double D ranch was in the *Chronicle* meant city folk like me should know about it, too.

"A cow there had triplets."

That was the last thing I expected her to say. In fact, it distracted me so much I sprayed sunscreen up my arm and into my hair. I now smelled like coconut and chlorine. I had to imagine triplets, then a cow giving birth to them. How big was a calf at birth? I couldn't picture the mother cow with three in there. Her belly must have grazed the ground.

"I didn't even know it was possible. Triplets?"

"I guess it happens on occasion, but not all three usually live. Some kind of mother-rejecting-the-extra-calves-thing. Who knows, but it's rare enough all three lived that the paper picked up on it."

"Huh." What the hell did a vial of bull semen in a gnome have to do with triplet cows?

# 6

"Absolutely nothing," Ty said that night after dinner. He'd come over to check on me. Which I didn't mind. Not one bit. "No one can plan a cow giving birth to triplets. It just happens. It has nothing whatsoever to do with the vial."

"Triplets or not, the vial most likely came from the Rocking Double D ranch. It makes sense. Morty Moore must have stolen it from there."

We sat on my front steps. They led to the front door painted a deep pumpkin, which stood open. Two planters were on either side filled with bright geraniums and other plants I couldn't name.

I'd showered and changed back into shorts and a T-shirt after the pool, but skipped shoes. Ty sat close to me, his hands resting on bent knees. I could see the small scratches on his forearms from the explosion and our dive into the ditch. He smelled of soap and clean laundry. It was hard not to look at his mouth, not to lean in and kiss him again. The attraction was almost too strong to resist. His kisses were like a drug and I wanted another hit, but being chaperoned by two kids kept things G-rated.

"You're probably right. He may have been trying to make a

little money on the side. But we don't know what his job is at the ranch or how he had access to the vials. And, why the hell did he stick the vial in the gnome?" His eyes dropped to my mouth as they seemed to always do. Maybe he was having a similar affliction. "You smell good." He reached up and ran a hand over my hair.

"Chlorine," I murmured as I leaned into his palm. It was warm, calloused, and the simple gesture was soothing, like a hug.

The boys were in the garage puttering around, one minute pulling out their scooters, the next getting a soccer ball to kick. They were self-entertaining and being creative. No TV or video games in sight.

The street was quiet except for a lawnmower in the distance and the smell of cut grass in the air. The crows had set up home in the pine tree across the street and their cawing or whatever their talk was called could drive someone to drink. The Colonel took his slingshot out at least once a day to scare them off. Right now though, they were quiet.

The dinner dishes were done, the evening had cooled down and my skin glowed pink from the inside out thanks to the sun. I heard the boys chattering away. It was a simple summer night and I was content. After the crazy morning and the insanity of the pool with nine kids, it was calm and quiet. Peaceful.

"What are you guys up to?" I called. I didn't want to move away from Ty to find out. His hand ran absently over my knee. Zing! If the boys weren't yelling at each other or crying in pain, I tended to keep out of it. Especially now when a hot guy told me I smelled good, his hand was on me and his mouth within kissing range.

"Working on our bikes!" Zach hollered back.

"Great. Occupied kids." Ty leaned in and kissed me at that soft, highly sensitive spot behind my ear. I couldn't help but gasp at the contact. Heat shot straight south.

"Um...any word on Morty Moore? Has he shown up yet?" I

asked Ty, trying to keep my sanity. It was one thing to practically climb him like a monkey behind a fire truck, another when the kids could pop out of the garage at any time. "We know he didn't die in the explosion and he was here running away from you last night. Oh, God." His warm hand moved up the bare skin of my thigh, his fingertips just below the edge of my shorts.

He nipped at the spot where my shoulder met my neck. Hot flash!

"The DMV provided us with his license photo," he murmured, as he kissed the sting away. "Morty Moore was definitely the man on your doorstep last night."

Ty would be able to identify him better than I. They'd stood face to face long enough for that. I'd only seen the man as he ran off down the street.

"The fire department talked with Moores in Arizona. Their son, Morty—"

I did all I could to keep my hands at my sides, even clenched them into fists. They wanted desperately to curl into his hair and pull his head about five inches lower. "What kind of parent names their son Morty Moore? He must have been teased mercilessly in school."

I felt Ty grin into my neck. He had to agree with me. "Morty has been living in the house. With the economy, the Moores aren't even trying to sell. They haven't heard from him in over a week. The whole business has been handed over to the police."

"The police?" I pulled his head back by the ears and looked at him as if he'd given birth to triplets. "I thought it was just a gas leak. You said it had been helped, but I figured you meant someone bumped into a pipe and knocked it loose or something." My desire to be taken right here on the steps diminished almost completely by the thought of potential death by intentional explosion.

Ty shook his head, although I wasn't sure if it was from being separated from my neck or in response to my comment.

He sighed, stood up and went over and plucked a dead flower off my potted geranium. "The pipe that ran from the tank to the house had been damaged. Intentionally. There was a leak, which is how you smelled the gas. That's all preliminary. They'll investigate and let me know."

I could feel the blood—what was left of it—rush out of my head. "Someone was trying to kill us?" I squeaked.

"I doubt it was meant for us. Most likely Morty. He's in something way over his head."

"Semen."

A side of Ty's mouth ticked up. "Something like that. Listen, I have to work the next few days. I've got my shift, a fill in, then another shift. Think you can stay out of trouble?"

"Funny," I replied, rolling my eyes. I wished he was sitting next to me again, his mouth back on my skin. "I think I can do that. Besides, it's Wednesday. What can happen on a Wednesday?"

Ty didn't answer, possibly afraid to say.

Zach and Bobby wheeled their bikes out of the garage. They had their helmets on, ready to go. At the sidewalk, they carefully climbed on, Bobby on his red bike with training wheels, Zach on his garage sale mountain bike. I looked closer at the front of Bobby's bike. On the handlebars, two of his stuffed animals rode shotgun. Since he didn't have a basket I had to wonder how he'd rigged it.

"Is that the...um—" Ty stuttered, pointing to Bobby's bike. He started laughing.

There, attached to the handlebars of a four-year-old's bike holding Puppy Dog and Buddy the Bear nice and snug were the pair of black mesh pouchless briefs. They'd somehow wrapped the leg holes through the handlebars, several times so they were secure. With the pouchless part in front, Bobby squeezed in his two stuffed animals.

"Holy crap. I forgot all about the men's um...underwear. The boys must have found it on the counter when I"—I did a slingshot motion with my hands—"launched them over by the fridge."

The boys gave a quick wave and pedaled down the sidewalk past the Colonel's house. Ty tilted his head and grinned. "Those boys are pretty damn inventive."

I dropped my head into my hands in mortification.

---

"WHY THE HELL would someone blow up the Moore's house?" Goldie wanted to know. She'd waited all day for answers. Tonight, she wore a pair of black capri pants, black platform sandals and a white V-neck cotton shirt with gold sequins in a diamond pattern across the front. Her hair was pulled back in a ponytail, but fluffed or teased up in the front. Between the heels and the hair, she was almost my height.

"We think it's because of the vial of semen we found," I said casually, as if I was talking about getting eggs at the store.

Goldie tilted her head down to look at me over her reading glasses. They attached at the sides to a rhinestone covered chain about her neck. She didn't say anything, just turned back to ringing up her sale on the cash register. I knew that look. It was half *WTF*, and half *don't sass*. She wasn't done with me.

Ha! I had something she didn't know about. I smirked. I couldn't help myself.

"Excuse me." A couple in their twenties grabbed my attention. The woman wore a sundress that showed a tattoo on her upper arm of a geisha blended artfully into a raging sea that curled around her elbow. Her hair was jet black and she had a silver ring in her nose. The guy wore jeans that hung down past his butt so I could see blue plaid boxers almost in their entirety. I had no idea how he could walk, but at least if the woman wanted sex right away he didn't have to pull his pants down to get to his package.

"What can I do for you?" I asked, ready to serve.

"We'd like to try anal and we're not sure what would be best."

Was there something about the butt that everyone was in on but me? "Sure." I walked over to the appropriate section and started handing them the things they might need. "Lube. Get the big bottle. There's regular and the numbing kind. There are plugs and beads and vibrators to choose from here on display."

"I want something big. Something totally rad," the guy said. He took down a plug that looked like a grenade. "Like this." As a salesperson, I wasn't going to ruin their fun by sharing my thoughts on a grenade up the ass.

I looked at his girlfriend to see if she bought into his idea. She nodded her head. "Yeah. Big."

"If you've never done it before, you might consider starting small so you don't hurt yourself. Work your way up." I wanted to make sure she knew what she was in for.

Her eyebrows went up in surprise. "It's not for me! *He* wants to try anal. Since it's going in his ass, he can pick it out."

Worked for me. "Sure. You guys decide and come up to the counter when you're ready."

A few minutes later I rang them up. They ended up going with the grenade model after all and took my advice on the economy-sized bottle of lube. Goldie joined us and tossed a few condoms into the bag. "Just in case," she said. "Oh, wait." She reached behind the counter to Ty's box I'd brought back to the store. "Here. Try these beads, too. You might like them. Free of charge."

After they left the store, I turned to Goldie. "What is it with all this interest in butt stuff?"

"Don't think you can distract me. What vial of semen?"

I enlightened her to all that had happened in the past few days, highlighting the garage sale, the gnomes, the discovery of the vial, the return trip to the garage sale house and the explosion. I left out my attraction to Ty and the kiss we'd shared. No sense in getting her all wound up about my sex life worse than she already was. Besides, even though she'd promised, I didn't want any more boxes ending up on Ty's doorstep.

"Humph," Goldie replied. That's all she said on the matter for over an hour. A group of twenty-something women came in seeking ideas and gifts for a bachelorette party. One of the offerings Goldilocks provided was an in-home sex toy party. It was like a Tupperware party but for sex toys. Some ladies were too embarrassed or skittish to come in the store so it often led to a bit of Sex Ed for grownups as well. Sometimes a long winter makes for dull, dark nights and Goldie's parties could sure liven things up.

I'd shared the toy party idea with Goldie to drum up new clients a few years before. She took to it like a duck to water and I'd been volunteered into this new branch of the business. It kept me occupied a few nights a month.

I arranged with the ladies to show up at the bachelorette party next month and vowed to make it extra special. Another day on the job.

"I think you need to be careful. Someone out there isn't happy," Goldie said when we closed up. She turned off the lights and we walked out to our cars together. At one in the morning, all was quiet. The air was cool, probably in the low fifties, and I had goose bumps on my arms. A big temperature drop from the pool earlier. It had been a full day and I was exhausted.

"Nothing that's happened has anything to do with me," I replied. "I only found the vial. I didn't try to sell it. Besides, there aren't any more vials. It's all over. I'm not getting any more gnomes." I wasn't going to tell her I'd already decided to go out to the Rocking Double D ranch and talk to the owner. Some shady things were going on and I wanted to warn whoever ran the place about Morty, tell them how I'd gotten involved and that I wanted to steer clear in the future. Maybe I could watch them fire the thieving Morty while I was there.

Goldie pursed her lips, but didn't say more. "What time do you want the boys in the morning?"

I usually slept late and enjoyed some quiet time to myself when she and Paul had Zach and Bobby sleep over. Maybe I could make the morning more productive by heading out to the Rocking Double D instead of hitting the snooze bar on my alarm.

"I might go for a run and get some errands done. Think you can keep them until after lunch?" Run! Ha! Maybe I'd run out to the ranch and do some investigating. In my car.

---

THE NEXT MORNING, after a peaceful and child-free night, I stood at the kitchen counter and sipped my coffee. I'd showered and dried my hair. The door to the covered patio was open, fresh air coming in. The cool night had turned into a soft, clear morning. Blue sky. The weather was perfect. It was supposed to be in the eighties today, although it was barely seventy so far. Usually I'd wear my typical shorts and T-shirt but since my plan was to visit a working ranch, I knew long pants and sturdy shoes were practically required. I wore jeans, a white tank top and my Frye boots. Hopefully, they would keep the horse poop and whatever else was in the dirt out there from getting on me. Besides, it was the closest to cowgirl-wear I had.

I did a search for the Rocking Double D ranch on my cell and was surprised to find it had an actual web site. It was said to be a premiere horse ranch, raising quarter horses, breeding and selling them. I knew nothing about horses other than identifying one when I saw it. They came in brown, black, white and some were spotted. No stripes, as that was apparently reserved for a zebra.

I called Kelly and she answered on the first ring. Kids screamed in the background. "Hey," I said.

"Hang on a sec," she replied. "Liam threw up on Hank's toy truck an hour ago and he hasn't recovered." I didn't know if she was talking about Liam or Hank. A door slammed, then quiet. "Okay, I went out front."

"I just wanted you to know I'm going to go out to the Rocking Double D ranch this morning. I need to find Morty and get to the bottom of this whole vial thing. Meet the owner of the ranch, tell him what I think is going on. I wanted at least one person to know who wouldn't yell at me."

"Be careful. Just because I don't yell doesn't mean I don't worry about you."

"At least your worry doesn't come with shouting and a guilt trip."

Kelly laughed.

On my phone, I pulled up a different link about the ranch, the one from the *Chronicle* which talked about the birth of triplet cows. "I see the article about the triplet cows," I said with the phone on speaker. "You were right about all of it. It says the ranch belongs to Drake Dexter. Know him?"

"Only as the owner of the ranch, nothing else. Sorry."

"This is a horse ranch, but there's got to be a cow or two in order for the blessed triplet birth to have occurred. So what do you think? Was the semen in the vial from a bull or a horse?"

I heard Kelly's muffled voice and something about ice cream for breakfast. "Sorry. Um, if the ranch is famous for its quarter horses and offers studs for breeding, I'd have to assume it was from a horse."

"Would fancy horse semen bring in lots of money?"

Kelly snorted. "Make sure you don't say 'fancy horse semen' when you meet Drake Dexter. You might insult the man, and your intelligence."

"Good point. Would horse sperm bring in more money than bull semen?"

"I have no idea."

"I could ask Ty's parents. They're cattle ranchers so they'd be the experts."

"Speaking of Ty...why don't you just ask him?"

"Because if he knew I was going out to the ranch today he'd get angry. He doesn't want me messing around with all of this."

"Aww, so romantic!"

"Romantic? I don't like being told what to do," I grumbled.

"He's just being protective. It's that alpha male testosterone that he's got tons of. Be careful, he may drag you by your hair back to his cave."

The image of being manhandled and dragged anywhere by Ty made me hot all over. "I met him for the first time last week. He has no claim over me or what I do."

"Then it shouldn't bother you to tell him you're going to the ranch. Why keep it a secret?"

Good question.

---

THE ADDRESS LISTED PLACED the ranch west of town, near Norris. It took me close to thirty minutes to take Norris Road all the way past the hot springs. I'd been stuck behind a pickup towing a trailer loaded down with a float boat, ATV and several coolers. Someone was going camping, hunting and fishing. I turned south toward Ennis and took a dirt road left, then right.

The ranch, like many in the West, had a huge log archway at the start of the drive. Two D's sitting on a curve like the bottom of a rocking chair was the symbol for the ranch and placed with honors front and center on the arch. I slowly followed the dirt drive back about a half mile to the main parking area. It was impossible to miss the horse buildings. The main one itself was an aircraft-hangar sized monstrosity. There had to be an indoor racing ring inside. That or a 747.

Gray metal siding with forest green trim all around. A cupola with a weather vane graced the top. It was a no-

nonsense building but obviously high-end. The minimal landscaping around it was tasteful and well-maintained, the building clean and only a faint scent of the horses lingered. No poop to be seen. The building had to have some kind of special horsy name but I didn't know what it was.

A large house sat on a ridge in the distance. A Montana mansion made of logs with big windows and expansive views. Land all around spanned to the mountains, the scenery beautiful. The house could be a cover home for *Architectural Digest*. If you liked the middle-of-nowhere mega mansion with stinky horses and cows roaming around. Some people loved it. Whatever floated your boat.

Next to the main building stood the stable, this much I could tell. Almost a football field long, it was narrow with big doors that slid open on the short end. I could see inside a little way and make out a few stalls. A horse or two had their heads over the half-doors so I knew I was in the right place. I parked and went in search of Drake Dexter—and Morty Moore.

It was darker in the stable than I expected and it took a few moments for my eyes to adjust from the bright sunlight. It was warm inside, dusty and smelled of hay and horses. Several people worked forking hay, some hefting something else, most likely poop. Lots of it. A brown horse was being led outside by a bridle about its head. It seemed a precision operation. All employees appeared to wear matching green polo shirts with the Rocking Double D logo embroidered in white on the chest. The facility was clean, well-kept and obviously a money maker.

"Excuse me." I stopped one of the workers who pushed a wheelbarrow with a pitchfork handle sticking out the end. "I'm looking for Morty Moore or Drake Dexter."

The man was shaped like a keg of beer with strong meaty arms from hauling poop all day. He wiped his brow with the back of a hand. "I haven't seen Morty in about a week, ma'am, so I can't help you there. Mr. Dexter should be over in the horse arena."

I'd been ma'am-ed. Holy crap, all of a sudden I was old enough to be ma'am-ed. It was all downhill from here. "The horse arena's the big building?"

"That's it. Go through the door on the west side. Can't miss Mr. Dexter. Big cowboy hat and a mustache."

I thanked him and left the building. Sounded like I was searching for the Marlboro Man. Shouldn't be too hard to spot, although in Montana, and on a ranch, there were probably a lot of Marlboro Men. But, as I followed the instructions and went through the west door, hello! There was Mr. Drake Dexter, Marlboro Man. Yup, he was the epitome of every woman's romance novel fantasy cowboy. He must have made lots of money from the royalties off all those cigarette billboards.

Tall, whoa, well over six feet. Solid, built as if he drank lots of fresh mountain water and ate lots of good meat growing up. Maybe some Wheaties, too. He wore Wrangler jeans, work boots, a long sleeved white western shirt with snap buttons. He had a honkin' silver belt buckle probably won doing something ludicrously dangerous, most likely on the back of a live, ornery animal. The hat was huge. It was definitely a five gallon one. White and well worn.

When the worker had said mustache, I instantly thought a caterpillar above the lip. This was a full-blown caterpillar above the lip plus handlebars down the sides to his jaw. The man could grow a mustache. His skin was tan, slightly weathered from being out in the elements. His hair was dark, although most was hidden beneath the super-sized hat. He was crazy handsome in that rugged, cowboy sort of way. The man you dreamed about riding his horse, scooping you up with one arm, placing you in front of him in the saddle and riding off into the sunset.

This guy gave me an instant zing, although this was a fantasy zing. No way in hell was I compatible with a man who dealt with horses and cows all day. Drake Dexter turned and saw me. His eyes roamed over my body. Not casually, but boldly, as if he was admiring a new piece of horseflesh. Okay, a fantasy zing felt pretty darn good as I had a hot flash that burned in all the special places.

"Mr. Dexter?" I asked when he came and stood close to me. A little too close. He put one arm on the rail that ran around the ring. I had to look up to meet eyes. It was like being sucked into a black hole. There was no oxygen.

"Dex." He smiled. Yikes, he was intense. His look, his stance, his entire being exuded power. Cockiness.

I held out my hand. He took it in his large, dinner plate sized one, his grip strong and forceful. He held on a tad too long for my comfort level. "Jane West. I...um...." Now, standing here with his brown eyes on me, it was hard to put into words what I wanted to say. "I believe I have some sperm...semen that belongs to you."

Dex raised one eyebrow. "You believe? I guarantee you'd remember if you had some of my sperm." His eyes roved over my body once more as if looking for where the sperm was.

I blushed from the roots of my hair to my toes. I couldn't see it, but I felt the flush everywhere. I wanted to sink into the floor and die. Had I actually said that? To a complete stranger? *I believe I have some sperm that belongs to you.* It couldn't get worse than that. "Let me start over. I found a vial with semen in it and I think it came from your ranch."

Dex smiled. "That's something different entirely. I don't forget where I put my sperm."

Ewww, gross.

# 7

Dex's smile changed to a leer. "I don't put my sperm in a vial." He didn't say more, although obviously he was making a point by what he didn't say. As if I didn't know where he *put* his sperm. "Our stallions are some of the best and *their* sperm...semen is put in vials. We provide stud services to other ranches who want superior bloodlines in their quarter horses by bringing their mares here to be inseminated. We also ship semen to ranches around the world when it's too far to travel."

"So it's likely I ended up with a vial that was to be shipped out?"

"Where did you find it?" He ran his hand over his mustache.

I looked at the snap buttons on his shirt. "Um, in a garden gnome."

Dex's eyebrows shot up. "Excuse me?"

I looked him in the eye. "I bought the gnomes at a garage sale."

Nodding his head, Dex asked, "How do you connect a vial of semen inside a garden gnome, which you bought at a garage sale, and my ranch?"

I didn't blame him if he thought I was crazy. It sounded ridiculous. Ridiculous, but true. "I got it by accident, actually, from Morty Moore. I've been told he works here."

Dex looked over his shoulder and gave a casual wave to a man leading a horse out of the ring. "I have over a hundred employees working for me. I don't know everyone by name. It's certainly possible this man, Morty Moore, works here." He pushed off the railing. I stepped back. "Let me make a call." He pulled a cell from his shirt pocket and did some fancy dialing.

It was plausible Dex didn't know the name of every employee, but in a ranch of this caliber, a man who was clearly in charge—of everything—it would seem likely he'd be very familiar with all of his workers. He didn't seem like the kind of guy who left anything to chance. There was something really off about Dex, something a little creepy. Make that a lot creepy. The way he looked at me, the snide sexual comments. They weren't flirty, they were possessive, overly aggressive, and not just dominant, but disrespectful.

I listened in as he asked someone about Morty Moore, then hung up. "Morty worked seasonally with the cattle. Spring season is big for when we brand and castrate the calves."

Chopping off calf balls. Good times.

"Is he here today? I'd really like to talk to him." I knew he wasn't here as I'd talked with the man in the stable. What would Dex say?

"The resource manager said Morty hasn't shown up for work in over a week." Dex shrugged his shoulders. "It happens. Turnover around here in some jobs, like working with the cattle, is pretty high."

I was disappointed. A dead end. Or was it? I'd seen Morty two nights ago fleeing my house. Ty had confirmed that Morty's parents hadn't heard from him in a week. He hadn't been to work in a week either. Were Ty and I the last to have seen him?

"Sure. Thanks for your help." I offered a quick smile and turned to walk away.

"Where's the vial now?" Dex asked in a friendly voice.

I turned back around. "Freezer. I'm guessing it's no good for you anymore so I'll just throw it out." I lied. I hadn't put it in my freezer. I'd have to buy a new one if I had. To save myself the expense, I'd chucked it into the trash can.

He gave a brief nod and gently took my arm. He obviously didn't care one way or the other about the missing vial. "I'll give you a tour before you go."

It seemed Dex didn't ask, he told. He steered me away from the ring and toward a side door. "Um, okay." Looked like I was going to get a tour of a horse ranch. Whether I wanted to or not.

Although if I put up a stink I knew Dex would let me leave. He didn't seem like the kind of guy who liked to make a scene. The tour probably wasn't a bad idea though. I might learn something about the vial and Morty's interest in it. I knew less than nothing now about the whole business. I wouldn't have minded being asked though. Bossy, bossy.

"So did you start this ranch all on your own? It's very impressive," I asked, trying to make small talk. Nothing like boosting up a man's ego. If I was going to stick around, it made sense to learn something, and do it with a man willing to talk. Dex might help me, unknowingly, learn more about Morty and help track him down.

Dex still had his hand on my arm, his skin warm in contact with mine. The initial attraction, that fantasy zing, was all gone. He might be super handsome, but that was it.

"My parents were cattle ranchers on this land since the fifties. I found a passion for horses and added the equine enterprise to the ranch."

"Are your parents still involved in the property?"

"They've been dead a long time. What about you? What do you do with yourself? I don't see a ring on your finger."

We'd left the horse arena, cut through the bright sunshine and approached a third building. This one was smaller, about fifty feet square. It too, had gray siding and green trim. All of the buildings matched.

"Um, no. I'm a widow."

Dex stopped in his tracks and gazed down at me. "Good. Wouldn't want to fight a husband for you."

My brain stalled. Good? That I was a widow? He didn't want to fight a husband for me? Yikes! I'd known the man less than ten minutes. He was serious. I could tell from the look in his eye. Like a predator ready to pounce on his prey. Gross.

"Boss!" a man in a green ranch shirt called from the door. "We're ready." Dex let go of me and raised his arm in response. The man ducked back inside.

Dex broke eye contact with me. Phew!

"I really need to get back," I said. "I don't want to interrupt your day."

"You're not interrupting anything. I don't get beautiful guests very often." He smiled down at me then started walking, heading toward the man who called to him. "What do you do for a living?" he asked over his shoulder.

Obviously, I was supposed to follow. "I…um…run Goldilocks in Bozeman." I had to walk quickly to keep up with his long stride.

"Goldilocks?" he asked.

"Adult store."

He stopped and looked me over again. How many times was he planning on doing that? He grinned and a new light came to his eyes. "Really? Then you're sure to find this part of the tour right up your alley."

I wasn't sure what running an adult store had to do with a horse farm. He held the door for me and I entered first. Skeptical.

"This is the breeding shed where we provide our stud service."

Shed was not the word I'd use to describe the place. I had a shed in the back yard I used to store the lawn mower and yard tools. Some people used the proverbial woodshed to spank their kids when they were bad. This was something else entirely. The room was large with a strange stand in the middle. It was well lit and operating-room clean. One area off to the right was a horse stall with a half gate and straw on the ground. No lawnmower in sight.

"This is the room where we collect semen on the phantom mare for artificial insemination. Mares are brought from all over and come to the Double D to be bred with our studs. Instead of the old-fashioned way, they're inseminated via pipette directly into the uterus to avoid being harmed by a rough stallion."

Okie dokie.

Wide double doors directly across from us opened and a horse was led in by a man in the green ranch shirt and jeans. I didn't know what kind of horse it was besides being brown. "That's a teaser mare. She's in heat and will be in the stall to help the stud."

Hmmm. Ick. Why on earth did Dex think this was *right up my alley*? What did running an adult store have to do with breeding horses? Did he think since I dealt in sex I'd be interested in horse sex, too? Within a minute I'd already learned way more than I wanted to about horse breeding. Ever.

The mare was led into the stall, the bridle removed and the half gate closed. "The stud will sense the mare, smell her and know she's in heat. This will build his need to copulate."

I assumed the phantom mare was the thing in the middle of the room. It looked like a pommel horse from gym class. About a foot wide and four feet long and cylindrical in shape. It was mounted on two metal posts at about four feet high. It was kind of like a horse body without any legs or head.

"Our studs have been trained to mount the phantom mare, although they'd much prefer the real thing." He winked at me. "We don't have a choice when it comes to a client's mare."

Another horse was led into the room through the same

double doors. This one was black and about a foot taller than the mare. He was frisky, moving his head back and forth against the bridle. His rear legs kicked as he pranced. The really large black penis hanging straight down about a foot near his hind legs was what clued me in on his gender. I was starting to catch on to what was going on.

How on earth did I make it just in time for horse porn?

"I've…I've got to get going," I said, starting to back away. "I think maybe the horse might want some privacy or something."

"Stay." He took my arm again, looked down at me. His gaze was powerful, his voice rough and deep. "It's like a man and a woman. Some stallions are downright barbaric with their mating. They're only focused on their needs, so single-minded in their desire to breed they forget about the mare. But when she's manhandled, treated roughly, she can't deny how, deep down, she really wants to be treated. When the mare submits to the stud, ultimately her needs are met."

I must have had a confused look on my face because he continued. "A woman likes a man to take control. Possess her body. Show her what she wants by doing what he needs."

Ding, ding. Drake Dexter was a Dominant. He liked to control women, use them. Treat them like a…like a piece of horse flesh. And he was showing off his prowess through a horny horse. To me. The widow who worked at an adult store.

"Oookay." I didn't feel threatened, just ludicrously uncomfortable. I wasn't into domination. Sure, I liked a man who took charge, made me feel feminine. I just had no intention of wearing leather, being bound and calling a man Sir. And I definitely wasn't into Drake Dexter. But it was probably easier to play along, for now.

"The stud is going to be led over to the mare. He'll smell her, sense she's in heat. This will ready him. There, see. He's smelled her." The stud was indeed checking out the mare.

The handler circled the stud around the phantom mare while two other men came into the room. One went and reached beneath the contraption and pulled out a white object. It was about eighteen inches long and cylindrical with a hole in the middle.

"That's an artificial vagina, or AV, Robert is holding."

Great. An artificial vagina.

"Now watch," Dex whispered. "It's always amazing to watch a stallion's power. His sexual intensity and need to expel his seed."

If I hadn't felt weirded out before, I officially was now. Dex was way too into this. He watched as if mesmerized. Probably fantasizing about a woman being strapped down to the phantom mare and taking her from behind like a horse. Was a woman just a vessel for his 'seed'? The answer was most likely yes. Hopefully I wasn't the woman he had in mind. Then I remembered what I'd first said to him. *I have some of your sperm.* Great.

The next thirty seconds were like watching a car crash. You couldn't look away from the carnage. The stud mounted the phantom mare and Robert, the AV holder, quickly placed the AV over the super-sized equine penis. The horse didn't really thrust as much as stand there, his hind legs adjusting to the position of his upper body across the phantom mare. The noise of horse pain—or possibly lust—filled the room. I winced as I watched. Moments later, Robert pulled the AV off, the horse dismounted and was led out of the building.

I felt like I needed a cigarette.

"Wow." I didn't know what to say. *That was great*, or *That really turned me on*, definitely didn't work.

"Amazing, isn't it?" Amazing wasn't the first word that came to mind. I nodded my head weakly. "The AV has a sterile tip that collects the semen. Then it's put into a vial, like the one you said you have, and frozen. It's stored until needed and sent around the world."

"Is there a big market for it?"

"Absolutely. My studs are famous for their speed, their

exemplary genetic qualities and are much sought after. So much so that the stud you just saw, his semen brings in over $10,000 a vial."

"Holy crap." No wonder Morty wanted the vial. It would be quite the side business for him.

Dex laughed. "You find this interesting." He still held my arm but now he moved in close, close enough to invade my personal space. "I knew you would." He brushed a strand of hair behind my ear. A chill ran down my spine at his creepy touch.

I stepped back. "Yup, it's been interesting." I looked at my watch. I didn't care what time it was, I just wanted out of there. I'd had enough for one day. Maybe a lifetime. "Boy, look at the time. I've got to run."

---

NORRIS ROAD WAS KNOWN for crappy cell service so I had to wait until I got closer to town to call Kelly.

"Remember when I told you my dream cowboy was Bobby Ewing?" I asked when I was finally in range. When I was eight I'd fantasized about marrying Bobby Ewing from the TV show *Dallas*. I wanted to be Pamela, his wife, with her beautiful hair and clothes. Bobby wore cowboy hats, lived on a ranch and drove that fancy red Mercedes convertible. He was the bomb. Ever since then I'd dreamed about marrying a cowboy. Maybe deep down that was a reason I'd moved to Montana. But Bobby Ewing lived in Texas. Obviously, I'd picked the wrong state since I'd ended up marrying Nate the Jerk instead.

"Yeah. Please tell me Drake Dexter was super-hot like Bobby." She sighed. "You get all the cute ones."

"Tom's a super stud and you know it," I countered.

"Yeah, but he's my husband. Not the same thing at all."

"This guy looks nothing like Bobby Ewing. Definitely Marlboro Man."

Kelly sighed again.

"But he's a total perv."

"Oh." Kelly sounded deflated. As if her dream man turned out to be gay. You only dreamed about guys who would have sex with you.

The gas warning light on the dash came on accompanied by a ding. "Crap. I've got to get gas." I hung up and drove to the nearest station on Huffine by the mall.

I fed the pump my credit card, then my car some gas. I was dying of thirst so I went inside to get a drink. I meandered through the fridge wall of the convenience store checking out all of the beverages. It smelled like hot dogs and buttered popcorn and the A/C felt good on my dusty skin. I opened the fridge and picked out a tea with ginseng and lemon when I heard, "Give me all your money!"

Holy crap.

I turned around and saw a man in a bright yellow wife beater holding a knife up to the cashier. Angled off to the side, I could see his crazy black hair standing every which way about his head. His eyes had a crazed, glassy look. Drugs. Definitely drugs. He looked like death warmed over, his skin color a funky gray, an open sore on his lip. If he was stupid enough to rob a convenience store in the middle of the day, his brain cells must be occupied with trying to score more drugs. Stupid, but dangerous.

Three other customers were in the store, two with the utility company with their neon orange T-shirts. They were further down the fridge wall that lined the back of the store. Another man, in his fifties, stood about five feet away from me. I was closest to the robber.

The store clerk looked panicked. He had to be eighteen and just out of high school. Pimple faced and a patchy attempt at a beard coated his cheeks like mange. He may have peed his pants with fear. I couldn't blame the kid if he had. He didn't make enough money to be held up by a deranged lunatic.

"Now! Open the register and give me the fucking money!" the robber shouted, his knife waving wildly about. It was a bowie knife used to gut animals during hunting season. Hopefully none of us were next.

I slowly stepped back, moving further and further from the register trying to breathe through my fear. I had that instantaneous hot flash that came with panic, kind of like just avoiding a near collision while driving. The utility workers charged past me. One pulled a gun from the back waistband of his pants. The other one held a knife that had been in a sheath attached to his leather belt. Obviously, working with the utility company required being armed at all times. No telling what type of customers they dealt with every day.

They approached Robber at the same time as a man threw open the door to the store armed with a rifle. At first, I thought he might be another bad guy, but then he yelled, "Put it down, Fucker!"

It was like living in a demilitarized zone with all the weaponry around. Montanans and their guns. Never get between them. All three Good Samaritans ganged up on Robber.

"Don't even think about it, asshole!"

A click-click of a rifle being cocked. "Drop the knife!"

The weapon fell out of Robber's hand onto the ground as one of the utility workers clocked him on the back of the head. He was then forced—at gunpoint—to the ground. I could practically see little birdies circle around his head. The fifty-something man had his cell out and talked with the police.

I stood there gawking and quickly closed my mouth which had fallen open. I grabbed a roll of duct tape off the shelves in front of me and handed it to one of the utility workers. He gave me a brief smile. Big and burly, he looked like he hauled a lot of cable. "Good idea." He started rolling the man's wrists and ankles in the gray tape and had him trussed up like a

Christmas goose in seconds. Must've done calf roping on the rodeo circuit.

"Lucky you had your gun," I commented once he'd finished.

"New wire's going to the new subdivision out on Huffine. Prairie dogs are all over the place. Thought we'd get a little target practice in over lunch."

Prairie dogs were everywhere in the West. They tore up open fields by burrowing entire towns underground and were shot for fun on private land. Barbaric, but natural selection at work.

The rifle stayed right on Robber until the cops arrived. The fifty-something guy on the cell must have updated the police to the various weaponry in the store and how they had Robber contained. Thankfully, they didn't shoot all of us and ask questions later.

Two minutes after the police swarmed in and took Robber into custody, the fire department rolled up, sirens blaring.

I was being questioned by an officer named Dempsey out in front of the building. Forty-ish and kind, he took his time getting my statement. Ty walked up in his fire uniform, navy T-shirt and yellow bunker pants and boots. Red suspenders. God, the red suspenders made my heart skip a beat. "Can you give us a minute?" he asked the officer.

Boy, I was glad to see him. My adrenaline had worn off and left me weary and shaky. It felt really great to see a familiar face. Comforting in all the insanity. I craved a hug and a kiss right behind my ear.

"What the hell are you doing here?" he asked through clenched teeth. Obviously, he was trying not to shout as the veins on his neck stuck out like he was about ready to stroke out.

"Getting gas."

He looked from the store to my car in front of one of the pumps. "That's it?"

I twisted my hand back and forth. "You know, the usual stuff that happens to anyone at a convenience store. I watched some lunatic hold up the store five feet in front of me with a bowie knife before three well-armed citizens cold cocked him and held him at gunpoint."

"Do you have a gun?" he asked as he looked me over, as if I had a holster like the Old West slung around my hips.

"Um, no. I don't *do* guns. My part in the whole thing involved staying out of the way, then handing over a roll of duct tape I found in the household section to tie him up."

Ty closed his eyes and I could swear I saw him counting to ten in his head. A vein pulsed at his temple. "Are you okay?"

He looked me over again. It wasn't heated, but clinical.

"Fine," I replied. "But I forgot my tea."

He lifted a brow and shook his head slowly. His hands went to his hips. "Jesus," he muttered.

We both watched Robber carried out by two officers, held up by his armpits. They hadn't traded the duct tape for handcuffs. Must've done a good trussing job. He shouted and ranted about needing money but was ignored. An EMT approached and the officers placed him face down on a gurney to be taken to the hospital.

"That guy's out of his mind," Ty commented as they slid the gurney into the back of the bus and shut the door. Quiet returned.

"He has to be on some kind of drugs."

"Meth. Word out is there's a new shipment around town. Churchill fire had a mobile home burn to the ground the other night. Meth lab. Something big is happening in the area but we don't know what yet."

Churchill was a tiny town fifteen minutes west of Bozeman. More Bozemanites were moving that way for cheaper home prices and a longer commute into work.

"Great. I'd hoped my kids would grow up in a safe, drug-free place."

"Meth's everywhere, even Bozeman," he commented. "This lunatic goes into the store waving a knife around and three men jump him with guns?"

"One of the utility workers had a knife, the other a gun. Another guy was getting gas, saw the man through the door and took his hunting rifle out of the window rack of his truck."

"Shit," Ty said. He stepped back and walked around in circles swearing. He returned to face me and ran his hands over his face. "I can't do this. You're like a magnet for disaster."

"Me?" I asked. My voice rose as much as his.

He poked a finger into my shoulder. "You! Who else would have a man steal something off their doorstep, practically get blown up and then get involved in a holdup?"

Was he losing his mind?

"It wasn't my fault the guy robbed the store. I was just getting a tea!"

"Exactly," he countered immediately. "You weren't even *trying*. I can only imagine what kind of disasters you can create when you actually try!"

I was stunned and angry. Hurt. Now Ty was turning into a lunatic.

Before I could even think, he grabbed my shoulders and pulled me in for a kiss, one with a really good amount of tongue. It was fierce and possessive, wild and untamed, as if the action told me everything he felt when he couldn't say the words.

I heard some catcalls in the background, probably from his fellow firefighters. And a few policemen. Some bystanders, too.

He pulled back, but held onto me. Good thing, as I wasn't steady on my feet after a kiss like that. "I can't keep my hands off of you." He sounded mad about that. "Fuck. But I can't do this anymore. I can't watch someone else I care about get hurt. Or killed."

Ty walked off and climbed into the back of the fire truck. I watched it pull away, frozen where he'd left me.

# 8

"What?" Goldie practically shouted when I shared the news about the robbery. We stood on her front porch. She and Paul had bought a small bungalow when Nate and I married. It was one story, over a hundred years old, and just three blocks from the store.

"Everything turned out fine," I replied, downplaying the entire incident.

"But it might have turned out far worse." She had a hand to her neck and some color drained from her face underneath her bronzer.

I gave her a quick hug when the boys stampeded out onto the front porch. I figured the conversation was over...for now.

"Mom, guess what?" Bobby asked.

"What?"

"We got to go in the hot tub in our underwear!"

Goldie and Paul had a hot tub in their backyard. They used it all year round, but it was fabulous for the winter. It held eight people and had special colored lights under the water. Zach and Bobby considered it their own mini swimming pool. And they didn't have to wear swim trunks.

"GG got us tickets to the demolission dervy!"

I eyed Goldie, also known as GG. It stood for Grandma Goldie. Goldie, of course, refused to be called Grandma so we compromised on GG. "Tomorrow night at the county fair. We'll go early and do the rides," she said.

The 'we' in that statement didn't include me. I was never psyched about spending time in the hot sun at the county fairgrounds waiting in line for deathtrap rides that were ludicrously overpriced. Top that with overheated, cranky kids and it made for a day in Hell. Obviously, I had very negative feelings about the county fair. I didn't mind walking around and seeing the animals and watching the auctions, but the rides, ugh.

"Demolition derby? I love a good demolition derby!" I told Bobby. I really was excited about a demolition derby. Who could deny an interest in cars smashing and ramming each other? And the mud! Now I just had to get out of the fair part.

"We'll talk more about the other stuff later," Goldie said as she gave Bobby a squeeze.

"You can just watch it on the news."

---

WHEN I GOT HOME, I stood under the shower until the water ran cold, the boys parked in front of the TV watching the original Star Wars. I used the bath salts Goldie had given me for Christmas last year but never opened, hoping it would scrub off the layer of sleaze that had built up at Dex's ranch. I let my hair air dry while I carried a laundry basket around the house picking up dirty clothes that had been scattered on the boys' bedroom floors and in their bathroom.

I had to admit my feelings were a little hurt. Okay, a whole lot of hurt. I felt a funny pang of regret, a loss of something that hadn't quite started. Ty didn't want anything to do with me because I was a threat to myself. Ha! Nothing, I meant nothing, exciting happened to me—until less than a week ago when I'd purchased two gnomes at a garage sale. Getting myself hurt was a silly idea because I did nothing crazy. Nothing over the top. Ever. No rock climbing, no sky diving, no crazy adventures of any kind.

Sure, there was a definite spark and connection on a sexual level with Ty. Make that raging inferno, but Ty didn't really know me. Just as he didn't know much about me, I didn't know anything about him. I knew he had parents and grew up in Pony on a ranch. I knew he'd been in the service. I didn't know what he'd done in the service. I didn't know how his deployments had affected him. He must have had friends and fellow soldiers who'd been hurt or even killed. And it had impacted him to such a level that he'd rather push me away before he could care about me, just in case something happened. He'd said as much.

Was it up to me to change his mind? Or was that too much for one man to handle? Was it even fair to try? Did I even want to? I'd already had one lying cheating husband die on me. Did I want to go through that again? Did I want to get in any deeper with a guy who might walk away? Ty wasn't the only one with scars.

But then I smiled to myself as I poured laundry detergent into the machine. I realized he cared about me enough to push me away, and that had to be a lot. And that warmed a place in my heart I thought long frozen over like a Montana winter.

---

KELLY CALLED ONCE the laundry was in the dryer.

"I saw the robbery on the news. Are you all right?" she asked, her voice laced with worry.

The local TV station was small-time. As in teensy tiny. Not that they weren't good. They, thankfully, didn't have a lot of news to cover. Not much bad stuff happened in Bozeman, one of the reasons I liked living here. It hit on the current news around town, which, most of the time involved crop rotation, deep freezes and triplet calves. The excitement of the day had been a toss-up between the Best in Class awards for poultry at the county fair and the convenience store robbery.

"I'm fine. Scary." I was in the kitchen getting a snack. Cheese and crackers. I had the phone tucked between my ear and my shoulder while I sliced some Monterey Jack and laid it out on a plate with a bunch of Ritz.

"It said the man was on meth."

"Looked like it to me," I replied. "He was completely wigged out."

"My next-door neighbor's son was arrested on Monday for possession of meth."

"Really? Mrs. Tanner's son?" Mrs. Tanner taught at the university. English professor, if I remembered correctly. Her son had to be in his twenties and obviously up to no good. God, I hoped my kids wouldn't turn to drugs and blow all the hard work I'd been doing.

"He worked at one of hot springs, I can't remember which one, and someone discovered him selling in the men's locker room."

"A hot spring?" That was surprising. Natural hot springs were all over Montana, several within an hour's drive of Bozeman. One was just down the road from Kelly's house so she went often with the kids. So did lots of other families. Most have four or five pools, each with a different temperature ranging from average pool water to just-before-scalding. They always smelled faintly of rotten eggs.

"It's weird there were two meth incidents within a few days. It's getting a little too close to home for me," Kelly said.

With seven kids, I couldn't blame her.

"Oh, I forgot. When Ty came to get Bobby's arm out of the patio umbrella stand, he said they went on a few meth calls. He told me today a meth lab burned down in Churchill. And, there's something big going on but they don't know what it is yet." I poured apple juice into plastic cups and called for the boys to come in from the backyard to get their snack.

"In about ten years we're going to be dodging all kinds of teenage crap without having to deal with drugs, too."

"I don't know if I'll be able to handle drugs, but teenage s... e...x, no problem," I spelled out as I handed Bobby his cup.

"Yeah, we'll just make them sit down with Goldie for The Talk. I guarantee she'll embarrass them into staying virgins until they're thirty."

"Don't forget Paul. He'll probably take them to watch a teenager give birth and scare the hell out of them."

"Ah, you've got the best family."

---

EVERY YEAR IN JULY, the Gallatin County Fair is held at the Fairgrounds, a few blocks north of Main. Contests gave blue ribbons in all kinds of categories. Horses, cows, chickens, rabbits, sheep, pigs. Quilts, pies and jams. Displays for each category were spread across various buildings of the Fairgrounds. The buildings reminded me of the old National Guard stations, built decades ago with vintage drab gray sheet metal siding. They were all shaped the same, long and narrow. Some were specifically for animals with pens running the length of the building in four long rows with two aisles to walk. The floors were dirt. The smells were intense and bad. In the chicken and rabbit building, it was also incredibly dusty and hot with feathers, fur and shavings in the air.

Ranch life and town life mingled for the week. It seemed that night we joined everyone in the entire county. And maybe some from the next. Wranglers blended with Carhartts. Baseball hats and Stetsons. I dressed somewhere in the middle with jeans and sneakers with a pink tank top. The dust kicked up with your every step so I learned the hard way years ago to skip flip-flops or sandals. Your feet got filthy dirty and covered in all kinds of animal poop bits. I had a serious thing about animal poop.

The sun tilted over the Tobacco Roots, the evening still warm. I had my hair up in a ponytail to keep my neck cool. I'd joined Goldie, Paul and the boys at seven after the heat of the day had passed and the boys had burned off most of their energy on rides. We had a little time to kill before the derby.

I kissed everyone and we started our meandering, checking out the animals. "I want to see the cows," Bobby said. "Some kids get to have one as a pet. I want one, too."

"Those are farm kids with lots of land. Where would you put your cow?" Goldie asked.

"In the back yard."

"There'd be lots of cow poop. Everywhere!" Zach added.

I didn't want to share with Bobby what happened to the 'pets' once they grew big enough to eat so I decided to distract. "Let's go check out the horse auction." I pointed to the building nearest us.

"Yeah!"

The boys ran ahead, Goldie following as best she could in her gold toned pumps. They didn't go well with the dust and uneven ground, but they definitely matched her black Capri pants and tank top that had been attacked by the Bedazzler.

"I delivered Joann Jastrebski's baby yesterday. A boy," Paul said. I'd been friends with Joann in college and kept in touch through social media and every once in a while, saw her around town.

"That's great." I was excited for other people to have babies, but it had been a hard time for me when I had Bobby. A three-year-old and a newborn without a dad. By that point, Nate had lived in Hamburg and a few months away from being dead. But even with the joy of a new baby, I had been heartbroken for what could have been.

Paul touched my shoulder and gave me a smile. A knowing one. What I liked most about him was his ability to understand, to have an entire conversation with just a brief touch or eye contact. He, too, remembered what his son had done to me.

The horse auction was in full swing when we took our seats on the bleachers. The stands circled the room and looked down on a center ring with a packed dirt floor. Plenty of people were there to buy, sell or just watch the action. Obviously, I had no plans to buy a horse so I fell under the *watch* category. After my unusual and graphic lesson the day before, I'd seen more horses in two days than I had in my entire life.

Horse sex didn't appear to be the main attraction, at least. In fact, it all looked fairly boring. Someone rode a horse around the pen, slow and fast, for those interested in buying to see what they'd get while the auctioneer did his fast-talking routine. I couldn't tell what made one horse better than another, but they seemed to sell for all kinds of prices. From several hundred dollars on up. Paul took the boys to stand down at the fence for a close-up view. Zach and Bobby stood on the bottom rail and Paul stood between them as they talked and pointed at various things.

Goldie and I sat quietly and watched first one horse, then another go up for sale. As the third horse came in, the announcer called, "This quarter horse is from the Rocking Double D ranch." My stomach lurched when I saw Drake Dexter ride his horse around the ring. He was definitely at home in a saddle, that was for sure. He wore jeans and boots and the same hat from the other day. Today's shirt was navy blue and the sleeves were rolled up to show his strong, tan forearms. Out of all the people in the audience he had to hone in on me as if he had some kind of weird ESP-type skill. His eyes met mine and he tipped his hat, old fashioned style.

"Well, well," Goldie said, looking the man over.

"That's Drake Dexter."

"That's one handsome cowboy. He melts my butter."

I had to admit he was handsome, but butter? He more like

curdled my milk. But looks were only skin deep. When he opened his mouth, the man gave me the creeps.

I wasn't paying any attention to the auction. My thoughts drifted to Dex and our first, very weird meeting.

"Sold!" the announcer shouted over the loudspeaker. Dex guided his horse over to the fence and lifted his arm in a casual wave to me.

"He wants to talk to you. Mmm, mmm. Go on down. Talk to the man. Maybe I'll send him a box of goodies."

"I have a feeling he already has a goodie drawer," I told her. Probably an entire goodie room, like say, a dungeon.

I smiled, admittedly weak, as I carefully stepped down from the bleachers and approached Dex.

"Hello," he said. "You look nice in pink." He stared at my tank top which meant he was taking in the cleavage. Being large-chested, I tried to buy the most modest tank style I could find with a higher scoop neckline than most, but when a man sat atop a horse he could see right down to your belly button.

"Um, hi." I crossed my arms over my chest and realized too late that only made things worse. I hadn't learned from the last time with Ty. Did I look as awkward as I felt?

"I'm surprised to see you here."

"I'm with my family."

He handed the reins to a man who'd joined us at the rail. Dex climbed down and the man and horse walked off. Dex put his forearms on the top bar and leaned in. I could smell some kind of spicy aftershave, which I had to admit, smelled nice. He held a short riding crop in his hands. I hadn't noticed it before.

"I didn't realize you whip your horses."

Dex looked at the whip. "Sometimes they need a little gentle prodding."

"Ah." I didn't know what else to say. This was one uncomfortable conversation and it had only just started. I wasn't a fan of hurting animals...or people.

He leaned in and almost whispered in my ear. "A crop can

be used for pleasure, too. If you're interested." His aftershave was stronger, almost cloying, once I processed his words.

I turned to Goldie and gave her a look. I darted my eyes from her to Dex and told her via female telepathy that I needed rescuing.

"Interested?"

I feigned ignorance once I turned back to face Dex. He smiled, his teeth super white against his tanned skin.

"If a woman is unsure of what she wants, a little redirection can help." He slapped the crop gently into his palm.

"You mean what you want."

He gave a quiet laugh, his breath warm against my face.

"A man knows what's best and it's important for a woman to remember that."

"So you beat her into submission?"

Dex tsked me. "Submission, yes. Beating? No. Punishment for forgetting her place."

And there you had it.

"Hello," Goldie said. Finally. She took her sweet ass time to get over here. She held out her hand daintily.

Dex smiled at Goldie and shook hands. "Drake Dexter."

"This is Goldie, my mother-in-law," I said in way of introduction. We weren't lingering, so I didn't think last names were necessary.

"Pleasure," Dex replied, his voice deep and rich, eyes penetrating on Goldie. It was obvious to me he could suck a woman in with his gazer beam. Hopefully, Goldie had her force fields up.

"That's a lovely horse you rode."

"Thank you."

I wanted this conversation over so I moved things along. "Dex was telling me the various uses for a riding crop."

Goldie lifted an eyebrow. "Oh?" She looked to Dex and the crop in his hand.

"Sometimes a mare needs a little help remembering where I want to go."

I gave Goldie a pointed look, hoping she'd read between the lines. She was always quick on the pick-up.

"You're absolutely right. It's important to keep your horse in line. If they get out of hand, they'll nip you in the butt."

My mouth dropped open in surprise. It amazed me both could speak double entendre. Or were they? I couldn't keep up. I obviously wasn't as skilled.

"A woman after my own heart. You've experienced this yourself?"

Goldie patted Dex's hand with her manicured one. "Honey, I'm old enough to have experienced everything. Oh look, Paul's ready with the boys to go to the derby. It was nice meeting you."

"Bye," I said to Dex, past ready to flee.

I turned to follow Goldie but Dex grabbed my wrist, kept me in place. His hand was warm against my skin and I felt the roughness of callouses. Goose bumps popped out on my arms. I looked up into his dark eyes. Deep and intense. Yup, gazer beams. "You know where to find me when you're ready." He let go of my wrist and slapped the crop against his palm again.

Thwack. That broke the stare. I mumbled something unintelligible and scooted off.

Once outside, Goldie stopped me, letting the boys go on ahead. "That is one handsome piece of man. Mmm, mmm."

"Uh, yeah." He was handsome, but that was as far as it went.

"And he's very interested in you. Should I send him a care package, too?"

"Only if it includes whips and chains," I grumbled.

Goldie nodded. "Oh, sweetie, I'm so glad you're willing to try new things, but isn't that a little out of your element?"

"If I threw a fit about anal beads, do you think I'd go for bondage and sadism?" I asked.

"Good point. That man screams Dom. But, you might be

able to tell him your limits up front. You know, no painful punishment but you'd be interested in being a sub. Following his commands. It can be quite liberating."

How the hell did she know that? I had split second visions of Paul wielding a riding crop and Goldie submitting and I shuddered, forcing my thoughts elsewhere. I didn't want to go there. Ever. Besides, I wasn't going to *submit* to anyone. As if I hadn't given enough control of my life over to Nate to have it yanked out from under me when he'd cheated. *Happy place, go to a happy place!*

"No way."

Goldie nodded her head. "You're right. You need sex, honey, badly. But not that badly. I'll get you the fanciest vibrator out there to use until you find the right man."

"Great. Thanks." It was better to go along than to argue. Maybe she'd forget. Doubtful.

She gave me a hard look. "You weren't seriously considering that man to scratch your itch, were you?"

"Only if I up my insurance premium first."

Goldie kissed my cheek. "All right then. What about Ty? I thought there was something there."

I briefly told her about how he'd reacted at the convenience store and whatever spark there'd been was gone now.

"Ty Strickland cares about you. It's obvious. He wouldn't have walked away otherwise."

My thoughts exactly.

"He just needs a little nudge."

"Not another box," I groaned.

Engines started to rev. Applause carried out of the arena.

"Competition," Goldie replied. "His testosterone level is through the roof. It's okay for him to walk away from you, but I can guarantee he's not going to be happy about some other guy filling his spot."

"You mean make him jealous?"

She pointed her finger at me like a gun and fired. "I knew you were the smart one."

We handed our tickets over for the derby and looked for the boys. "And Little Missy, you need to tell me how you got to calling Drake Dexter by his nickname, Dex, if you aren't performing sexual services for him."

Shoot. Nothing got by that woman. "If I was performing sexual services for Dex I'd be calling him Master."

"Don't distract me from the original point by making sense."

# 9

"Wow! Look at that upside down car!" shouted Zach.

We were all into the crash and burn portion of the derby. Cars were mangled on the mud track, some with steam coming out of their radiators, two cars stuck together in a T-bone gunning their engines, wheels spinning in the mud with the hope of separating. The latest excitement was a car pushed up a berm and flipped onto its top. It slowly came to a standstill after spinning around in circles twice.

"Cool!" Bobby added.

Goldie, Paul and I sat with little yellow foam earplugs sticking out of our ears, the boys with the large earmuff style to muffle the unbelievably loud engine noise.

The arena was an outdoor venue, rectangular shaped and open to the elements. No roof. Similar to a high school football stadium. It was used for everything from rodeos to demolition derbies. No restrooms, no food vendors. That was all outside the arena, part of the fairgrounds. Running down the long sides of the event area were the stands, all concrete steps and wood bench-style seats. Room enough for about three hundred. We sat most of the way up the stands so the boys had a good view. Couldn't miss any action. I could see the sun setting on the Gallatin Mountains from our seats.

Zach and Bobby held red and white striped bags of popcorn. I had the super-sized soda to wash it all down, which was now only half full. The smells of animal, mud and buttered popcorn mingled in the evening air.

I was mentally betting how long it would take for the boys to need the bathroom. I swear they had bladders the size of walnuts and it was a haul to get there. You had to leave the stands, go outside the arena and over to the small, squat buildings that served as restrooms. They'd miss all the demolishing. So would I.

Goldie caught my attention by giving me a little finger wave, and then tilted her head to the right and down a few rows. I followed her gaze and saw Ty and the Colonel. Both wore white shirts—the Colonel's had a collar—and the similar close-cut hair. Based on the smiles on their faces they, too, were enjoying the smash-up. Even from my side view of Ty, I felt that excitement, that zing, course through my blood and travel to all the important sexual places on my body.

Damn small-town life. If the man wanted to avoid me, why would he show up exactly where I was? The state was six hundred miles wide. Couldn't he be somewhere, anywhere else? It wasn't fair for me to have the zing if he didn't have it, too. Equal opportunity zing.

Goldie did a couple weird gestures with her head and eyes which I translated to be: *Here's your opportunity. Make the man jealous!*

But how? Where I sat—high up in the stands—no man was going to turn around and look my way, let alone flirt with me while cars rammed each other in the mud. It was a demolition derby! Hell, I could walk around stark naked and all a guy would see is big tires flinging mud. There was no separating men from their machines.

Fine, I'd trek to the ladies' room while I contemplated my

first move in Operation Make-Him-Jealous. Goldie would think I had a plan. It would give me at least ten minutes to come up with one. If there was no line, otherwise it might be longer.

The boys were mesmerized by the carnage before them. Zach had forgotten the popcorn that was halfway to his mouth. After I gestured to the ladies' room and Goldie nodded in understanding, I handed her the soda and maneuvered down the stands and out of the arena.

I took the east exit, away from the fair. The ground was packed dirt, the air cool as the stands blocked the sun. Not many people milled around. All were either at the fair or at the derby.

"Jane!"

I turned.

Ty.

"Hi," I said, nervous. He looked really good up close. As usual. I could see some dark blond stubble on his chin and I wondered what it would feel like against my skin. The underside of my breasts, my stomach, the inside of my...stop! I felt my face flush.

"Yeah, hi." Ty stared at me. Looked at my mouth. Looked at the ground. Looked at me. He leaned in.

He was going to kiss me!

He lifted his hands to hold my head. To pull my hair from the ponytail and run his fingers through the silky tresses. Yes!

But, instead, he lifted his hands to pull the little ear plugs from my ears. Crap. I held out my hand and stuffed them embarrassingly in my jeans pockets. "Thanks," I grumbled.

"So, that guy from the auction."

Holy crap. Goldie was right. Replace First Guy with Second Guy and First Guy would be jealous. Regardless of the fact that Second Guy was way too kinky/creepy for me to be cool. That didn't matter. The fact that he had a penis was enough to make Ty strut around like a rooster.

"What about him?" I tried to sound nonchalant. I wasn't

very good at it, so hopefully I seemed way more confident in my feminine wiles than I felt.

"He looked at you like you were a piece of meat." Ty didn't need glasses, that was for sure. To Dex, I was nothing more than an object. "I swear I saw him wipe drool."

"And?"

Ty ran a hand through his hair. "And? Jesus, Jane."

I wouldn't put the man out of his misery. He had to come to me. "What are you doing here?" I lifted my hand in an all-encompassing gesture. "You walked away from me the other day at the convenience store. Said I'm a...what was it? Oh, right, a 'magnet for disaster'. You have no say in who I see or what I do."

Ty didn't like being told off. His jaw clenched tight and his face reddened. Clearly, he was angry, although I wasn't sure if it was directed at me or himself for being such a dumbass.

"Look, Goldie came over to say hello to me and the Colonel in the stands and asked how we were enjoying the derby. She said you were leaving and told me to give you a ride."

Ah, Goldie-the-Meddler. She obviously didn't say why I was *leaving*. The old omit-the-important-parts trick.

"Why didn't you just tell her no?"

Ty lifted an eyebrow. "Have you ever told that woman no?"

He had a point.

"Besides, she gave us the tickets to the derby so it was the least I could do."

"So you're going to give me a ride because Goldie is making you, not because you want to?"

Ty opened his mouth to say something, and then shut it, smart enough to recognize he couldn't answer that question without stepping in a pile of horse poop.

"It was nice of Goldie to give you the tickets," I commented.

That woman. I swear I'd strangle her one of these days. Or kiss her. I wasn't sure which at the moment. She'd planned the whole thing! First, she probably bought extra derby tickets so

Ty could be in the same place as me. That was even before Ty walked away and at that point, she just wanted us to be around each other as much as possible.

Only an hour ago, she'd put the bee in my bonnet about making Ty jealous. She must have seen him at the horse auction watching me with Dex. With Ty at the derby, it would have been child's play for her to have him follow me. Goldie had a twisted, devious mind when it came to matchmaking, even more so at making men suffer. The least I could do was to keep the pain going for the man. All of Goldie's hard work demanded it.

"So who was that guy?" Ty asked, venturing back into Jealousy Territory.

I shrugged. "Just a guy I met the other day."

"I didn't think you went for cowboys."

"You never know who you're going to be attracted to."

"Yeah." Ty looked at my mouth with longing, as if he couldn't help himself. I almost succumbed to making the first move. I remembered his taste, how his was a mixture of gentle and demanding all at the same time.

I ran my tongue over my lower lip, wetting it. Right then, I wanted him to kiss me so badly I couldn't stand it. I felt heat flare beneath my skin. Who could blame me? Any single woman would shoot me dead for not giving in to the obvious want I saw in his gorgeous, blue eyes. I was a piece of meat and he wanted to eat me up. That was the look on his face, not Dex's. That was A-OK with me.

I didn't mind if *Ty* wanted to eat me. *He can eat me all he wants. Oh God! Did I just think that? That meant I'd feel his stubble on my thighs, his face buried...No! Stop! Don't think about him nibbling there!*

"You never know who you'll be attracted to," he repeated, eyes now on my breasts. My nipples hardened involuntarily.

The man was ridiculously attracted to my breasts. I was

attracted to his attraction to my breasts. The man wanted *me*. Me!

Yes!

Kiss him!

No! No. Be strong. Make him suffer. Only then would he come back.

Goldie didn't mention how much I would suffer, too. How my panties would be ruined and I ached for him to discover that. I might take her up on the offer for the top-of-the-line dildo to ease my need. And boy, did I need!

I gave him a friendly pat on the shoulder instead of yanking him into my arms and kissing him. It was one of the hardest things I've ever had to do. What kind of crazy woman turned down a guy who wanted her? Especially when you wanted him right back. I could be in bed with him, hell, pressed up against some hidden wall at the fairgrounds with my legs wrapped around his waist in minutes. But noooo, I had to do the right thing, the stupid thing—push him away. "I'm...I'm glad you're my neighbor. I'll definitely knock on your door if my snow blower breaks."

I walked off, headed to the ladies' room. I swear I could feel Ty's eyes boring into my back. I looked forward, focused on the women's restroom, a gray squat building. I whispered to myself, "Do not turn around. Do not turn around." I missed the smashed-up derby car barreling down on me until the last moment. I turned and saw one broken headlight and cracked grill. For a split second, I felt like a deer ready to be run over, literally, before strong arms pushed me out of the way. I fell to the ground with a thunk, felt a heavy weight land on top of me —not heavy enough to be a car—before the world went black.

---

I CAME to with Ty's face looming over me. Not a bad image when returning to consciousness. But the concern I saw there was something I wouldn't soon forget. He was so close I could feel his warm breath on my skin. I noticed the scent of peppermint.

I blinked.

"Jesus," Ty whispered before closing his eyes briefly.

I started processing other things besides Ty. I saw the small crowd that had formed around us, heard the engine noise from the derby, smelled sausage and peppers from the fair's midway. "I remember a derby car trying to run me over."

Ty nodded his head. "I remember that, too." His voice was grim and angry, his jaw clenched tight.

I sat up.

"Don't. Just lie there until the paramedics come."

"I'm fine. No little birdies flying around my head." I carefully stood up but Ty kept a firm grip on my arm. I brushed dirt off my jeans hoping to hide my wobbly knees. "I don't need —or want—the paramedics. Besides, aren't you one?" At Ty's nod, I added, "You know I'm fine."

Ty contemplated my words for a moment as he looked me over. Not the same heated look as only a minute before, but now in a clinical, assessing way. "How many fingers am I holding up?"

"Two," I grumbled. "Four. Stop switching it!"

Ty rolled his eyes. "Show's over, folks," he told the few still concerned. Once we were alone again, Ty pulled me tightly into his arms.

"I can't breathe," I gasped.

"Sorry." Ty loosened his grip but still held me close.

"Mmm, you feel good." His body heat seeped into me through his rock hard, muscled chest. He smelled like...Ty. Rugged male, soap and something else I was learning was just his own scent. I heard his heartbeat beneath my ear and it raced like a thoroughbred. Clearly, he wasn't as calm as he appeared.

"Was that a crazy driver or was he trying to run me over?" I asked.

Ty gave me a quick squeeze then loosened his hold, although he kept his hands on my upper arms. Either he didn't want to let me go, which was a very romantic thought, but more likely he wanted to make sure I didn't fall over on my face. "It looked to me like the bastard was trying to run you over."

I was dumbfounded. "Wh...why?"

"I have no idea, but a crazy driver would have at least stopped and said he was sorry. You have to admit a lot of weird things have been happening. Even for you."

I snorted. Not very ladylike, but neither was the topic. "I told you these...weird things are not usual. Something is going on and it all started with those stupid gnomes."

Ty's eyebrows went up. "You think all of this is tied in to the semen, the gnomes and Morty?"

"It makes sense, doesn't it? I think something's happened to Morty. No one's heard from him. He was desperate for that gnome. If someone hurt Morty because of the gnome, it's not hard to follow they might come after me."

Ty thought for a moment. "It actually makes sense. We should check and see if that derby car was stolen."

We?

"Great. So you're saying someone's trying to kill me? With a derby car?"

"Not anymore. That didn't work."

"Neither did the explosion."

Ty clenched his jaw. "Christ, neither did the explosion. This is nothing to feel proud about!"

"I'm not proud," I muttered. "Relieved I'm not flattened."

Ty kissed the top of my head, probably not remembering he'd put a ban on kissing. It was as if he had to do it. "The gnome's glued back together, the vial is in the trash, Morty's gone. The question is: Why the hell does someone want you dead?" His voice was frustration, anger and worry rolled into one.

I pulled back and looked him in the eye. His face showed the same mixed emotions. Obviously, he wasn't sure if he should hold me or push me away.

Someone wanted me dead. *Someone wanted me dead.* Who? Why? What was so bad that someone hated me so much? "I...I have no idea." My voice was shaky. "I lead a boring life."

Ty laughed humorously. "Boring? You're the least boring person I've ever met. I've known you less than a week. You had a person roam around your yard, a missing man on your doorstep, an explosion, a convenience store robbery, and now are almost run over by a derby car in that small window of time. Is there anything I've missed?" He raised an eyebrow, daring me to add something else.

No chance I'd tell him now about visiting Dex at his ranch. It had been a dead end in finding Morty, hopefully no pun intended. He hadn't been there shoveling poop like I'd wanted. He hadn't lifted a pitchfork all week.

Dex didn't want me dead, he wanted me in his bed. And that wasn't something I was going to share with Ty.

I hoped my face didn't give my thoughts away. I tried to look all innocent and clueless like Zach and Bobby when they broke something special.

"Nope." I heard applause from the crowd and saw people filing out of the arena.

"The derby must be over." Ty finally released my arms. I brushed the dust off my jeans. "Let's not tell Goldie or anyone else about this little incident. I don't want to scare them. Especially the boys. Besides, we don't know for sure someone wants me"— I gulped— "dead." It was hard to get the words out. *Someone wanted me dead.*

"The only way we'll know for sure is if you're actually dead," Ty grumbled, angry. "Which I don't want to verify. But I agree. We won't tell your family, but I'm going to talk to some cops I know and look into all this. Morty, the explosion, the goddamn derby car. We can't do nothing and wait for someone to try again." He took my hands in his, rubbed his thumbs over my palms. I felt the caress all the way to my hooha. "But you have to lay low. Promise me you won't take any unnecessary risks." He brought my knuckles up to his mouth and kissed one hand, then the other. "Don't do anything crazy."

Just his lips on my knuckles gave me a zing. Like mini lightning. If Ty only knew how much I felt like a wanton hussy by a simple brush of his lips, he'd probably toss me over his shoulder like a caveman and haul me back to his man cave and do stuff to me so I couldn't walk right for a week.

Oh, boy. Please!

Focus. I lifted my chin defiantly but was content keeping my hands in his. "I never do *anything* crazy. That's my problem!"

Right then, my sexual control snapped. That last zing had done it. I kissed him. Right there with the crowd parting around us. A quick, hard kiss. Not too quick, as I was able to tangle tongues with him before I pulled back. "There. That was crazy."

So much for making him suffer, waiting for him to come to me. Let's face it, I sucked at it. But I'd almost been run over by a demolition derby car. Probably not many women trying to make a man suffer were almost run over during the suffering process. The rules had changed when my life flashed before my eyes. I realized I hadn't kissed enough yet. Life was short and I needed to squeeze in all the extra kissing I could. Besides, Ty had pushed me out of the way and saved my life. He deserved a kiss for that. A mulligan. That's what it was. A mulligan kiss.

Ty had a deranged look on his face. Half lust, half insanity. "Promise me," he repeated before pulling me back into his arms for more.

I had no doubts if we hadn't been standing out in public at

a county fair I would have had my panties around my ankles within five seconds. Fortunately, we both had a smidge of self-control—and a desire to avoid being arrested.

"I'm going camping tomorrow," I said, breathlessly. "What can happen in the woods?"

# 10

After two nights of roughing it up Hyalite with two RVs—the Colonel's eighteen-foot-long monstrosity and my more modest pop-up—I'd had enough of wilderness fun. Sure, there were real beds with sheets, air conditioning and heat, a kitchen, pots and pans, a fridge and all the other accoutrements that went along with fancy RV living. But I longed for a real shower. The closest thing to that had been walking under the mist at Palisade Falls the day before.

My curly hair never looked great after a night of sleeping on it. Usually, it resembled a bird's nest when I woke up. I didn't dare get in front of a mirror now. I could only imagine what it looked like after two days outside in the wind.

I reached my camping limit and was desperate for a break from my children. I loved my kids, but I needed a time out. A time out from boys who fell into icy streams. A time out on gutting fish. Bug spray. Sunscreen. Dust. If that wasn't enough, I smelled like a cooked ham from all the campfire smoke.

Hyalite area was Bozeman's backyard playground. Only fifteen miles south of town, it was a quick trip up the canyon to the reservoir and extensive trails. You could hike, fish, kayak, mountain bike and in the winter, ice climb. In my opinion, it was one of the prettiest spots in Montana. Rugged mountains curved around the reservoir that reflected their snowcapped peaks. Aspen trees dotted the water's edge and meadows. In the fall, their leaves were bright yellow. At night, it was so dark the Milky Way spanned the sky.

Our traditional camping spot was on the east side, right on the banks of the reservoir with views to the south of Hyalite Mountain. I loved the outdoors and I loved the quiet, but I loved my bed, too.

Goldie and Paul had joined us the day before, towing their own home on wheels. They'd come late since Goldie'd had to work Friday night at the store. Paul had rolled out early this morning because he was on call and needed to be near the hospital.

Goldie stayed behind, getting a ride back to town with me and the boys. For a woman who was high maintenance and a serious primper, Goldie loved to fish. In fact, she put everyone around her to shame. Sure, she wore designer jeans and the least wilderness-worthy shoes a woman could find to camp in, but once she slipped on a pair of waders and picked up a rod, she was a different woman. Fly fishing was her favorite. She said it calmed her, just like golf did for my mom. She easily picked up the plastic Mickey Mouse rod of Bobby's and would hook a worm for him.

Goldie and her grandsons were up at the crack of dawn and spent the morning fishing in the reservoir in front of our campsite hoping to pull out a whopper or two. I wasn't quite as worm friendly, so I left the three to their fishing fun while I packed up.

Even after two days, my body was sore from the full body slam I'd taken at the fair. Ty had felt like a ton of bricks when he'd landed on me and my muscles still complained about it. I'd wanted to have Ty on top of me, but not like that.

Anything was better than being run over by a car, so I was grateful for my aches and pains. My mind had spent the weekend processing the fact that someone was trying to kill me. I'd tossed and turned reliving the terrifying moments. I'd woken up in a cold sweat dreaming about the car's broken grill. Someone hated me enough to want me dead. But why? My brain spun its proverbial wheels in the mud trying to answer that question.

"The only thing I caught this morning was a four-foot wiggle-fish," Goldie said, laughing. They'd returned from their fish catching mission. Next to her stood a grinning, wet four-year-old who had clearly fallen into the reservoir. His shorts and T-shirt clung to his skin and his dark hair stood up in wet spikes.

I'd put all the cooking gear back in plastic bins and had been rolling up the last sleeping bag.

"Ah, so do we get to gut him and eat him?" I asked as I hugged and tickled Bobby, all the while he shrieked with laughter. I felt my front get cold and damp from his clothes. Oh well, at least he didn't smell like dead fish. A shower was only a few hours away.

"It will go well with the Jell-O mold I plan on making for dessert tonight," the Colonel added, joining us in front of my camper. "Lemon and whipped cream." He wore his usual tan shorts and white collared shirt. Somehow, his clothes were pressed and starched. How he looked immaculate after two days I'd never know. He didn't have a speck of dirt on him. I, however, probably looked like I'd wrestled a baby black bear.

"Man, we didn't catch anything," Zach grumbled. His hair was tousled, his cheeks a rosy hue of exertion and exercise.

"Good thing we've got carrots and celery for snacks then," the Colonel replied, half joking.

Zach and Bobby both grumbled some more, debating what was worse, the lack of fish or the lack of junk food to eat.

"It's hard to catch fish when you yak all the time and someone falls in," Goldie commented. "We'll have to stop and try a spot on the creek as we head home. Maybe those fish won't recognize us." She wore gray neoprene waders which came up waist high, held up with a pair of black suspenders. You could wade into water up to your belly button in them and stay dry. With the water around Bozeman all fed by melting snow, it was never warm fishing around here.

A hot pink short sleeved shirt looked strange beneath the waders, especially with bits of thin gold chain that hung in swags about the round neckline. Goldie wore a matching hot pink visor, her blond hair teased into a poof out the top and a full ponytail curving down the back. It wouldn't surprise me if the blinding bright pink and gold bling had scared the fish away instead of the boys. "After that we'll stop at the Dairy Queen on the way home."

A smile lit up Zach's face as he fist-pumped the air. So much for eating carrots and celery. "Go get dried off and cleaned up while I finish packing up," I told them. More fishing. Yippee.

---

AFTER PACKING AND LOADING UP, we found another spot at a pull-off about a mile down from the reservoir. Goldie and the boys spent another hour attempting to hook something besides overhanging tree branches and rotting sticks without success. The Colonel joined them, although he chose a deep swirling eddy upstream. Without the ruckus of Goldie and the boys nearby, he caught three small rainbow trout before releasing them. Not to be a party pooper, I joined them at the water's edge, but found a nice big boulder in the sunshine, laid back and savored the rock's warmth against my back and the sun on my face. I promptly fell asleep.

"I swear I've seen old people climb a hill faster," Goldie said once we were on the road. "You could barely make it up the river bank to the car. What's wrong with you?"

It wasn't hard for Old Eagle Eye to notice how gingerly I'd

moved up the steep bank to the car. All I needed was a cane and I'd be ninety. Muscles I didn't even know I had were sore. "I think I pinched a nerve sleeping last night."

Goldie nodded sympathetically. "Sciatic. Sometimes happens during more"—She lowered her voice—"intimate moments, although I'm guessing that's not the reason in this case."

"GG." I used my warning tone and the name the boys called her, reminding her of their presence.

"Mmm, right," she replied, obviously remembering herself. "When you play *field hockey* with someone else, sometimes you hit the *ball* too hard with your *stick* and you get hurt."

I peeked in the rearview mirror. The boys weren't listening. "Like you said yourself, I wasn't playing *field hockey* last night, I was camping."

"Camping's a great place for *field hockey*. Especially when you have a really good stick. You can definitely score. Sometimes you feel like playing more than one game."

"Mommy, what's field hockey? Is that some kind of sport?" Zach asked. Apparently, he had been listening after all. I gave Goldie a pointed look.

"Yes, it's a sport you can play when you're thirty," I replied. "And married."

"Huh. I thought you used to play soccer. You don't need a stick for soccer," Zack added.

"You're right, love, I did." I gave Zach a quick smile in the rearview mirror, then darted a look at Goldie. "I don't have lots of experience with games that use sticks."

"Then maybe you should find someone who does," Goldie added. "I bet Ty is really good at games, and I'm *sure* he'll let you use his *stick*."

I thought of the feel of Ty's *stick* when he'd pressed me up against the fire truck.

"Yeah, Mommy, Ty told me he played lots of sports as a kid.

I bet he'd teach you!" Bobby added, breaking off that line of thought.

I rolled my eyes at Goldie.

"Use a heating pad when you get home." Obviously, she, too, thought it was time to drop the subject.

After that fun-filled conversation I stayed quiet. I didn't need any more talk in code. Or talk, period. Since the road twisted and turned for ten miles following the banks of Hyalite Creek back to town, I wanted Goldie to think my silence was due to my focus on the driving. Which in part, it was. With a camper, top speed maxed at thirty-five going down due to having to deal with the steep decline and narrowness of the road. Take in lack of guardrails and potentially falling rocks, I kept both hands on the steering wheel and both eyes on the road.

The Colonel followed behind us in his truck, blissfully unaware of my ridiculous conversation with Goldie. I couldn't tell either of them the real reason I was sore. The last thing I needed was for them to go off the deep end about someone trying to hurt me.

The boys were in the back staring out the open windows. The gnomes, brought along for the weekend, were in the middle between Zach and Bobby, the lap belt securing them in place. The hot breeze blew the hair on their sweaty heads. They were both in almost vegetative states after a weekend of camping fun and hours of fishing. I wouldn't be surprised if they fell asleep before we got home.

A few minutes later, Goldie piped up. "Whatever happened the other night with Ty? At the demolition derby."

"Mmm?" I tried to remain mute, but I knew it would be impossible. She wouldn't shut up until she'd wheedled it out of me. And the last thing I wanted to bring up was the other night. I'd end up blurting out about the derby car and possible death. That would not be a good thing.

We came around a right turn and hit a small stretch of straightaway. I felt a thunk and took it for a pot hole.

Goldie turned to look at me, settling in for a good long chat. "Don't *mmm* me, missy. You know very well I gave you an opportunity and I want to know if you grabbed the bull by the horns."

I smiled to myself thinking of grabbing Ty by the....

"*Holy Mary, mother of God*!" Goldie pointed out the driver's side window in utter disbelief. Her mouth hung open, her eyes wide. What on earth could make Goldie speechless?

"Mom! What's the camper doing over there?" Zach yelled.

I yanked my head to the left. There, moving parallel to the car, was the pop-up camper. All white and shiny. Even the black pin stripe down the side was clearly visible...since it was only four feet away.

I shifted my eyes off the camper for a split second and back on the road.

I was going straight.

The camper was going straight.

The road curved to the right.

"Holy crap!"

My brain finally kicked in and I yanked the wheel to stay on the road. Both feet slammed the brakes. All four of us, as well as two gnomes, whiplashed in our seat belts and watched, stunned, as the camper rolled right past us, off the road, across the dirt shoulder and over the edge into the creek.

# 11

"What the—" Ty yelled as he stormed through my backyard over to the patio. The Colonel was here. So were Goldie and Paul. We'd just finished a late dinner, the dirty dishes still on the table in front of us. He wore his fire uniform with a pager and walkie-talkie still clipped to his belt. Obviously, he'd come over directly from work.

I cleared my throat and tilted my head toward the boys playing in the sandbox with their gnomes.

"—*heck* is going on? We're wrapping up a gas leak on Durston and a county sheriff tells me this insane story about a call he just came from. It was a runaway camper up near Hyalite. I started laughing as it sounded so insane, hilarious even, but then I got this crazy feeling." He ran a hand over his face as if trying to remain calm. "I asked him if the camper by any chance belonged to a woman named Jane West. The sheriff starts laughing. You know what he said?" His voice started to get even louder. I'd never seen Ty so flustered. "He said I sure know how to pick a girlfriend!"

Out of the corner of my eye I saw Goldie's brows go up. I ignored her.

"Girlfriend?" I squeaked. I never knew he thought of me as his *girlfriend.*

Ty shut his eyes. I guessed he was counting to ten. When he opened them, he said, "You. Only you would pick out that word from everything I've said." He swiveled and pointed at Goldie. "Okay, maybe you, too." He shifted back to me. "Your camper disconnected, ran off the road and into the creek!"

"If I hadn't been there and seen it first hand, I wouldn't have believed it either," the Colonel said. "I think I'm calm in most situations, say, war for example, but I tell you, when I saw that camper alongside their car, I almost had a heart attack. Jell-O?"

The Colonel scooped up his lemon and whipped cream concoction onto a plate and held it out to Ty. For about five seconds, Ty just stared at the yellow and white jiggling glob. He had no choice but to take it. He dropped down into an empty seat and started shoveling it in. With a full mouth, he couldn't do a lot of talking.

After a few bites, he pointed his spoon at me. "How does a pop-up camper with only two wheels manage to stay upright long enough to do"—his wrist rotated his spoon around in circles—"whatever it does to roll down the road and into the creek?"

"That's the part that bothers me," Paul added, holding Goldie's hand. He'd switched his on-call shift with another doctor after he heard of our camper fiasco and stuck like glue to his wife's side. "Jane said she raised the wheel jack and connected the safety chain to the hitch on her car before they pulled out of the campsite."

Ty looked at me and I nodded.

"I checked it, too," the Colonel said. "It was hooked up just like it's supposed to be."

I looked at him, surprised. He smiled at me. "I like to make sure everyone's safe."

I smiled back.

"Then how? If the hitch didn't hold, the chain would have

caught the camper and kept it from rolling away. Besides, the front jack would have hit the ground and just dragged. There's no way anyone could miss that. The sound would have been terrible and sparks probably would have shot up in the air."

"The wheel jack was down," I said. I poked at the remainder of my Jell-O. "When the tow truck pulled it out of the creek, it was down, not up like it's supposed to be for travel."

Ty sat forward in his chair, placed his arms on the table, gazed at me with a new intensity. "Are you telling me someone tampered with the camper?"

"Looks that way," Goldie added. She'd been unusually quiet since the incident. It was a treat to have her off my back, but I could live without the reason why. "We stopped to fish at the bend above the beaver dam. We were all down by the water for close to an hour. It could have happened there."

"I didn't see a thing. I fell asleep," I told Ty.

"Let me get this straight. Someone disconnected the safety chain and unlatched the hitch so it would come loose around one of the turns or over a bump. They lowered the wheel jack so that when it did come loose, it wouldn't tip over, but ride on three wheels, at least for a little way."

I nodded.

"The question is: Why?" added the Colonel. He looked between me and Ty. He was a smart man. He'd been to war. He knew when things had been left out. People didn't just sabotage a camper for the hell of it.

I glanced at Ty. He grimaced, nodded his head but stayed quiet.

"In this particular case, someone wanted to scare me, but I think someone is trying to kill me."

---

I RELATED ALL that had happened over the past week, sharing

the details about the gnomes, the vial, Morty Moore, the explosion, the convenience store holdup and the derby car. No one said a word. Goldie's mouth clamped tighter and tighter as I went on until her lips were barely visible. Paul remained quiet. Most likely contemplating all the details.

"The only thing that doesn't fit is the convenience store robbery. That was happenstance, although I have to say you have a knack for finding trouble," said the Colonel.

Ty looked at me as if he wanted to say, *I told you so.*

"Everything that's happened up until today has all been directed at you," Paul pointed out. "Your gnomes, your doorstep, your camper. Even the derby car. Ty was there too, but he aimed for you."

"At work today, I had time to check with the fairgrounds and friends with the police." Ty scraped smears of yellow on the plate with his spoon. "A derby car was stolen from the ready area. A driver was pistol whipped and left behind a hay bale."

"Is he going to be all right?" I asked, alarmed. It only confirmed it hadn't been an accident. It also confirmed whoever wanted me harmed was serious, hurting some innocent person like that. Besides me, that is.

"Just got his clocked cleaned. Concussion. He'll be fine in a few days."

"Unlike the derby car, the camper today seems more like a warning. Like someone's trying to tell you they're watching you," said the Colonel.

I didn't like the thought. Someone had been there in the canyon, following us. Watching us. Not just me but Goldie, the boys, the Colonel. My family. They'd seen me napping, and then messed with my camper.

"Exactly," Paul continued. "It wasn't meant to kill you, just shake you up. To make you know their intentions. Thankfully, no one was driving the other way and got hit."

"The boys," Goldie said, her voice rough.

Just what I'd been thinking. I hadn't decided what to do with them yet, but I knew they needed to be somewhere safe, somewhere away from me. And that ripped my heart out, knowing we had to separate. I hadn't been away from them for more than a day or two since they were born. The farthest I'd ventured was to an adult merchandise convention in Vegas with Goldie when Bobby was one.

"The boys were in the car. That's where I draw the line. We need them away from here until all this is settled," Paul added.

"I'll take them to your mom's. The boys will think it's an adventure and you know she'll be thrilled to have them. She's coming next month anyway so we'll bring them back then," suggested the Colonel.

Relief washed over me at the idea. In Georgia, they couldn't get any further from the danger. "Thanks, Colonel. It's a great idea. And reassuring. I'll feel better knowing they're with Mom. And you."

"I've wanted an excuse to get down there. And stay." A small smile played about his lips. Maybe a few weeks with my mom could move their romance along. "Now I've got one." The Colonel patted my hand again. "Get the boys packed up. We'll fly out tomorrow."

---

Ty and I were sitting on the couch in my living room watching TV, although I didn't think either one of us was absorbing anything about the ballgame. I didn't even know which team was ahead. I didn't even like baseball. But I did like sitting near Ty. Over a foot of empty couch separated us, but felt like a mile. I knew if I crossed the line, I'd never go back. Figuratively and literally. Ty probably had the same thought, so we kept the No Man's Land there between us. For now.

I had two dark green couches in an L shape facing the TV. Two wood end tables with lamps on the far ends, another one in between. An area rug was beneath a wooden coffee table. On the other couch sat the gnomes, watching the game. The boys had propped them up to watch TV and left them there before they went to bed. They'd said the gnomes were going in their suitcases to Georgia but I planned to change their minds. The gnomes carried some bad mojo and I didn't think it was best to move the mojo across the country. Besides, they'd definitely break. Again.

Goldie and Paul had left. So had the Colonel, to pack. The boys were in bed, asleep. They'd burned off all the excitement from the camper incident and then the news of their trip to see Nana and crashed hard.

I'd spent over an hour talking with my mom on the phone, getting her updated on the whole fiasco my life had turned into. Agreeing the boys would be safest with her for the time being, she immediately hung up on me to book flights online. Beneath her worry, I figured she was secretly excited about seeing the Colonel. For three weeks.

At least they'd have two boys as chaperones. But I wouldn't. I'd be on my own, without any supervision. I could do things I would never do with the boys around. Like fulfilling Goldie's hopes for my non-existent sex life. I wouldn't even have the Colonel in his house separating me from Ty.

"I guess I owe you for saving my life," I told him, beer in hand.

"Which time?"

I stopped to consider. It seemed I had quite a bit of thanking catch-up to do. "I'm thinking of the derby, but I guess the explosion, too. Thank you."

"Great. You're welcome. You owe me dinner. Tomorrow night." Ty slouched down, feet up on the coffee table, arms crossed.

I tilted my head. "For saving my life? That's all you want?" I flushed realizing what I'd said.

I could tell he had more on his mind than just dinner. "For

now." He had that look in his eyes that I was starting to recognize as the I'm-going-to kiss-you look.

I hopped up from the couch. "Well," I said, nervous. I did not want him to kiss me now. Not with the kids in the other room. Not when we couldn't finish what came after a kiss. Besides, I didn't know if Ty had decided to put a kybosh on his kybosh of our friendship, relationship. Whatever he called it.

Sure, we'd kissed at the derby. But I'd kissed him first. And there'd been tons of adrenaline pumping through our veins along with lust. Maybe I'd get the answers at dinner tomorrow.

He stood up, both of us close and fenced in by the coffee table. His hand came up, brushed gently over my cheek. "Tomorrow. Definitely tomorrow."

And he wasn't talking about pizza and beer.

---

"How long did you cry?" Ty asked the next night at dinner. We sat at a four top at a brew pub on Main. I had the chicken burrito, Ty the steak. The building was an old warehouse, brick with turn-of-the-century photographs on the walls. A vintage train car was built into the side to add ambiance, and history dating back to the golden age of railroad. Since it was a nice night, we'd ridden our bikes down the Galligator Trail, past the new library, to the restaurant.

"What makes you think I did?" I asked.

Ty didn't reply, just took a sip of his beer.

I rolled my eyes. "An hour," I admitted.

I'd dropped the boys and the Colonel off at the airport after lunch. The entire morning had been spent running around trying to find a missing flip-flop, packing enough snacks for the plane and crazily searching for medical release forms. I'd tried my best not to cry until I got home and made it as far as the garage before I'd lost it. I didn't know how long I'd sat and cried into the steering wheel. After that, I climbed in bed and threw the blankets over my head. I woke up ten minutes before dinner with Ty.

I'd rushed to pull myself together, splashing cold water on my face to reduce the puffiness around my eyes. I'd run a brush through my hair, pulled it back in a loose ponytail so some curls hung around my face. Swiped on some tinted lip balm. I'd thrown on a pair of black Capri pants with a white cotton shirt, slipped on simple black sandals and called it good.

My babies had left the state for weeks and it hurt. Who cared about makeup and pulling myself together for a date when my children were hurtling through the sky in a tin can at five hundred miles an hour...without me to protect them?

Ty took my hand and squeezed. The simple touch felt good. Soothing. Reassuring.

"I heard from the fire investigators about the explosion at the Moore's house. As we thought, there was a propane gas leak."

"Duh," I said. I tucked a curl behind my ear.

"At first, there was talk about a homemade pipe bomb in the garage."

I looked at him blankly. "You mean like extremists in Idaho?" We never mentioned extremists in Montana like the Unabomber. They were all in Idaho now.

Ty smiled, but didn't comment on that touchy subject. "That was nixed pretty fast. A propane tank is usually positioned away from the house and down a hill or embankment of some kind to prevent a gas leak from filling the house. The Moore's tank was next to the house, which is rare. Should have been moved years ago." Ty took a sip of his beer.

"Okay, go on."

"Propane inside the tank is liquid then converts to a gas when it mixes with air. Propane gas is heavier than air so it settles low to the ground. It should have spread into the basement and to the hot water heater or furnace where it would ignite."

"Right," I said. This whole gas thing was a little over my head. I knew he was speaking English, but not all of it made sense. Some of it. But I never really thought about blowing a house up before. "Go on."

"The Moore's water heater and furnace weren't in the basement, but in a closet off the garage. Not uncommon, although most are in basements. I guess since the house didn't actually have a basement, they were given a space off the garage."

This I understood. "My friend Kelly's house is like that." I suddenly had a really crappy thought. "Should I be concerned about her house blowing up?"

He casually pointed his fork toward me. "No. She doesn't use propane, nor did someone tamper with her gas pipe."

Thankfully true. "How did they tamper with the pipe?"

"Pipe wrench." Ty took a bite of his steak.

I nodded my head envisioning someone with a huge wrench crouching down behind the Moore's house. Conceivable since the yard was lined with very mature lilac bushes. Definitely shielded from neighbors.

"Long story short, we smelled gas because we were downwind. Whoever did it must've assumed the water heater was in a basement or a lower portion of the house where they hoped the whole house would be launched to Kingdom Come. But they were wrong and it didn't cause a huge explosion."

"This wasn't a big explosion?" I asked, amazed.

Ty shook his head. "This one just flung crap through the air and made a huge mess."

"Huge," I added, thinking of the collapsed garage and Ty's smooshed truck.

"Huge," Ty repeated. "But the idiot didn't know about the water heater off the garage, and when the gas seeped in, it filled just that area and the pilot light ignited it quickly. There wasn't time for the gas to fill the lower area of the house. Besides, the propane tank itself was almost empty. The Moores never had it refilled before they moved to Arizona. That's why the most damage was to the garage and the left side, nor overly big. He didn't make a real explosion, thank God. He just wrecked the house."

"Like I said, that wasn't a big explosion? I don't have a lot of comparison here," I added, sarcastically.

"Let me put it this way. If it had been a serious propane tank explosion, instead of the fridge being on top of my truck, it would have landed on someone else's a mile away."

Okay, that's a big explosion. "So you're saying this was done by an amateur."

"I'd say an Internet-savvy, anti-social person intent on hurting someone."

"I'm an idiot when it comes to gas, although I can light my grill." I sipped my iced tea.

Ty nodded. "Yeah, I'd say you're at least that smart."

I smacked him on the shoulder. "Funny. But we still don't know Morty's whereabouts. All we do know about whoever's trying to hurt me is that he's some half-cocked person spending too much time online. That's probably half of the population of the US."

"True. But he was obviously trying to blow up the Moore's house. And just that house. As I said, Mr. and Mrs. Moore have been out of town for a while. They weren't the target. Someone wants Morty dead, someone who knew he'd been staying there." Ty ate a couple of bites. "The real worry is when whoever's doing this decides to get smart."

"Because they're trying to kill me now, too," I added. We didn't comment more on that but ate instead. My burrito didn't taste as good as it had a minute ago. Or maybe it was the whole death and destruction thing that put me off my food.

My cell phone rang. I jumped in my seat and grabbed for my bag, frantic to find the phone.

"Relax, the kids are fine."

I gave him the evil eye. I looked at the caller ID. Phew, not CNN calling about a downed commercial airliner.

"Hi, Goldie," I said. I took a deep breath, my heart rate slowly dropping back into normal range.

"We've got a doozy of a problem."

"Okaaaaay." That could mean a thousand different things.

"No, no, don't worry, I'm fine. You're the one with all the secret admirers," she said sarcastically. "Remember the bachelorette party we arranged to do?"

"Sure, it's next month." I absently forked up a bite of burrito. Ty watched me as he ate some fries.

"Actually, it's tonight. It's a surprise party. The bride was at the store with her girlfriends and they couldn't blow it by giving the actual day. So, they told us next month. Unfortunately, dingbats that they are, they forgot to call us and tell us about the real date. Until now."

I looked at my watch. Six thirty.

"What time's the party?"

"Eight."

"Holy crap."

Ty perked up at that.

"I've got everything organized and in boxes here at the store. I just need you to pick them up and get to the party."

I took a deep breath. "Fine. Call Dingbat back and tell her we won't be there until eight thirty. She can make do until then. We'll be by the store in an hour to get everything. And Goldie, make sure you get good directions. The last time I drove all over trying to find the place."

Goldie hung up. No goodbye.

"Dingbat?" Ty asked.

"Don't worry, you'll meet her."

"Huh?" A fry was halfway to his mouth.

"How do you feel about bachelorette parties?" I scarfed down a bite of my meal.

"Never been to one."

"That's about to change."

"Oh really? Male stripper call in sick or something?"

I contemplated that for a moment, the image of Ty stripping like a Chippendale dancer. It actually wasn't a pretty thought. I've never been big on strippers. Didn't do a thing for me. Seeing Ty naked though was something entirely different. And maybe watching him take his clothes off might not be so bad either. The idea made me hot all over. I took a sip of my iced tea to cool off. As long as when he finished he was naked instead of wearing some pouchless briefs or banana hammocks. Gross.

"Have experience with that? If you do, you may not want to mention it to Goldie or you might have a side job." I paused to let Ty consider this back-up career. "Actually, we scheduled a toy party for a couple of bachelorettes last week. There was some confusion about the dates. It's tonight. We've got two hours to get there."

"We?" he asked. I could tell he was a little nervous. What guy wanted to break the invisible barrier between men and women and end up at a bachelorette party? He had every right to be anxious. The few males who ended up at one were only wearing neon yellow nut huggers and a pair of cowboy boots.

"Don't worry. You'll keep your clothes on. I thought you didn't want me going anywhere by myself. Besides, I'm your *girlfriend*." It was a perfect time to throw that word out there. See what I might reel back in.

Ty took a swig of his beer. "You're right. I don't want you going off by yourself with everything that's happened, but I draw the line at stripping in front of a bunch of women, especially one named Dingbat. If you want me to take my clothes off, we can go back to your house—or mine. You can even help." He lifted his eyebrows rakishly and took another swig of beer. "But here's the thing you need to know if you're going to be my girlfriend."

He looked me in the eye. I was practically hypnotized by their blueness.

I licked my lips in anticipation. I hadn't been a girlfriend since tenth grade. And that consisted of holding hands while walking through the mall. I dated. I married. There had been no girlfriend status ever with Nate. "What's that?"

Ty's mouth twitched. "I can cut my own meat."

I looked down at my fork and knife. I was so flustered by the boys' departure, the night's change in plans, the imagery of Ty getting naked, I didn't even notice what I'd been doing.

I had cut up Ty's steak into little bite sized pieces, just like I did for Zach and Bobby.

# 12

"Oh shit," Ty mumbled as we rolled up to the house for the bachelorette party. You couldn't miss it. Unless the house had penis-shaped balloons attached to the mailbox just *because*. "This can't be good."

We were in Belgrade, near the airport. The subdivision was brand new with matching street lamps all the way down the road. The house had two stories, painted a cheery yellow with red shutters. The two-car garage took up most of the lower floor except for a tiny porch and front door. The yard had been put in by landscapers but ended abruptly at the property line on either side as the home abutted two empty lots.

"Where's your sense of adventure?" I mocked. Secretly, I was enjoying every moment of this. His discomfort was comical and I tried hard not to laugh. Hell, I tried hard not to crack a smile.

"I will be the first man in the history of the world who's ever gone to a bachelorette party unpaid."

"I think you have enough testosterone to make it out alive." My mouth twitched.

Ty popped the trunk of his rental car. He'd insisted on driving as his car was unfamiliar to anyone who might consider following me and doing me harm. It was a pale blue two door and small enough to fit in the bed of Ty's pickup truck. It was a clown car and he had to practically fold himself in half to fit behind the wheel. Its only saving grace was a remarkably large trunk. Ty was a big man and he needed room. Lots and lots of room the rental could not provide. I could imagine him standing on the curb waiting for the mailman to arrive with his insurance check just to be rid of his pint-sized rental. Images of the boys waiting for the ice cream truck came to mind.

I started digging through the boxes Goldie packed for me.

"What the hell?" Ty asked as he picked up a rubber dildo from the box. The tip of it jiggled like the Colonel's Jell-O. "What on earth do you guys do at a bachelorette party?" he snapped.

"What do you guys do at a bachelor party?" I countered.

Ty's eyes lost focus as he most likely imagined strippers, porn and lots of liquor. "Never mind. Please explain." He couldn't figure out where to hold the dildo, his hands shifting from the shaft to the balls to the tip.

I took it from him. His face looked as if he'd swallowed a bitter pill. "I believe that's the All-American Whopper Dong and friends."

Ty shuffled through the box. Inside were at least ten dildos, all identical. He mumbled something I couldn't catch, but I did hear the words 'women' and 'insane'. I decided to let it go. We weren't even through the door yet.

"You're here!" A woman—from the looks of her—the bride, squealed. She weaved her way down the walkway, most likely very tipsy. Although, if I wore the black patent stilettos she had on, I'd be weaving around, stone cold sober. She wore a white tank top that showed off her youthful breasts. I'd bet my paycheck they'd been medically enhanced. Somehow, she wore a jean skirt that was as big as a Band-Aid and kept everything legally covered. I'm not sure what would happen if she sat down.

Her hair was long, straight and dark. A little poof in the back gave it lift that only came from a half can of hairspray. On her head was a plastic diamond tiara in the shape of the word BRIDE. To accompany this, she wore a Miss America sash that read *Bride To Be*.

"I can't believe the surprise! I thought it was next month! I'm sooooo excited!" She even came up and hugged me. Yup, drunk. She smelled of rum and something fruity. "OMG, we're going to play with dildos! That's great because it matches the party's theme!" I had a pretty good idea what that was. "We've got a penis cake and penis shaped ice in our drinks. This is going to be amazing!" She grabbed the dildo from me and ran back up the walk. As she entered the house I heard more screams than at a ninth-grade sleepover.

We grabbed the boxes and headed inside.

The front door opened onto a family room with two tan couches, a wide screen TV and a fake plant. White walls and bare floors. Probably recently moved in. I quickly counted heads. Nine women of various ages were drinking wine from the box on the coffee table and eating chips and salsa, gabbing like sorority sisters. They ogled the dildo as if it were the Lost Buddha from the Ancient Empire. They sat on the couches, squeezed in like peas in a pod, with one or two ladies on chairs probably pulled in from the kitchen.

All heads swiveled to us and it became as quiet as church on Sunday.

No one looked at me. I could have been naked twirling batons of fire. No one would have noticed. They were all looking at Ty. Like a piece of meat. Okay, I now knew what Ty had been saying when he told me Dex had looked at me that way. These ladies would eat him alive if I wasn't here.

I actually thought I heard Ty gulp. With a shaky smile he said, "Ladies."

"This is Ty," I replied by way of introduction.

"A stripper! I didn't know Goldilocks did that!" A

bridesmaid I recognized from the store squealed with delight. I figured this one was Dingbat.

Ty took a step back.

"No, he's not a stripper," I clarified.

They took in his faded, well-worn jeans and how they hugged his really nice ass. They admired his button-down gray shirt and how it showed off his broad shoulders. It was rolled up at the forearms to reveal tanned and toned muscles. His hair was still cut short and he was clean shaven. I could even smell the soap he used. I didn't blame them the ogling, or taking him for a stripper. He was a man at a bachelorette party, and he'd come with me, the woman who ran the adult store. And of course, he was hot.

A chorus of "Hellooo, Ty" rang out.

He pointed his thumb at me like the Fonz. "She's my girlfriend."

So *now* I was his girlfriend. The ladies looked at me, sizing me up. Was I worthy of a hunk like Ty? Some of the mean looks the women gave me said no.

"Hi, ladies!" I said brightly. "Let's get started." I slid the box of dildos in front of me. "If you each will take one and pass the rest around, great. No, there's enough for everyone. Tonight, you're going to learn how to give your man the blow job of his dreams."

Ty coughed. I looked at him and I swore he choked on spit.

I dug back in the box. "Oh, here, the plastic plates are for you to suction cup your—"

"Cock!" one woman shouted out.

"Dick!" Another.

"Man part." Another.

I laughed. "—whatever-you-want-to-call-it to. You want to keep your hands free. It's all about the mouth."

I should have been mortified I was talking like this in front of Ty. I wasn't because I knew the more I talked on the subject of dildos and BJs and mouths, the more embarrassed he was going to be. And I thought that was hilarious. Goldie would be mighty proud.

The ladies shouted out while they were laughing, wielding their rubber phalluses like swords. This was a typical reaction to this activity. No chance of getting their full attention. I didn't take it personally. I just let it go. It reminded me of Zach's kindergarten class and trying to get them to glue cotton balls on Santa's beard during craft time. Half the Santa's went home with cotton ball pants.

I demonstrated how to do the suction cupping.

"Here, can you hold this for me?" I passed Ty the cock on the plate. He looked at it, the tip jiggling back and forth. Goldie didn't pack the little guys, she went for the eight inchers.

"Uh, sure." Ty started to look panicked. His expression was a cross between extreme embarrassment and intestinal cramping.

"Ty, come sit next to me," a woman who looked a lot like the bride, but thirty years older and wearing a longer skirt, purred.

Between the ladies ogling him, the super-sized man part on a dinner plate and the cat calls, I wasn't sure what was worse for him. "Ladies, leave Ty alone," I scolded gently.

"Now, don't worry, all of the dildos have been washed and sanitized." I grabbed for the condoms at the bottom of the box. "So, if you can each take one of these, I'm going to show you how to roll a condom on just using your mouth."

The ladies hurriedly passed the foil packages around then heard several thwaps where the rubber smacked the plates.

"If you're at the coffee table, you can just stick them on there instead." Some ladies ran with this idea.

I ripped open a foil packet and pulled out the condom, then held my hand out to Ty to get my plate back for the demonstration. I looked at him and smiled. He winced back.

I sat down on the arm of the couch. "Stick the condom, all rolled up on the tip like this. Good. Just like that." I paused and waited through the sexual banter, laughing and talking until almost everyone had finished. "Now, you'll use your mouth and tongue to slowly unroll the condom as you move down your man's penis. Like this."

I leaned forward to demonstrate.

"I'm out of here," Ty said as my mouth was almost on the dildo. He was halfway out the door before I got the plate onto the coffee table.

"Ladies, you try it. I'll be right back."

I walked out onto the front porch and heard the ladies laughing and chatting behind me.

"I thought you didn't want me left alone just in case someone...you know." I tucked a stray curl behind my ear.

Ty stood on the front walk, stuffed his hands in his jeans pockets. "Sweetheart, no man is going to come to a bachelorette party to hurt you. After what I saw in there, he'd kill himself first."

"So where are you going to go?"

"There's a ballgame on somewhere." He looked at his watch. "How much time do you need?"

"Mmm, can't say for sure."

We both heard a woman shouting, "My man's gonna get some tonight!"

"Right. Just call me when you're done."

---

It was late when we pulled into Ty's driveway. I wasn't the least bit tired even though it was after eleven. I was hyper-aware of him sitting next to me, his body only inches from mine. A tiny car sure came in handy at times like this. It was easy to brush up against each other. Which happened a few times on the way home. It had been accidental the first time, but the second, I had to admit I faked it and leaned in. I couldn't help myself. I needed body-to-body contact. A girl had to fake it every once in a while. Although I hoped I wouldn't have to fake it much—or ever again—with Ty.

"Let me help you get these boxes into your garage."

"Is that a euphemism for something?" I asked, coyly.

"You've been hanging around Goldie too much. It means, I have to work tomorrow and I can't have adult sex toys in my car at the station."

"Right," I replied, mollified. Huh. Shot down. He must still be grumpy from the bachelorette party ogling. I wanted him to kiss me, to *touch* me!

We both hefted a box to carry to my garage, trudging across the Colonel's front yard. The air was cool, a slight breeze made the leaves rustle in the ash tree above our heads. Ty waited patiently as I glumly punched in the code to the door opener. The single bulb popped on, giving us just enough light to dump them unceremoniously in a free spot. "I guess I don't have to be as careful as you, or as I usually am. With the boys away—"

One second I was talking, the next Ty's hands were on my shoulders pushing me roughly against the side of my car. His mouth was on mine before I could even make an umph. Huh, rough was a major turn-on. Who knew?

I could feel every inch of Ty's body pressed into mine. A knee nudged my legs apart and he was even closer. I could feel the muscled slab of chest against my breasts, his hips against my stomach. Hello! I could feel something else against my stomach and it wasn't made out of rubber, nor did it have suction cups, but it felt like a solid eight inches.

His tongue plunged into my mouth, his hands moved to my hair.

I was pinned. There was nowhere for me to go. Not that I was complaining. Why would I want to go anywhere except to my bed? *With Ty.*

"This," he shifted his hips, pressing his man part, his cock, his dick, up against all the right places, "is just the beginning of what I want to do to you."

Ty started kissing my neck, nibbling at my ear.

"Beginning?" I whispered, angling my head.

"Mmm hmm." He started telling me all the dirty things he was going to do to me, with me. Thank God he held me up or I would have melted into a puddle on the concrete floor. I felt the ache, the need for him...*everywhere*. Who knew he could be so creative?

"You can do that with a chair?" I asked. Wow.

"Uh huh." He whispered more.

"On my knees?" I gasped.

And more.

"With your tongue?"

"Fuck, yes." I could feel him smile into my neck. "And sweetheart, toys sure are fun, but I don't need them to get you off."

"Okay," I replied breathlessly, before I pulled his mouth back to mine. Yes! I was ready. My body was more than ready. No toys. I was fine with that. I could hear an orgasm calling my name. Maybe more than one! A chorus of orgasms singing in my ears.

The timed light on the garage door opener clicked off. Darkness.

We progressed from there, right against my Jeep. Ty's hands were on the buttons of my shirt, his fingers fumbling slowly with one button at a time. My hands slipped around his waist and down to his butt while we kissed.

*Briiingg.*

No! Not Ty's cell! We ignored it, his mouth too busy locked to mine to answer it.

*Briiingg.*

"Shit," Ty said, our foreheads touching, breaths mingling, his hands on the second button down on my shirt, or was that the third?

He pulled his cell from his pocket, leaned back. “Hi, Dad.”

I gently pushed him off and gave him some room. I didn’t need his hands on me while he talked to his father. Being interrupted by a parent was close to the best libido killer ever. Even in your thirties with two kids.

“What?” he yelled. I couldn’t see his face, but from the tone, it didn’t sound good. “Where?” He listened. “When?” More listening. “Shit.”

He ended the call. “You’re not going to believe this. Morty’s turned up.”

I had a really bad feeling about this. “Let me guess, he’s dead?”

“Yeah. Someone dumped him on my parents’ ranch.”

“What do you mean dumped him?”

“You really want to know?”

I nodded, then realized he probably couldn’t see it. “Yes.”

“Someone put a bullet in his brain, chopped him up and fed him to my parents’ pigs.”

“Holy crap.”

“I need to go to my parents’ but I can’t leave you here all alone knowing there’s a lunatic who chops up bodies on the loose. You’re spending the night at Goldie and Paul’s.”

I wasn’t very interested in being alone with a lunatic on the loose either. The thought of being by myself gave me the willies. “No problem.”

“Pack a bag and I’ll follow you over there.”

I rang Goldie and told her I was coming. While I dug through my clothes, I listened as Ty called in to work to get the day off. It was a haul to get to Pony, close to two hours, and he’d have to deal with the police in the morning.

Any interest we might have had in sex had been killed off, just like Morty. It definitely wasn’t the right time for the two of us. We’d both given it the old *college try*, but something always seemed to get in the way. Dead bodies, homicidal maniacs, gnomes with semen inside.

Ty followed me the short distance to Goldie's in his rental car. All was quiet and dark. Goldie was at the front door waiting for me, the porch light on. She wore a thick robe. Her hair was mussed.

I climbed out of my car, went over to Ty who was in his loaner car. His window was rolled down.

"Later," Ty said. I read it two ways, as in *see you later* and in *later we will have sex.*

# 13

"I swear your life was as boring as could be before all this hubbub started," Goldie commented the next night while inventorying lickable body lotion at the store.

The phone rang.

"No kidding," I replied, taking over the lotion stocking. Goldie liked to answer her own phone.

"Goldilocks. We're open until midnight. Yes, we have bondage items. What are you looking for specifically?" Goldie pulled out a pen and scrap paper. "Uh huh, okay, right," she mumbled as she took notes. "If you're interested in all that, you may just want to start dating a police officer." Goldie laughed. "We have everything on your list. Stop in and we'll get you all set up."

She came back to the aisle and started stacking the dusting powders. Strawberry and piña colada were the current choices. "The boys called me this morning."

"I know," I said wistfully. "They called me, too. They were very excited about going to the beach today."

Goldie patted my shoulder. "They'll be fine."

Of course, they were having too much fun to be homesick, but what about me?

"So how was last night?" Obviously, Goldie decided to change the subject. She, no doubt, missed the boys, too.

I stopped shelving and grinned at her. "Ty came with me."

That stopped Goldie's hand mid-motion. "You're kidding me." She laughed again. "That man has a *thi-ing* for you. If you can't see it, you're an idiot. He went to a bachelorette party. That's love."

I put the lotion down. "No way," I said, nervous. Sweat formed on my upper lip.

"Have you ever, in your entire life, heard of a man going to a bachelorette party?"

"Well..."

"One who's not a stripper."

"No." I thought back to Ty at the bachelorette party, how miserable he'd been. Does miserable mean love? How the hell would I know?

"I'm surprised you didn't go with him last night to his parents instead of staying with us." Goldie stood, dusted off her jeans. She wore a matching jean jacket, white blouse and gold hoop earrings. Her hair was left down long, curling artfully about her shoulders.

I, on the other hand, wore jeans and plain shirt, this time in green. I had simple black flats on my feet. My hair, too, was left down, but I habitually tucked it behind my ears.

"I wanted to go with him. I was anxious to learn more about Morty and his gruesome death. But I wasn't prepared to meet Ty's parents."

The bell on the door dinged the arrival of a customer.

"Hello!" Goldie called out. "Let us know if you need any help."

She turned back to me and looked me up and down. "I'll say you weren't prepared. When you came to pick up those boxes for the party last night you wore black pants and a white shirt. You call that date-wear? Someone might have taken you for a waitress." She all but glared daggers at me. "How are you going to land a man in an outfit like that, let alone win over his parents?"

"I don't think they would have noticed what I wore with a chopped up dead body in their pig sty."

Goldie moved her head from side to side, contemplating. "You have a point there. But"—she pointed her finger at me —"you're not having sex with his parents."

"I'm not having sex with Ty either," I grumbled.

"I know how to take care of that."

"Not another box!"

"No, but that couldn't hurt either. Wear something sexy and I guarantee that will change."

A man wearing a camo T-shirt with jeans interrupted us. Mid-twenties. I pegged him for a video rental. "I'm looking for *Tappin' that White Ass 2*. Do you have that in stock?" Yup, video.

"Karl, how are you tonight?" Goldie asked the man, making small talk as she walked behind the main counter. "Have you seen the first one yet?"

"Yes, ma'am."

"All right then." She turned to the wall of DVD's, looked under the T's and found the film. "You know, I think there's something else you might like." She hadn't turned around because she was still searching. "Here it is." She placed it on the glass counter and smiled. "*Bubble Butt Buffet*. On the house."

"Thanks, Miss Goldie." Karl handed over his money and left, two videos in a brown paper bag.

Goldie liked to treat her customers right. She knew Karl would be back. She did the same for almost everyone. And almost everyone treated Goldie right. If they saw her in the grocery store, they said hello. If she needed help, people lined up to offer her aid. It paid to be nice. And offer buy-one-get-one-free porn.

A few more customers came through, buying and browsing.

After an hour, we were back to restocking, this time various tubes and bottles of lube.

"What did Ty learn about the dead man?"

I laughed.

"What's so funny?" she wondered.

"You. Only you would ask about my dating wardrobe before a dead body."

"Well?"

She wasn't deterred.

"Fine. It was Morty Moore. Ty said he could be identified, once the parts were cleaned off of pig junk, pretty easily. The hacker didn't do a very good hacking job." I grimaced. "Besides, I guess his wallet was left on top of one of the fence posts."

"His poor parents." Goldie took a moment to be sad, knowing what his parents were going through, but brightened back up. "That's some stupid killer. Why would you go to all the effort to chop him up and leave the ID? Even I wouldn't do that. I'd even chuck the head, the hands and feet in different places so he couldn't be identified."

I wrinkled my nose and looked at Goldie funny. "You're gross."

"Aren't I right?"

She was, but that was beside the point. "Yeah, but Ty and the police think he was meant to be identified. Morty had nothing to do with the Strickland's ranch. It's nowhere near where he lived or where he worked. Ty thinks they dumped him there as another message." I rubbed my finger over the letters on the plastic lube bottle absently. "Whoever is doing this knows Ty and I are...are something. They know the quickest way to get to Ty would be to mess with his family. He thinks the killer is telling him he knows about Ty's interest in me and what can happen. To all of us."

"Well, hell."

---

"Let me guess, Goldie called you," I grumbled when I opened my door to Kelly the next morning. I should have been surprised to see her, but I wasn't. I'd spent the night in my own home, doors locked. I liked Goldie and Paul, but I wasn't moving into their house while this fiasco was resolved. Ty had been home, but probably snoring by the time I'd gotten off work. Having him two doors down had been reassuring, although in my bed would have been better.

"Show me the coffee." She pushed past me into the kitchen and stopped short, pointing at the gnomes sitting on the counter. "What are they doing here?" Sounded as if they were some bad guys screwing up my life. Maybe they were.

"The boys wanted to bring them when we went to the airport. I brought them in from the car and left them there."

Kelly picked George the Gnome up and twisted and turned him around. Eyed him expertly. "Nice glue job." She put it down and turned to the coffee pot.

"Thanks." I'd had plenty of practice fixing things, doing craft projects and making Halloween costumes with the glue gun. Kelly trumped me by five kids and had a Masters' degree in gluing arts. When she gave glue compliments, it was serious.

Once she'd filled a mug, she opened the fridge. "Where's the milk?"

"All out," I said. She looked at me like I was crazy. I guess they never ran out of milk at her house.

She sighed, resigned to drinking it black, leaned against my counter and gave me the evil eye. "You wore Capri pants and a white T-shirt on a date? With Ty? I swear I don't know how you're my friend."

I felt contrite and defensive all at the same time.

"Do you or do you not want to have sex again in this lifetime?" She took a swig of coffee.

"Now you sound like Goldie." To deflect a response, I refilled my own mug. It was ten o'clock, early enough to keep pumping in the caffeine. "Yes, of course I want to have sex."

"With Ty?"

"Yes, with Ty. *Especially* with Ty."

Kelly nodded her head, her cute, perky haircut bouncing about. She wore multi-colored plaid shorts with a white cotton blouse with a small frill along the button line. I took stock of my own hair. Ponytail. My own clothes. Tan shorts, white T-shirt with a small flower printed on the front. Flip-flops.

"You look so cute." I pointed to her outfit. I looked down at myself and groaned. Realized the sad truth. "I dress like the Colonel."

"At least he presses his clothes."

I kind of felt like crying. "Hey, that hurt."

She placed her mug on the counter and gave me a hug. "You either need some cuter—and sexier—clothes or the next time Ty stops by, answer the door naked. This is an intervention." She put my mug down too, even though I hadn't even had a chance to sniff it, let alone drink any. "I've got the rest of the day. Without children. Let me reiterate. Without children. We're going shopping. We're going to find you a wardrobe that makes you look hot, sexy and totally fuckable."

This day was as much for Kelly as it was for me. The opportunity for the two of us to shop without any kids, hers or mine, was rare. She wanted out of her house and I was a great excuse. Besides, if I dressed like a sixty-something man, I needed serious help and answering the door naked wasn't an option. Or I didn't want it to be my only option.

"Okie dokie."

---

AN HOUR LATER, we were on Main Street checking out the shops. The business district was about ten blocks long, from the new library on the east to the old high school on the west. Red brick buildings from the late 1800s to more modern eras lined both sides of the four-lane road. Flower baskets hung from attractive street lamps. It had a quaint western feel. Very small town. Stores included restaurants to used book stores to baby boutiques. Not one chain store. The Parade of Lights, the Taste of Bozeman, the car show, homecoming and the Sweet Pea Festival race all closed Main Street down for family fun. I'd never seen another town that liked to close the main thoroughfare through town for the benefit of the community instead of motorists.

We were in a women's clothing store where I'd tried on three different fancy dresses, all with various parts of skin exposed. Fancy to me wasn't prom; it was when I had to wear earrings, makeup and heels all at the same time. I found a little black dress that had tiny buttons running up the front. It had a deep V neck and small capped sleeves. I felt covered, but feminine at the same time. There was not one speck of bling on it. Goldie wouldn't touch it with a ten-foot pole, but I liked it. Kelly approved, so it was a keeper.

Kelly was in a changing room trying on a pile of items from the sale rack and probably would be awhile.

"I'm going for coffee. I need energy," I called through the purple velvet curtain.

"You had some at home," she called back. Obviously, she was afraid I'd make a break for it while she was in her underwear and unable to chase me down.

"No, you had some," I grumbled. "You took mine away and pushed me out the door. I'll be back in ten minutes. Want some?"

"Usual."

I shoved the bag with my new dress under the curtain for Kelly to keep with her. I heard a zipper so I figured I'd have some time before she redressed.

I made my way down the block to the nearest coffee shop, ordered our usual and waited. I had a mocha with skim, no whipped cream. Kelly got the fancier caramel apple latte, with an extra pump of vanilla, whipped cream, and soy milk. She ordered it because she knew I wouldn't drink it even if I was crawling through the desert and it was the only liquid in sight.

With the beverages in hand, I made my way out of the shop only to bump right into Dex in the doorway.

"That for me?" He pointed to the coffee.

I was completely flummoxed. His spicy cologne wafted up and mingled with the aroma of coffee. His broad chest was a millimeter away from mine in the doorway. A fly couldn't squeeze through. Boy, he was big. I had no choice but to tilt my head back to look him in the eye unless I wanted to stare at his shirt collar all day.

Wow. His brown eyes were really mesmerizing. I wasn't sure what it was about Dex, but he could suck you in. Really hot guys had a way of making your whole body freeze up, your brain turn to mush.

"Um, sure." I handed him Kelly's froufrou drink. He would change his mind about lingering once he took a sip.

Someone wanted in the coffee shop so Dex placed a hand at the small of my back and ushered us both out onto the pavement. Cars drove by. A woman with a screaming baby in a stroller dashed by, probably wishing they were at home for naptime.

"Jane, how are you?" Dex stood in front of me, still too close. His hand moved to my shoulder, as if to keep me from running away. I felt the warmth of it through my shirt. He wore jeans and boots as he had the other times I'd seen him but today wore a dark blue button-up. The sleeves were rolled up, the collar open. Not like a seventies-era swinger with a bunch of gold chains and ample chest hair, but just the right amount. As a rancher, I bet he didn't own a pair of shorts or sneakers.

I noticed a woman eyeing him as she walked past.

He didn't seem bothered by that, nor was he rude by giving her any attention while talking with me. Was there a hint of gentleman in there? He wasn't in any rush to move his hand. I stepped back, uncomfortable at his lingering touch.

I took a big swig of my mocha and burned my tongue. I winced. "Fine, fine."

"I saw you on the news about the gas station robbery. I have to admit, I don't like hearing you were mixed up in a dangerous situation like that. I wouldn't want to see you harmed." His words rang sincere, but from our previous sexually laced conversations, I couldn't figure out his angle. Or if there even was one. "You're much too special to get mixed up with the likes of that loser."

I thought back to the convenience store. The guy was definitely a loser. "I wasn't really mixed up with him, just wrong place, wrong time." I intentionally deflected his compliment, if that was what it really was.

"Yes, but you'd just been at my ranch with me. If you'd stayed longer, you would have missed it entirely. I feel it's my fault."

I bit my lip. "That's nice of you to be concerned, but I don't see how any of it is your fault. Like we both said, that guy was strung out on meth. It was his fault. Besides, nothing happened. I wasn't hurt or anything."

Dex ran a finger over my cheek. "I'm glad." He smiled. It was a killer smile.

I couldn't help but smile back, although I did take a small step back. In the few minutes we'd talked, I hadn't heard one peep of perv.

"Look, I've got to get back to my friend. She's waiting for me." I pointed over my shoulder.

"Would you go to dinner with me tonight?"

Wow. "Um. Really?"

"Really," he repeated.

"You do know I'm not interested in...in doing the things you like to do." I wrinkled my nose, worried I may have said something to make him feel bad. I couldn't help it. Good manners were ingrained.

Dex laughed. "Oh, I don't know about that. Do you like the outdoors, football, skiing?"

"I um…wasn't exactly talking about that."

He winked. "Maybe it would be best if we just start over."

I was completely taken aback. Did Dex have an identical twin? Was he schizophrenic? Was this Gentleman Dex as opposed to Creepy Dom Dex? Not that *all* Doms were creepy. I'd met some who'd come into Goldilocks and knew they adored their submissive. Cherished her. Put her first. I didn't get that vibe from Dex. Instead, to me he seemed both dominant *and* creepy, and that gave me the willies.

But, he could have new answers to the Morty mystery. Dex might know more about his death as his employer. I knew next to nothing, so any information would be helpful. It wouldn't hurt to try to learn something from him. Again. What could happen over dinner? Oh yeah, Ty. He would not be happy about it. Probably the biggest understatement of the year. But he'd be at work. Unless the restaurant caught fire, he would never know.

Then there was the sex part. Was Dex the kind of man who expected it on the first date? And if he did, what did he have in mind?

"Just dinner?" I asked cautiously. I wanted him to know up front where I stood on getting naked. If it was just dinner, it wasn't really a date, right?

"Just dinner," he countered. He put a hand back on my shoulder, leaned down a little so we were eye level. "You pick the place. We can even meet there, if you want." He smiled reassuringly.

I gave in, eager to get details on Morty. "Okay." I nodded my head. "Gilly's Grill."

"Great. I'll meet you there at seven." He gave me a quick, chaste kiss on my cheek before he turned and walked away.

I had to admit, I felt funny things at the brush of his lips against my skin. It might have been his mustache tickling me. I wasn't sure if I should feel creeped out or special.

---

HAVING the boys out of town let me eat what I wanted. I'd made a quick dash to the store after Kelly and I finished shopping to pick up a few essentials. Not graham crackers, macaroni and cheese or baby carrots. No sir. My taste buds were on vacation from kid food. I ran into Town and Country and picked up the milk Kelly had pointed out was finished off, cheese puffs, coffee ice cream, the funny, stinky cheese the boys gagged at, large baked potatoes and a jumbo shrimp ring. Sure, it was an odd combination. I didn't have to eat it all at once, but I'd sure try. As I put the frozen items away, Kelly called.

"Wear one of the dresses tonight with Dex or I will hear about it."

She would, too.

"Yes, ma'am."

"I mean it!" she yelled. A kid screamed in the background. "Shoot, I've got to go. Caroline blew a bubble and it popped all over her hair."

Click.

---

I FELL asleep on my bed, face first, with the bags from the shopping trip at my feet. I'd bought two dresses, a pair of black strappy heels, and underwear from Victoria's Secret at the mall. Kelly ordered me to get matching sets, so I ended up with black lace, red satin and an ivory pair that were made out of some sheer material that left nothing to the imagination.

Initially, Kelly had been disappointed I'd given her coffee away, but forgave me when she learned it was for Dex. Skeptical at first, she grew to the idea of me going to dinner with him. Although she was wary of me going out with a guy who gave me the heebie-jeebies, she'd chalked the whole date up to practice. The more I got out there with guys I knew weren't keepers, the better I'd be once I got to the one who was. Besides, all I had to do with him was eat. Nothing else. Gourmet sex was optional.

Maybe the keeper was Ty. At this point, I didn't know. I had feelings for him. All kinds of feelings. Did they include love? It was possible but, for now, it was all clouded by the whole someone-wanted-me-dead issue.

At six, I rolled out of bed, showered, shaved, primped and spritzed, and was out the door by seven. Only a little bit late. I'm usually a stickler for punctuality, but I took too long debating what to wear. Did I choose the new black dress or the new red one? The red one screamed fuck-me-now and I didn't think that was the image I wanted to get across with Dex. My other option was my usual black capris and white shirt, but Kelly warned me she'd shoot me dead if I went in that. So, little black dress it was.

Dex was waiting at the bar, but joined me at the hostess stand when I came in the restaurant. He wore clean Wranglers, boots and another crisp, white shirt. His brown hair was neat, his face shaven except for the handlebar mustache. I had to admit, he looked good. As he approached, his gaze raked over me from head to toe. From the look in his eyes, maybe the black dress screamed fuck-me-now, too. He leaned in and kissed my cheek. "You look lovely. Would you like a drink?"

He guided me by the elbow to the bar where he'd left his beer and white cowboy hat. The bar was crowded so Dex stood and gave me the tall stool. I sat and crossed my legs. Crap, my dress rode up my thigh just shy of slut. Dex definitely noticed.

I took a deep breath to try to calm my nerves. "Um, beer's fine."

He signaled to the bartender, and then turned to me. His leg brushed mine. "I'm glad I ran into you today. I've been thinking a lot about you," he said, without any of the nervousness most men had when admitting their feelings. Dex was one confident man.

My drink came in an icy pint glass. I took a sip. "Really?"

"Like I said at the coffee shop earlier, I think we should start again."

The hostess approached and showed us to our table. Dex, the gentleman, held out my chair for me. Gilly's was an upscale restaurant on Main, located in the basement of one of the older buildings. The ambience was warm, the lighting dimmed and the food excellent. We sat at a table in the back where it was quieter, a small candle between us.

Kelly had told me to use this as a practice date. I wore a dress and heels, had on makeup and earrings. This in itself was out of the ordinary. I definitely needed practice in the super high heels.

Usually I held my feelings and opinions close, especially with someone new. But with Dex, knowing this would be the first, and only, date, I could lay it on the line, stick it all right out there. Like the top half of my breasts in this dress.

It didn't matter what I said. I wasn't trying to impress him. I wanted to make him not like me so there wouldn't be another date. And this wasn't actually a date. It was dinner where I could learn more about Morty Moore. He was the key to finding out who wanted me dead. If dressing up and wearing high heels—and dealing with Dex—was the price for information, I could handle that. For about two hours. Then I turned into a pumpkin and went back to my regular life and comfy clothes.

"Start again? I think you made yourself very clear about what you wanted with me the other times I met you." I held the menu in my nervous fingers.

Dex nodded. "Yes, I did. I still think I'm right."

*Really?* I raised my eyebrows.

"Just hear me out. I took you for someone who was a submissive or possibly interested in being one."

I was offended because that was *soooo* not me. "How could you tell by looking at me? You didn't know anything about me. You still don't."

The waitress came for our orders.

"What would you like?" Dex asked me.

"The fish," I said as I looked at the waitress.

"She would like the fish and I'll have the steak, rare." Dex took my menu and handed them both to the waitress.

"I can order my own food," I commented, my hackles raised. I'd never had someone order for me, except my mom when I was six.

"I have no doubt. But why would you want to? Don't you find comfort with me taking care of your needs, protecting you?"

"From the waitress?" I asked sarcastically.

"Not her specifically, but from the hardships, the dangers in life. Giving the day to day challenges to someone else to handle frees you to take care of different, more appropriate things."

I didn't think ordering food was a hardship, but who was I to say? "What more appropriate things?"

"Your husband, family, home."

I smiled. "So this dinner," I moved my hand to indicate the table, "isn't really a date. You're looking for more, a lot more."

Oh, boy. I was way over my head.

"I admit, I've been with women and knew they were never worthy of being my wife." He took my hands in his large ones. "But the moment I met you, I knew. I want you to be my wife."

# 14

*oly crap.*

"Are you proposing?" I squeaked.

He shook his head, squeezed my fingers. "I'm sorry, I admit, I'm not doing this very well. No, it's not a proposal. I'm stating my intentions. Letting you know I'm serious about you, about us."

I pulled my hands free. "I have a life, a job, *children*." As I took a big gulp of my beer, I wished I had something a whole lot stronger.

"Yes, you do. But your job, you work for your mother-in-law. She would understand your need to care for your family first. And I'm sure your children are wonderful, just like our children will be."

This got weirder and weirder. I actually thought it was funny, and I tried not to laugh. This was every woman's dream! A man who stated his intentions on the first date. Who wanted to commit. To have children. To provide for them in every way. A man who had a job, who was attractive, had all his hair, and most likely would for years to come.

To top it off, out of all the women out there, he wanted me! This was not good.

I didn't want to live out in the boonies. I didn't want more kids. I didn't want to be Suzy Homemaker. I didn't want to be *his* wife.

"Before you said you would take care of things for me. Take care of me. What does that mean?" I wanted clarification and would I take mental notes for Goldie. She'd love to learn the inner workings of a pseudo-Dom—if she didn't know already!

Dex smiled, leaned forward. "If you were my wife, I'd expect you to manage my home, raise our children, be the proper, respectful wife at all times, especially in front of others."

I could only imagine what that meant. And he was *sooo* not a Dom. He was a faux Dom.

"Behind closed doors," he continued, "obedience, the ability to recognize my needs and take care of them immediately."

Um. Hunh.

"And you, as husband and provider, what would I get from you?"

The waitress brought our salads.

Dex didn't touch his but looked at me, intently, seriously. "I will take care of you financially, emotionally, physically. I will make decisions for you—"

"Like what to eat?" I interrupted.

"I would offer my suggestion about what you serve, what you wear, where you go."

Finally. The good stuff.

"These would all be things you like. A rare steak, a revealing dress, things like that?"

He nodded. "That's correct. Wouldn't you want to please me by serving food I like, wear the clothes that make you attractive to me, go places I feel are safe?"

I took a bite of salad, chewed slowly, and swallowed. Stalled. "What wife doesn't want to do that for their husband?" I had to admit, he had a point. When I'd been married to Nate,

I wanted to cook things he liked to eat. I often picked clothes that I knew would turn him on. I called him when I would be out late so he wouldn't worry. "I did that for mine."

Dex pointed his fork at me. "Exactly. When you came to the ranch last week, you were nervous, skittish."

True. But that was because Dex was way more man than I could handle.

"Your husband—I remember you said you'd been married —dominated your spirit, the very essence of who you are. He took that from you, without providing in return."

I swallowed hard. "How do you know that?" Wow, I was having dinner with Dr. Phil.

"I can see it in your eyes when you talk about him." Dex put his fork down, focused on me. "What did he do to you?"

What the hell, I thought. *Practice date. Practice date.* It was the weirdest practice date I'd ever been on. Although this was the first. I sighed. "He cheated on me. Said things that made me feel bad about myself. Left me for another woman."

Dex's jaw clenched in anger. "If he wasn't already dead, I'd kill him. You should not be treated that way." His voice confirmed it.

I smiled weakly. "That's...in a weird way...nice of you to say."

The waitress traded salad plates for entrees.

"He should not have needed to seek out other women. When you are mine, I will make sure you are pleasured sexually, just as much as you will pleasure me. I guarantee there will be no reason to stray."

"And what would happen if I did stray?" I dared to ask.

Dex smiled again, this time without any warmth. He cut his steak. It was so rare I waited for it to moo. "You won't." He put his silverware down and leaned close, his voice a husky whisper only I could hear. "I'll give you the best orgasms of your life. You'll be begging for more."

I blushed. I could feel it to the roots of my hair. This

conversation was going completely the wrong way. How had we gotten this far into what it would be like if I married Dex?

As if!

I wanted to find out about Morty, not Dex's fantasy marriage. Maybe going along with him would get him to share more about himself. It had worked so far. Maybe he'd be compelled to share about Morty. Maybe.

*Okay, play along. Play along.* "Multiple orgasms sound... appealing." I tilted my head and attempted my best flirtatious smile. "Tell me more," I tried to sound seductive, although to my ears it sounded as if I needed a cough drop.

Dex's eyes flared at my sudden interest. He was still close, our conversation intimate enough not to be overheard. "You submit to me in every way, every sexual way, and I'll make you come. Hard. Every time. Once my ring is on your finger, I'll train your body to be constantly aroused. You won't have time, or want to do anything else but pleasure me. I doubt I'll even let you get dressed the first few weeks."

Somehow Dex's dirty talk sounded creepy, not arousing. And I was super creeped out. I *liked* to wear clothes. And he'd forgotten there would be two kids under foot. Sexy times weren't the same with children.

"This is um...a lot to think about." Truest statement I ever made. "But I want to know more about you. About your work, your ranch."

Dex must have felt he'd given a good sales pitch toward marriage as he'd returned to his dinner. After taking a few bites of meat, he asked, "What do you want to know?"

"I heard about the poor man who used to work at your ranch. You know, the one I asked about when I first met you?"

"Right," Dex said, bitterly. "I heard about that, too." I could practically see Dex take a step back emotionally.

*Change tactics! Think!* I reached out and placed my hand on top of his, pinned him with my gaze. "I just worry that something like that might happen to me if I lived with you.

Someone was murdered!" I tried to sound like a complete wuss.

Dex brought my hand up to his lips, kissed my knuckles. "Thanks to you I learned Mr. Moore stole from me and was obviously involved in criminal activity. If someone hadn't already killed him, I assure you, I would have taken care of him myself. No one messes with my ranch, with what's mine."

I could tell that was all I was going to get from Dex about Morty. Which was nothing. Crap. He'd turned all possessive and was smart enough to know I was fishing for information if I asked more.

We finished our meal and Dex walked me to my car. It was almost dark, the sky a deep purple. The air was surprisingly cool. I opened the door and turned to him. He'd moved in close, pinning me between the open door and his body. I could smell his cologne, feel his body heat. "You'll consider all we talked about?"

I nodded. My palms were sweating. My heart pounded in my ears. He was too close, in my circle.

"I'll call you later this week. Dinner again? This time at my house."

He didn't give me an opportunity to answer. His lips found mine before I had a chance to say no. I'd never kissed a man with a mustache. It was odd, ticklish. Like kissing a man and a caterpillar at the same time. Definitely weird. His mouth was warm on mine, tender. It wasn't a possessive kiss, surprisingly gentle considering his size, his dominating personality. I thought about how it must be hard to keep a mustache clean when you ate soup. Was it hot having a mustache? My mind wandered, clearly not into the kiss.

I didn't pull back, didn't push him away either. *Practice date. This was a practice kiss.* Would I ever kiss another guy with a mustache? Was this my last mustache kiss? It was brief, no tongue. Pleasant. And pleasant wasn't the word you wanted describing a kiss with a man. Unless it was your grandpa.

I wanted the zing I'd discovered with Ty. When I kissed Ty I forgot everything, forgot even to breathe. Ty! The image of him popped into my head and made me pull back from Dex. I felt my stomach do a somersault with guilt at letting Dex kiss me. I wanted Ty's mouth on mine. Only Ty's.

"I...I have to go," I murmured, lost in my thoughts of that sexy fireman.

Dex stepped back, let me get in my car and close my door. I let out a deep breath and drove off. I was definitely in over my head with Dex. He wanted to marry me and have mustache kisses the rest of my life. This was bad. Really bad. I had to figure my way out of this. But not tonight. I wanted Ty and I wanted him...now.

---

THIRTY MINUTES LATER, Ty knocked on my door and took in my outfit. His jaw tightened. He pushed past me and into the kitchen. "Russell Hosanski was at Gilly's and said he saw you. With a man. Based on what you're wearing, it must've been some date."

Oh crap. "Who is Russell Hosanski?" I asked. Damn small towns. Of course, he'd find out. What had I been thinking? Unless Dex and I had a picnic in the woods, someone who knew me was bound to be around.

"Works B shift at Station Two."

I followed him into the kitchen. "That doesn't explain how he knows me." My hands went to George the Gnome and fiddled with him, my finger running over the pointy hat.

Ty rolled his eyes. "I told him the same thing. He finally admitted to being a customer of Goldilocks on occasion."

"Ah." That clarified everything.

He made a circular motion with his hand. "So, Gilly's?"

"Yes. Gilly's."

He went to my fridge, pulled out a beer, popped the top and

drank half of it in one swallow. He wore his fire uniform, although he must've dumped all the electronic paraphernalia off at home because his belt was gizmo free.

"So who was this *date*?"

"Drake Dexter. He has a horse ranch down by Ennis."

I wasn't going to share the fact that he was the same man from the horse auction at the fair. Definitely a bad idea right now.

We stared at each other, his gaze so intent, so dark I swallowed. It was blatantly obvious Ty was jealous. His body was tense. He practically ground his teeth to dust when I'd said Dex's name, making the guy real for him.

*This was so cool!*

I'd never been the kind of woman who made men jealous. Now, I had two men interested in me. Dex wanted to marry me and make babies. He also wanted to take away my own free will and keep me naked all day. The only thing I knew for sure about Ty was that he cared about me, wanted me, and was not planning on taking over my life. We'd never talked about babies. The idea of being naked all day with him didn't freak me out at all. In fact, it made me hot all over. Zing!

"It must have been some date if you wore that," Ty grunted his response. "Is he still here?" He looked over my shoulder toward the living room.

Now it was my turn to overreact. I had planned to tell him I wanted to have sex with him right this very minute. Now, I just wanted to be pissy. "No, he's not in there. The bedroom actually. You caught us just before he ripped my clothes off."

"Funny," Ty said sarcastically. He ran a hand over his face.

"You're jealous because I went out to dinner with another man!" Okay, screw being pissy. I just wanted him. I fisted my hands at my sides ready to either punch him in the face to knock some sense into the man or pull him in for a kiss. I took a step closer. The nearer I got, the more turned on I became. Something about arguing made my adrenaline, and other juices, flow. Made me want to rip the uniform off his hot body. This past week had all been foreplay.

He felt enough for me to be jealous! It sounded kind of stupid, but it felt wonderful. Ty was being possessive and not in a creepy, chain-me-to-the-bed sort of way. My heart might burst with joy and excitement. Need. I'd never had that happen before. I felt like a teenager, but wiser.

Ty's feelings probably came from the genetic makeup of his ancestors, the caveman. He needed to beat his chest, stake his claim. Mine were newer to me. I just learned I had power over a guy, over Ty. Who needed a box of Goldie's toys when I just needed confidence in myself to make it happen?

"Hell, yeah, I'm jealous." Ty shook his head. "I want you to go out with me, have my friends mention seeing you on *my* arm. Do I feel threatened you went out with another guy?" He shook his head. "There's some reason why you did, I just don't know what it is yet. I know enough about your past to know you're not a cheater." His eyes raked over me in my new dress.

The light bulb went off. "Oh." I smiled at him. A full wattage smile. "You're jealous because I wore this"—I moved my hand in a sweeping gesture over my new dress—"for another guy. It bothers you I put effort into a date with someone else."

"You look hot as fuck in that dress. But if the guy you were with needs that dress to get him interested, he's not the guy for you." He pointed his beer bottle at me. "You don't need to wear that to turn me on."

I angled my head to the side. Looked at him. Really listened to his words. Goldie and Kelly had been right. I'd needed an update to my wardrobe. But they'd been wrong about part of it. I'd needed a makeover for *me*, not for Ty. Ty wanted me just as I was, uninspiring clothes and all. He'd seen me at my worst and wanted me.

"I know." All my doubts, my insecurities about getting close to a man were gone. Poof! Just like that. Knowing Ty liked me for me, not for a smokin' dress, was all the help I needed to let go of that last little bit of insecurity.

The slow burn for him had grown to forest fire proportions. I thought about what Kelly had said about answering the door naked.

I took a deep breath. It had been years and now, it was Go time. With a man in uniform.

"You know?" He looked confused. "Know what?"

I slowly undid the top button at the front of my dress. Ty's eyes dropped to watch my hands.

"You're the kind of guy who goes for a little...less."

He cleared his throat. I saw his hands clench into fists. "Less?"

I undid the next button. "Less clothes."

He swallowed. "Less is good."

And the next until enough buttons were undone that I could slide the dress from my shoulders. Ty's eyes stalled at my lace covered breasts when the dress dropped to the floor. I stood there in front of him in only my newly purchased red lace bra and panties and my strappy heels.

"Holy shit," Ty murmured.

His eyes raked over me and I felt my nipples harden. I was unbelievably nervous under his scrutiny, but the look on his face got rid of that. Fast. I was starting to get to know Ty's various expressions, but this one was new. I recognized it as pure, unadulterated lust. Completely out in the open. No hiding it to keep me from chickening out.

And it looked damn good on him.

His pupils dilated to make his eyes even bluer. A muscle ticked in his jaw. The fingers of his free hand were clenched at his side. I took in the front of his pants. Hello! Ty had a Whopper Dong of his own.

"You're right. Less is fine with me," he replied as he placed his beer bottle roughly on the counter, and then took the two steps that separated us. One finger lightly brushed over my breast above the red lace.

I sucked in a breath. Fire! *Fire!*

His hands moved up to tangle in my hair as he pulled me into a kiss that was all tongue. Worked for me.

It sent a lightning bolt of need straight south. There was the zing again that had been missing when Dex had kissed me. *This* was the difference between Dex and Ty. Dex who? Once I felt the zing, there was no going back. And I intended to go all...the...way.

I tasted beer, smelled it as well as soap and something I recognized as pure Ty. He slowly backed me up into the fridge and leaned into me. Ty's hot body pressing into me from the front, cold steel against the skin on my back. I gasped at the shock. I was so turned on, so needy. God, yes, I wanted this. I wanted him.

Ty spun us around until my butt was against the kitchen table. "Better," he murmured between kisses. He grabbed my hips and lifted me up so I sat on top without breaking the kiss. His hands pushed my knees apart so his legs fit between mine. I felt open and exposed and oh so good. "Yeah, better."

My hands moved to frantically work the buttons on his uniform shirt while his reached around behind my back and unhooked my bra. The straps caught at my elbows and my breasts tumbled free.

He broke the kiss for his first glimpse of them, to watch his hands cup them, his thumbs brush over the hard nipples. Then he traded his hands for his mouth, sucked on one nipple. Then the other.

My fingers tangled in his hair, holding him there.

"Um." I had a thought, but it was gone. He looked up at me through his lashes. The thought was back. "Remember when you told me that guy looked at me like I was a piece of meat?" He didn't say anything, only circled his tongue around my hard tip, so I continued. "You have that look right now."

He gave a quick grin as he stood up straight. With one yank he pulled my hips so they were at the edge of the table. I cried out in surprise, grabbed hold of his firm biceps. Another yank and my brand new lacy panties were a scrap on the floor.

"So you're saying I should have a taste?" he quirked a brow as he looked at me. *There.*

"Um," I said again as I leaned back on my elbows. His mouth moved lower, made a path with his tongue to my belly button while his hands pushed my knees wider.

"Like this?"

His mouth moved lower still and his tongue went for a ride up one side of me and down the other. HOLY CRAP! I hadn't felt a Super Zing like that in...I couldn't remember ever feeling a zing like that. My head fell back and I saw the red spaghetti sauce stain on the ceiling Zach made when he was two. I would never look at that mark in the same way again.

"Oh my God!" The tips of my ears tingled. I took a few deep breaths trying to get enough oxygen to my brain so I didn't pass out as Ty settled his mouth on my pussy, lapped at my entrance then flicked my clit.

I pulled on his ears and Ty came up for air. He had that crazy grin on his face. His mouth glistened and I'd never seen such need before in his eyes.

The need was mutual. "Inside of me. Now!"

Slowly, he shook his head. "Not until you come on my face first."

My eyes fell closed and I dropped back on the table as he put his mouth on me again. And added a finger. I gasped when it slipped inside, curled over a spot that had my back arching, my heels digging into his ass. "Yes!" I cried.

He was so skilled and I'd been horny for him for long enough that he pushed me right into my first man-made orgasm in...oh, who the hell cared? I screamed his name, writhed on my kitchen table, naked, as he got me off with his head between my legs.

Once the pleasure ebbed and I released my tight grip on him, Ty stood up.

He had a smug, satisfied look on his face as he wiped his mouth with the back of his hand.

I was too sated to care. He'd earned that look. I just wanted more. I was naked while he was dressed. I had to have my hands on him, on his bare skin. I roughly spread his uniform shirt to reveal his chest, lightly matted with hair that tapered in a line down to his pants...and beyond. I ran my hands over his hot body, reached around to his butt and pulled him into a kiss. I could feel the hair on his chest tickling my breasts, making my nipples ache. Much lower pulsed with need while my fingers fumbled with his belt buckle. I all but cried with frustration when I couldn't get it open. Ty took over, undid the button and unzipped his pants in record time.

I had to have him in my hands. I reached inside his boxers and pulled his erection out into my palm. He was big. Big enough to ruin me for all dildos in the future. Eight inches, easily. I slid my hand gently up and down. Once, twice, felt the little spurt of pre-cum coat my palm. Now it was his turn to gasp.

"Shit." He pulled back out of reach of my hands. I saw him now, long and thick, a ruddy red color, the crown broad. It curved up toward his belly. It was a gorgeous cock and I'd seen plenty. Not personally, but professionally.

"This is going to be fast. And we're going to do it here," he told me as he pushed on my shoulders so I lay back on the table once again.

I was naked, sprawled across my kitchen table with Ty's fiery gaze raking over me. He'd been too far south to look at me all of me before. He ran one palm from my neck, between my breasts, his long fingers brushing tauntingly over a nipple, past my navel and lower still. One finger, then two slid back inside. Yes! I made some kind of sound in the back of my throat and my eyes rolled back in my head.

Ty did the same come-hither motion with his fingers. I arched my back into his touch. Yeah, the g-spot did exist.

"Please," I begged.

He fumbled with his pants and pulled a condom from his back pocket, his cell phone falling out and onto the floor with a clatter. In seconds, he was sheathed and ready. In one thrust, he was inside. I stretched around him, my inner walls clenching and squeezing to adjust. I wrapped my legs around his waist, my ankles crossed behind his back. Ty was all the way in, his hips pressing my thighs wide. He stayed still and groaned. It felt so good, and he hadn't started moving yet.

But then he did and it was...mind blowing. I'd come once and that had gotten me all sensitive and easy, primed to come again for him.

I didn't consider myself an overly religious person and I never had a very close relationship with God. But I just shouted out His name a few times and hoped He wouldn't start paying me a lot of attention right now.

The feeling of Ty inside me, filling me, was...amazing.

He started moving. Hard. Fast. In. Out. Our breaths mingled. The look in his eyes, his expression, the pleasure, the intensity had me cupping his face. He turned his mouth into my palm, kissed me, as his hips pumped.

We worked the table across the room as he went harder, faster still. Keeping one hand on my hip, he used the other to touch me as he thrust deep.

Three, two, one. Blast off!

I saw rockets and fireworks and felt the whole parade.

I'd never had an orgasm like this, not even from his mouth just minutes earlier. Hell, I'd never had an orgasm with a man until him.

Within moments, Ty yelled, "Fuck!" and gave one last thrust, deeper than ever. He smacked his palms on the table, his rough breath mingling with mine, holding himself off of me.

I lost all thought besides how my body felt, savoring the last lingering aftershocks of pleasure. I couldn't help but smile. After a while, I opened my eyes. Ty too, had a very satisfied look on his face.

"I think we just gave the neighbors quite a show," I commented, looking out into the darkness.

My kitchen table was placed directly in front of the floor-to-ceiling windows that faced the back yard. Now it was about two feet further to the left. "Good thing the Colonel's out of town."

Ty chuckled as he pulled out and I hissed. "Those gnomes, they're checking out my ass."

I looked up at the counter. Yep, the gnomes had their beady eyes glued to Ty's butt. Better thinking it's his ass they were staring at than my....

"Smart gnomes," I told him.

I sat up. Mortification could have swept in faster than the passion receded. I'd just had sex on my kitchen table, with the lights on. Anyone in the back yard would have had a live-action porno. But I didn't care. At all. I'd just had the orgasm of all orgasms. To hell with everyone else.

Goldie would be so proud!

"That was—" I couldn't finish. I wasn't sure of the adjective that might work.

"Fast," Ty answered. He buttoned his pants but left his shirt undone. The look really worked for him. "But sweetheart, we just got started."

"I don't think my table can take anymore."

Ty grinned. "Good, because I want to try a bed next. I want you to ride my face. I want you to grip my headboard as I fuck you from behind. I want to take you in my shower. The list is long."

Oh. A long list. Worked for me, and my pussy.

In one swift motion, Ty bent down, picked me up and threw me over his shoulder in a fireman's carry. I got a good view of my kitchen floor and his butt as he carried me out the back door. "Where are we going?" I shrieked.

"My bed. I've got Goldie's gift box of condoms and we're going to use every one of them."

"I don't have any clothes on, just my heels!"

"You won't need any clothes. And don't even think about taking the shoes off."

# 15

"It took most of the night but we made a good dent in that box of condoms," Ty said as he rolled onto his side to face me, one arm thrown over my waist. He grinned, obviously pleased with his extensive and thorough male prowess. Every inch of me was pleased with his male prowess, too.

"That's because you had me demonstrate the trick from the bachelorette party." I pushed on his shoulder sleepily. "Several times."

A hand snaked up into my hair, one of Ty's fingers wrapped around a curl. Pulled gently. "I love your hair." He looked enthralled.

"My hair?" I couldn't have been more surprised. "I figured you for a breast man. Or a leg man."

"Definitely a breast man." To prove his point, he moved his hand down to the top of the sheet, lowering it just enough to expose one. His fingertip circled my nipple ever so lightly. "Ever since that morning when you flashed me—"

I threw a hand over my eyes and chuckled. "Don't remind me."

He pulled my hand away, kissed my knuckles.

"—I dreamed of seeing you naked, touching your breasts." He looked at my hardening nipple like a boy opening a present from Santa. Mesmerized, obsessed. "Pink. The same pretty shade as your pussy."

Who knew a man's words could make you feel...wonderful. Sexy. A whole lot naughty. It was like a Band-Aid to my wounded libido. I felt attractive, alluring. And that was very empowering.

"But your hair, it drives me crazy."

I harrumphed. "It drives me crazy, too. I'm glad you like the one thing that's the bane of my existence. It's curly," I grumbled, as I pulled on a curl, let it spring back.

"Sexy."

"It's messy and lacks style."

"Wild."

*Wild.* I would never have used that adjective to describe it, but if it floated Ty's boat, it was okay by me.

"Save my spot." Ty climbed out of bed and went into the bathroom.

It was just getting light, the early morning sun coming through Ty's bedroom window. I could now make out what I'd missed the night before. I hadn't noticed his interior decorating skills at the time. I'd been too distracted by...other things. There was a bed, a big one, an oak dresser with a fichus plant on top, wicker laundry basket in the corner. The walls were a light tan, white trim. Rattan blinds on the windows. I hadn't seen or touched the floor yet as Ty had dumped me straight into bed the night before and hadn't let me up since. I rolled over now and saw refinished pine.

"Why do you think I left you there?" Ty asked as he leaned against the bedroom doorway, naked. Very, very naked.

I looked at him, confused. I didn't remember what we'd been talking about. "Where?"

"The damn bachelorette party. If you're going to put a dick in your mouth in front of me, it's going to be mine."

I remembered how it felt stretching my lips wide, against my tongue. The taste of it, the way it swelled even further just before he came. I looked down at his growing...dick. "So it's a good skill to teach?"

He yanked on the covers, exposing me to the waist, and climbed back in bed. Moved on top of me. I felt every hard, hot inch of him. "You might need to practice some more." His blue eyes crinkled at the corners as he grinned.

"You didn't think I was skilled enough last night?"

His eyes went all out of focus as he remembered back to the multiple times I'd helped him with a condom.

"This is where I get jealous and possessive knowing you did this with some other guy."

I smiled up at him. His beard had grown in surprisingly quickly and he was on the way to being Grizzly Adams. "Then you'll probably be happy to hear I learned it, not from being with another man, but from Goldie."

"I don't know if I should be creeped out you learned that from your mother-in-law or thankful."

I ran my hands down his lean back to his butt and pulled him closer. "I'm thankful for the gift box of condoms."

I opened my legs so he fit in between, felt his hard length pressing against my entrance.

Ty shifted slightly and I moaned. "What about the toys?" he asked.

I reached down and took him in my hands. Ty sucked in a breath. "Like you said, who needs toys?"

---

"I THINK we should talk about your husband," Ty said, awhile later.

We were still in bed, the sheets a tangled mess, although we'd eaten, showered and returned to make a bigger dent in the condom box. I was insatiable. I couldn't get enough of Ty, of his hands on my body. But with those words—

"I don't usually take two men to bed, even if one's dead."

I wore one of Ty's fire department T-shirts and nothing else. I sat up, propped by pillows against the headboard.

He smiled, ran a finger up my bare arm. I swatted his hand away.

"That first time I met you at the pancake breakfast, you said he'd been with another woman."

I sighed, tucked the sheet and blanket around my waist, worried the edging between my fingers. "I found Nate cheating on me the day I learned I was pregnant with Bobby. They'd been fucking—there's no other word for it—for over a year. I had no clue, until I found them in the storage room at Goldilocks."

Ty lay on his side, propped up on his elbow.

"He used to travel a lot, specifically to Germany. He *said* there was a dealer of very unique and high-end glass toys he wanted in the store. Back then, he helped run it with Goldie. I guess they'd met online. Turns out he was demo-ing the toys with the dealer. Her name was Annika. She'd flown into town under the guise of a sales trip, touring the US with her specialty items. She was supposed to hit stores all over the West, but didn't make it any further than Bozeman."

I gave Ty a wistful smile. I didn't like talking about this part of my life. It was a painful time, but Ty deserved to know. I didn't want it to come between us.

"After I kicked him out, he moved to Germany to be with her. The story goes, she was married. Her husband didn't freak out about the extramarital activities like I did. Instead, he joined in."

Ty half grunted, half laughed. "Go on."

"Nate died of a blood clot that went to his lung, they think from flying. He'd just arrived in Hamburg the day before."

"Ah, yes, hamburger."

I laughed, remembering Bobby's words. "Right. He was in bed with Annika and her husband and just died. Poof."

"Holy crap."

Ty placed a hand on my thigh and I felt his heat through the covers. "So you were married to an asshole. Do you still miss the bastard? Do you still—"

"Love him?" I ran my fingers over Ty's head, loving the feel of his soft hair. "After I kicked him out, I was sad. Depressed. Hormonal and nauseated for months. More angry than anything else. I filed for divorce. By the time Bobby was born, Nate had moved out of the country. Out of my life. But when he died, we were technically, legally still married. It's hard to divorce a dead man. So I'm his widow, not his ex."

Ty slid up the bed to kiss me on the mouth. A gentle, soft kiss.

I looked him in the eye. "Looking back, I'm not sure if I ever really loved him the way one should love their spouse. I'd been young. Naïve."

A side of his mouth ticked up. "And now?" One of his hands tugged gently at the blanket, lowering it so he could kiss a little lower. My left nipple, to be precise. Right through the T-shirt. He bit down gently.

"Now?" I asked, my voice breaking. I forgot the reason for the question.

He yanked the blanket down to the foot of the bed. And kissed a little lower, below the edge of his shirt. He pushed it up and moved between my legs. I shifted to let him.

"Now?" he asked again. His hands followed his mouth until they were doing very special and exciting things to very special and exciting places on my body.

"Now!" I yelled.

---

THAT NIGHT, after dashing through the Colonel's backyard in

Ty's T-shirt, I found four messages on my phone. With Ty doing his caveman routine, I'd left my cell at home the night before. Standing in the kitchen, I listened to them. Kelly called first to hear about my date with Dex, which I'd completely forgotten about. While my mom told me about her day with the boys and asked me to call them back, I noticed the gnomes were missing. Hadn't they been on the counter watching us have sex? Now where were they?

The last message was from Goldie to call her when I'd taken a break from sex with Ty. The gnomes were the least of my concern. I had to deal with a sex curious mother-in-law before I dealt with wandering gnomes.

I called Goldie. "Hi!" I said brightly. What did one say to someone when they knew you'd had sex? Lots and lots of sex.

"I knew it. I can hear it in your voice."

I wedged the phone between my ear and my shoulder as I pulled the kitchen table back in place. I had a hot flash remembering how the table got moved. Could I ever eat there again without breaking into a hormone induced sweat?

"All I said was hello."

"I know about these things," she said sternly.

"I could have been having sex with Dex instead of Ty! He was the guy I went out with last night."

"I hear the sass in your voice, but I'll forgive you this once since you did good. I bet Ty was, too." Goldie chuckled at her own pun. I rolled my eyes. "Of course, you wouldn't have sex with Dex. You love Ty."

I dropped the phone. It bounced off the kitchen table before I was able to grab it back up.

"Um, love?" I gurgled and plopped down into a kitchen chair, the wood cold on my butt. I wasn't prepared for that. Sure, there was definitely something special between Ty and myself, but love? I just chalked the butterflies in my stomach up to lust.

"I *lust* Ty."

"Sure, you do. If I was thirty years younger, I'd lust Ty, too. Hell, I lust Ty at seventy."

I smiled. I saw Ty cut through the back yard. I gave a little wave and felt those butterflies. Was that love?

*Oh, my God.* Why did Goldie always have to be right?

I was in love with Ty. I was in love with the man coming in my back door in rumpled shorts and a gray MSU T-shirt. No shoes and wearing the look of a man who'd had lots and lots of sex. *Holy crap.*

Thank goodness Goldie couldn't see him now. I put my finger to my lips to keep him quiet. He came close and dropped a kiss on top of my head.

I smiled at him. A sappy smile of a woman in love. "Um. I've got to go."

"I don't want to keep you from ripping Ty's clothes off," Goldie said.

*Not a bad idea,* I thought as I eyed Ty's body.

"But I just wanted to tell you I've got Veronica coming in tomorrow to help me out. She's back from her trip to the Alamo and needs some extra shifts."

I'd forgotten about work. Hell, I'd forgotten about everything except putting Tab A into Slot B with Ty.

"Thanks," I said, meaning it. I ran my hand up under Ty's T-shirt to feel the soft hair, his hot skin. Why couldn't I get enough?

"By the way, do you know anything more about the dead guy in the pig pen?" Goldie asked.

Oh yeah, that. "Haven't heard a thing. When I hear something, I'll call you."

"Ha! Sure, you will. Tell Ty I said hello. Say, want me to swing by with another gift box for you? Just tell me what you need and I'll leave it on your doorstep."

My hand dropped lower to press against his erection. "Ty's got everything I need."

---

One quickie later, we were finally able to control ourselves. I showered, put on a pair of sweats and hoodie, and pulled out the shrimp ring from the fridge.

We sat shoulder to shoulder on my couch watching a James Bond marathon, Ty's arm thrown over the back of the couch. His hand rested on my shoulder. The shrimp, cheese puffs and beer were spread out on the coffee table in front of us. Ty turned down the stinky cheese with a similar face the boys made. Must be a guy thing.

"Goldie wanted to see if I knew more about Morty's murder."

Ty tossed a cheese ball in the air and caught it with his mouth. He crunched a few times then said, "I called my parents when you were in the shower. They said the police have no real leads as there's no way to take fingerprints. There aren't any footprints or tire tracks to give someone away. It must have been raining when Morty was dumped there."

"Are your parents all right?" If my mom had found a hacked up body in a pig sty, she'd probably have a nervous breakdown. But, she'd probably have a nervous breakdown being near a pig sty.

"They're fine. Taking it all in stride. They're more worried about you."

"Me?" I raised my eyebrows. "Really? That's sweet."

He popped another cheese ball, had a swig of beer. "I called the sheriff who I met that night. He didn't have much new either. The only thing they've been able to say definitively is that Morty had meth in his system."

I wondered which body part they'd analyzed to discover that and cringed at the thought. I grabbed a shrimp, ate it, and tossed the tail onto the plastic tray. Not very ladylike, but I'd already gotten the guy. With all the unladylike stuff I'd done already, tossing a shrimp tail wasn't going to make much of an impact.

"Meth, meth, meth. Everything's meth around here. Crazy robber guy, Kelly's neighbor's kid—"

"The house in Churchill, about five or six calls in the past two weeks."

I pointed my beer at him. "Exactly."

Ty's cell rang.

"Strickland." Ty listened. "Where?" Listened some more. "I can't come now. I've had a few beers. Right. Seven. I'll be there." He hit End and turned to me. "Wildland fire. In the National Forest north of Big Sky."

"Do you have to go? Now?" It was dark out. Late. "Sorry, I forget fires don't stop because it's nighttime."

He smiled. "I can't go now. I've had too many beers to head out but they want me in the morning. I'll meet up with a crew coming in from Helena and go down."

"How big is it?"

Forest fires happened all the time out West. Lightning strikes, negligent campers, tossed cigarettes could create a catastrophic fire that burned acres and acres of wilderness. If it was big enough, firefighters from all over the country came to help fight it.

"So far, just a few hundred acres, but it's going to be windy up there. It'll grow more before it's contained."

"Do they know how it started?"

"No bad weather in the area, so it wasn't lightning. Probably a camper, but they won't know for a while."

I stood up and started cleaning up the food debris. "You should get some sleep. Sounds like you're going to need it."

Ty stood, too. Turned off the TV. "Your bed or mine?"

# 16

The sun just came up when the alarm went off. I groaned and burrowed deeper under the blankets. Ty moved in close and let his hands roam over my body. "I can't get enough of you," he whispered.

I half groaned, half sighed. His hands felt good, but I was sore in places I hadn't known existed. "When I get back, love, I...." He kissed the back of my shoulder. "Remember we talked about sex versus relationships?" His voice was rough from sleep.

My brain was mostly asleep. "Mmm?"

"This isn't just sex, Jane." Ty sighed. "I've...I've fallen for you."

I smiled, savoring the cocooning warmth of the bed and Ty's words.

He rolled out of bed and I heard him rustle into his clothes.

I vaguely felt his knee press into the bed. "Please, be careful while I'm gone. I have plans for you, for this *relationship*, when I get back." He dropped a kiss on the top of my head and was gone. Left for the burning Montana wilderness. I missed his body heat for about thirty seconds before I fell into REM sleep until nine when I woke with a start.

He loved me? Had I dreamed that whole conversation? What were Ty's exact words? *I've fallen for you.* Why the hell hadn't I woken up? That's right, having sex for two days straight wore you out. One of the most important conversations of my life and I'd slept through it. When Ty got back, I'd just blame it on him. It was his fault I missed it. *Right.*

I showered and dried my hair, the whole time with a silly grin. I went extra fancy and did my hair, which meant putting it up in a ponytail. I threw on clean shorts but I put on Ty's T-shirt I'd worn the night before. I was being a sap, but it smelled like him. And because my lips were worn out from all the kissing, I treated them to some lip balm. And I smiled some more.

Thanks to Veronica, Goldie's trusty employee, I had the day off. I ate stinky cheese and watched morning talk shows in between bouts of napping. I had no idea a sex marathon could be so exhausting.

My cell phone beeped from the bedroom signaling a text. Sighing with laziness, I went to read it.

*Ty: new info re Morty @ DD ranch. meet @ 1*

I perked up at his message. I'd all but given up ever learning anything new about Morty, knowing I'd tried all I could, just short of sleeping with Dex. What had Ty found out?

I looked at the time. 11:30. I had just enough time to change into jeans and boots to protect myself from animal poop—or dead bodies.

---

I SPENT the hour driving to Dex's ranch working through everything I knew about Morty Moore. It wasn't much and I'd finished that train of thought by the time I drove by the mall. Morty had worked at the Rocking DD Ranch and had a side job selling stolen horse semen. Someone blew up his parents' house. He'd been killed for some reason, by somebody. That's it. That's all the definitive information I had.

After that I thought about sex with Ty. I had a mental porn movie going, starring the two of us. It lasted until I was south of Norris. I was smiling to myself and felt surprisingly horny as I drove through the Rocking DD archway. I was eager to see Ty even though it had only been a few hours since he'd left for the wildfire. Must have been put out much quicker than he'd thought.

I followed the driveway like I'd done the last time up to the large horse arena. I intentionally skipped Dex's mega-mansion first, not super interested in seeing the house Dex intended for me, as his future wife, to clean every day. As if. The house had to be over five thousand square feet. No chance in hell I could keep that monstrosity clean.

The sky was big and blue, the sun bright. It was exactly the same as my previous visit, although there appeared to be less action. I parked and got out. I didn't see anyone else around, although the side door to the stable was open. I smelled hay and horses. No Ty. In fact, I didn't see his rental car.

I held my hand up to my eyes to shield the sun and looked around. Where was Ty? I ventured into the arena first, taking time for my eyes to adjust. Only half the lights were on, the building cool and quiet.

"Hello?" I called out. Nothing.

I returned outside and looked around again. I heard some nickering and horse snuffling coming from the stable and headed that way. A few horses had their heads out over their half stall doors. Nothing else was going on down the long central aisle. No one on poop patrol with a wheelbarrow. No hay tossing. Nothing. I pulled my cell from my pocket to see if I'd missed a message from Ty.

"Crap," I muttered to myself. No service.

I returned to the car to consider my options. My watch said

1:15 and Ty wasn't here. I didn't have much choice but to go up to Dex's house and knock on the door.

I pulled up and parked in the circular drive. The house was much larger up close than from the main driveway. It was two stories; a large porch ran the length of the main section with a wing off to the left. A four-car garage was to the right. Shake shingle roof. Stained siding and deep eaves. Tall pillars made from roughhewn pines graced the entry leading to double wooden doors ten feet tall. The home was what Donald Trump would build if he wanted to live in Montana and get horse poop on his shoes.

I rang the doorbell.

"Hello, Jane," Dex said as he opened the door. He stepped back. "Come in."

I took in the large entry, two stories tall. Slate floors, several closed doors which I assumed were closets for winter coats and boots. Beyond was a great room facing west that had wall to wall windows with vistas of the Tobacco Roots. The furnishings were dark leather and lots of wood. An interior decorator had been through because there were unusual knickknacks and throw blankets worthy of a show home. A large elk head was positioned above a river rock fireplace big enough to stand in. I had to admit, it was beautiful.

"Hi. I'm supposed to meet a friend of mine here. Ty?"

"Would you like a drink?" He turned and walked toward what I assumed was the kitchen. Since he hadn't answered my question, I had no choice but to follow.

The kitchen was everything you'd expect. Stainless steel appliances worthy of Wolfgang Puck, a marble topped island the size of my kitchen, gleaming wood floors. By the time I'd taken in the views from the big windows—which were everywhere—Dex held a glass of red wine out to me.

"Thanks," I replied, not sure what to say. I wasn't a big wine drinker and it was a little early in the day. I took a polite sip.

Good stuff. There was no way Dex was a boxed wine kind of guy. "So, about my friend?"

Dex took a sip of his wine as well. "What do you think of my home?"

"Um, well, it's very nice." Dex made me nervous, but I couldn't put my finger on exactly why. He wasn't answering my question about Ty, although he never seemed one to like to talk about other men. I took another sip of wine to ease my nerves.

"I knew you would like it." He put his wineglass down on the counter. "Would you like a tour?"

A tour? "Sure. A tour." I started to put my glass down.

"No, you're welcome to bring your wine with you. Please, enjoy it. I have more." He took my free hand and led me through the downstairs. His hand was warm, his skin slightly rough with calluses. Dex talked about the building of the home, the details, and his plans for the future.

That was great and all, but I was getting worried about Ty. "Dex, I was supposed to meet my friend here. He's really late. Have you heard from him?"

Dex looked down at me and smiled. "Yes, sorry. He called and said he was running behind. Something about a fire?"

"Right. The fire." I relaxed then and took another sip of wine.

"Let me show you the upstairs while we're waiting for him." He led me through six bedrooms, a study, media room and laundry before ending at the master suite. It was bigger than my entire house. Lots and lots of cream carpet. Again, the views, the dark wood furniture. The bed. A great big bed.

I had this funny feeling in my stomach. This was not where I wanted to be with Dex. Alone. I swallowed. All of a sudden, I didn't feel so well. The bed started to lose focus. I blinked to clear my vision.

"Jane, are you all right?" He sounded concerned.

"I think I'm scared of your bed." I giggled. "Everything all of a sudden feels...groovy."

Dex took the wineglass from my fingers and placed it on a dresser. "That's to be expected." He didn't sound concerned anymore.

My foggy brain was slow to process. Next to the wineglass on the dresser were the boys' gnomes. "Whuh?" I looked at Dex and he was all soft around the edges. I was so confused. What were the gnomes doing in Dex's bedroom? "The gnomes....how?" I lost my train of thought. "I don't think I can feel my fingers. What's...what's wrong with me?"

I think Dex smiled. "You didn't think I'd let you taint my bedroom, did you? This is where I plan to bring my wife someday."

I felt wobbly, the room spinning. "I thought...." I couldn't formulate what I wanted to say. Something about Dex and a wife and me. Gnomes.

"You thought I wanted you to be my wife?" He yanked me by the hand he still held, pulled me close to him. "I did. Not now. I don't bring sluts to my bed."

I felt so funky, so spacey, so foggy, so...happy. Whatever was wrong with me didn't feel bad. It was like being drunk, but drunk on happy juice. My limbs were loose, my skin felt tingly. I swear I could feel each and every hair on my head. Even with the weird feelings, I could hear the anger, the evil in Dex's voice.

"You betrayed me and you will be punished." He released me and I stumbled, fell toward the dresser. I grabbed its edge with both hands to keep upright, the movement tipped over George the Gnome and knocked him onto the carpeted floor with a soft thump.

The lethargic feeling moved into my chest. My lungs felt heavy. It was difficult to breathe. "I...can't...catch my breath."

"Or you may just die. Who knows how much of the drug I should have given you."

With those words my body let go, and I fell without fear into blackness.

---

When I slowly came to, my first thought was about how dry and funky my mouth felt. It tasted like I'd eaten a wadded-up tissue. I slowly blinked, but my eyes flew open in panic when I recognized my surroundings. I was in a horse stall, lying on scratchy hay.

My body felt sluggish as if I'd had a fifth of whiskey and slept it off. I looked up and blinked some more, clearing the fog. I took in my surroundings. Cinder block walls on three sides painted white. A closed half gate on the fourth. Feeding trough in one corner. I stood up on shaky legs, wobbly like a newborn colt, and recognized the space outside the gate. I was in Dex's breeding shed.

This was not good.

I heard a door open, the clip clop of horse hooves. Dex walked up leading a big, black horse. The animal's large head came into the stall and he snorted. I stepped back, shaky and afraid. I could feel his hot horsy breath on my skin.

"Dex! What is going on?"

"You didn't die after all." He sounded as if this disappointed him. Leading the horse away, he looped the lead on the bridle to a ring on the...what had he called it? The phantom mare. Dex returned and leaned his forearms on the half gate, watching me. I backed up further, slipped on the hay and landed on my butt with a jarring thud. That hurt!

I remembered I'd first thought he was the Marlboro Man. He still looked the same, but now had a mental disorder to go along with his good looks. Ted Bundy came to mind. Handsome, yet completely psycho. Something dark and sinister lurked in his eyes which I hadn't seen before.

"I wasn't sure if the amount I gave you would knock you out, or kill you."

I closed my eyes for a second trying to clear the cobwebs. Slowly shook my head. "You drugged me."

"Ketamine. Also known as Special K." He smiled. A creepy, serial killer kind of smile. "Around here, it's also known as horse tranquilizer."

Oh boy. "Dex, you need to let me out of here!" I shouted.

"Scream all you want. No one's on the ranch to hear you as everyone has the day off. You will be punished."

Those words flashed in my mind. He'd said that right before I passed out. Right when I saw on his dresser...the gnomes.

"Oh my God. The gnomes. You stole the gnomes from my house." I rubbed a hand over my face, felt a piece of straw in my hair, tugged it out.

"A necessary loose end to clean up."

The gnomes were a loose end? Then that made me....

"Ty! Where's Ty?" I said, panicked. My skin broke out in a cold sweat. Was he a loose end, too?

Dex shook his head and tsked. "Ty's dead. Or soon will be."

What? A tightness spread across my chest, compressed my lungs so I couldn't breathe. Dead? I gulped in air trying to remain calm. "But he sent me a text to meet me here. He can't be dead! Where is he?"

Dex looked down at his fingernails. "I sent you the text from Ty's phone."

The phone Ty couldn't find because...he'd dropped it under my kitchen table when we'd had sex the first time. With the gnomes watching us. The pieces were starting to fall into place.

"You were there." I was mortified, but body-numbingly afraid. Afraid of Dex and the extent of what he'd done. And why.

"Saw you having sex in your kitchen? Right after you kissed me? Yes, I was in your back yard watching. You were to be my wife!" His voice changed. Angrier. "I would have shared everything with you. But you gave yourself to another man, out in the open for all the world to see." Dex's anger was controlled, focused. Not like a pressure cooker ready to blow sort of way. More like a snake that had been poked one too many times. Ready to strike. The man was mentally insane.

I was grossed out. Dex had seen something that had been private, something special between Ty and me. But that was quickly replaced by bowel liquefying fear. Ty was dead, and if he hadn't sent the text, then no one knew I was here. Being held by a crazy man in a horse breeding shed.

"I'm sorry, Dex." Placating him might work. "But I don't understand. Why steal Ty's cell phone? And the gnomes. Why the gnomes?"

"You wouldn't leave it alone," Dex growled.

I grabbed some straw, the rough edges poking into my skin. "What?" I wanted to cry from fear and frustration. "Leave what alone?"

"Morty Moore. You couldn't leave it alone." His hands gripped the gate rail until the knuckles were white. "I knew Morty was on the take even before you showed up. He'd been stealing valuable horse semen and selling it completely without my knowledge until about a week before you started nosing around. But you wouldn't leave it alone. The more you looked, the more you brought attention to me and my ranch. I didn't want anyone snooping around. Especially you."

"Why? Morty stealing horse semen isn't that big of a deal."

Dex grinned. "You're right. That's nothing. But millions of dollars of meth is."

"Holy crap." A wave of nausea curdled my stomach. I swallowed, trying not to throw up. "You shot me full of horse tranquilizer so my brain isn't working that well," I said sarcastically. "I think you're going to need to start at the beginning."

He shrugged his shoulders, contemplating as if he had all the time in the world. "No one steals from me, so Morty had to go."

I looked up at Dex from my seat in the hay. "The explosion."

"It would have been considered a gas leak, if it hadn't been for you."

"But Morty wasn't even there."

I heard Dex's horse snort behind him.

"Didn't matter. I got him another time."

My eyes locked on Dex's, realizing what he'd said. "You cut him up and fed him to Ty's family's pigs!" What kind of man was I dealing with here? All this time, I just thought he was a pervy Dom-wannabe who had a weird obsession with animal husbandry. That, it turned out, was nothing.

"I told you, he had to go. What better way to get rid of a body?"

"Why there? What do Ty's parents have to do with anything?"

"Nothing. But by then, I'd seen Strickland sniffing around you. I wanted him to know he was getting too close to something that belonged to me. To warn him I could get close, too."

My legs had fallen asleep. I straightened them out, the ginger ale tingles reminded me I was still alive. I thought through all the weird stuff that had happened. "The camper?"

He shrugged again. "Another attempt to show you how easily I could get to you and those you care about."

I opened my mouth to tell him off, but knew it wasn't worth it. This was not the time, nor the place to start practicing for the debate team. But I was getting the answers I needed to figure this whole mess out. Although I was sitting in a horse pen with a homicidal maniac who liked to chop people up for fun blocking my only exit. "Let's not forget the derby," I said.

Dex smiled. "I'd seen you with Ty again. You were mine!" He ran fingers over his mustache. "If you're not going to be with me, you're not going to be with anybody. And a hit and run with a derby car would never be linked to me."

I mentally tallied all the crazy stuff. Morty on my front steps. Solved. Explosion. Solved. Derby car. Solved. Camper.

Solved. Morty's body. Solved. The more he talked, the less killing he could do. "What I don't get is why you think I have anything to do with your um...meth?"

"You nosed around too much. You started to look at my ranch a little too closely. Meth is being made on a far corner of my land, near the national forest. Shipments are flown out of a hidden runway without any problems. In fact, since my property is big enough, no one knows the airstrip even exists. I can't have you jeopardizing all I've built. Besides, the only loose end with Morty is you. With you dead, no one can tie Morty to me except as an employee, which is easily explained away as a man quitting a job. Problem solved."

"I won't tell anyone about your meth," I assured him. "I can't anyway. I don't know anything about it."

"You'll be sampling some soon enough."

Huh? That didn't sound good. I felt green, like the first three months of pregnancy with Bobby. As if I ate a dozen oysters left out in the sun. The Ketamine and my stomach were not friends. I gulped in air, trying to ease the roiling.

"A horse ranch is a perfect cover for meth. Like I said, lots of land to hide a meth lab and a runway for small planes to carry meth out of state. Shipping boxes of horse semen is the perfect front to move meth to my overseas distributors."

Wow. I had to admit it was a pretty good setup. I burped up funky air.

"All that meth around town?"

"Mine," Dex boasted. "Except for the lab in Churchill. That was a competitor, but he had a little *accident* and the lab burned down."

Sure, an accident.

"To remove the competition. The wildfire Ty's fighting. Let me guess, you started that?" I asked.

"To remove the competition," Dex repeated my words. "Permanently."

What was his definition of *remove*? "Um..." I swallowed

down some bitter bile. "Why kill Ty?" Hot tears burned the back of my eyes. I blinked them away. If I started crying now, I'd never stop. I had to remain clearheaded to get out of this. To save Ty. Somehow.

Dex shrugged casually. "I hope you said your goodbyes." He pushed off the rail, ignoring my question. Uh-oh. Now what? He'd run out of story and I still hadn't figured out how to escape. My mind was spinning on a vision of Ty, lying hurt, flames fast approaching. Or was he already dead, chopped up into pieces to be burnt to a crisp? Dex opened the gate and stepped into the stall. I had to tilt my head back to look up at him. His body blocked most of the light. I crab walked away from him, sliding on the hay until I was forced into the corner. The cinder block was uncomfortable at my back.

He easily grabbed and lifted me painfully by the armpits. I wobbled on legs that were still unsteady. His cologne, which I used to find appealing, was now cloying and harsh. I saw the evil in his eyes up close. No warmth. The cold sweat returned. I felt the roots of my hair tingle.

"What...what are you going to do with me?" I asked, breathless with fear. I tasted bile again, acidic in the back of my throat.

"You saw the real side of me when we first met. I wanted you for a sub. I didn't care you were inexperienced in the lifestyle. I would have trained you, taught you to please me. You'd have been too busy doing that to ever learn about the meth." He gave me a little shake and my teeth clacked together. "I even tried a different approach, being a gentleman, courting you with dinner, words. You know where that led."

Right into the arms of Ty. I thought something had been off about Dex that night. He was definitely not a gentleman.

"Now...instead of being my wife or even my sub, you'll just be Jane, my little brood mare."

Brood mare? I didn't think so!

I didn't think my stomach could hold out much longer.

Even though I was scared out of my wits, I was angry. Smoke-coming-out-of-my-ears angry. Not just because he held me prisoner and had completely obscene plans for me, nor for the fact he'd either already killed Ty or was just waiting for the fire to finish doing his dirty work for him. It went even deeper than that. During my marriage to Nate, he'd molded me into what he wanted me to be. Of course, I let him. I figured doing exactly what he wanted would make him want me, love me. Need me. But I'd learned a lot since I kicked his sorry ass out, and that included never compromising for someone else. No one was going to boss me around again. I wasn't going to give in to Dex without one hell of a fight.

I glared at him. "Is that what the horse is for since you can't get it up?" I struggled against his grasp knowing I'd pissed him off. Good. I saw anger flare in his eyes before he quickly hid it. Direct hit.

"I had no idea how long you'd be unconscious. I was leading him to the corral when I heard you stirring."

I laughed, directly in his face. "Excuses, excuses."

Even though I was a little dizzy, I kneed him in his junk as hard as I could. Unfortunately, a woman must have tried this tactic before. His reflexes were quick and all I hit was his thigh, which did nothing but make him furious. Dex changed his grip into some kind of wrist lock. I winced, cried out. Any movement I made caused sharp pain.

"Don't worry. Meth will make you do lots of things. All kinds of things. And when you're so strung out and you're no good to me anymore, well, an overdose is not hard to accomplish."

It might have been sheer terror or the aftereffects of being tranquilized like a horse, but my stomach finally revolted. I threw up all over Dex. Projectile vomit famous with newborns. With babies, it was kind of cute. Me, not so much. His once clean shirt now had funky chunks and orange slime dripping down it. Hopefully, it felt as bad as it smelled.

"Shit!" he swore as he looked down at himself.

I had to admit I felt better in more ways than one. He released his grip so I tried to dash past him, my legs jiggly like the Colonel's Jell-O, but he had a long reach. He yanked me by the arm out of the stall and into the bright, sterile room. It felt as if my arm had popped out of socket.

The large horse startled, his big eyes bulging with fear. His nostrils flared, probably from the horrible smell emanating from Dex, and he pulled up on the lead. Unfortunately, the horse wasn't much help to me unless he could go and call the police.

Dex pushed me roughly against the phantom mare, my stomach pressed into the worn leather. The impact knocked the wind out of me. I didn't even want to think about the cooties that were all over it. So gross. I tried to wriggle free but Dex's large hand pressed into my lower back, holding me in place. Breathe!

"Struggle. I like it."

I stopped at once. Sucked in some much needed air, funky smell and all. Think. Think! I had no intention of being raped, now or ever.

Dex pressed his lower body into me, legs against legs, hips against hips. I felt his erection, hard against me. I heard him rip his soiled shirt off. It landed on the floor in front of me in a soggy heap.

"I think we can start our first lesson now," he said, grinding his hips into me. His hands moved to the waistband of my jeans.

I felt around beneath the stand frantically searching for something, anything, to use as a weapon. I wasn't sure what I grabbed but it felt like hard plastic. It was heavy and cumbersome, but I was able to get my right hand on it. In a firm grasp I swung it up and around, twisting my body, using all the adrenaline-induced power I had, and clocked Dex on the side of the head.

*Thwack.*

He gave a grunt and went down like a redwood tree in the forest, landing hard, right next to his horse, which whinnied at the near miss. I stood up shakily and stared down at his prostrate form. The spooked animal pranced in place, his lead preventing him from moving away. He tugged at the bridle, wanting to escape as I much as I did. I scrambled back. Put the phantom mare between us. No way was I going to approach the horse, to ease his fears. I was just as scared as he.

The animal reared, his front hooves going up and coming down hard on Dex's head and upper body. With a sickening sound, kind of like a pumpkin being tossed off a roof, I knew Dex wouldn't be bothering me anymore. No way could a man survive with a horseshoe shaped dent in his head. My stomach lurched, although it was already empty.

I realized I still grasped my makeshift weapon, the artificial vagina I'd seen in action the first time I'd come to the ranch. I placed it on top of the phantom mare, carefully fighting my need to giggle hysterically.

Dex had been knocked out, most likely killed. I'd been saved by an artificial vagina. Wouldn't Goldie think that was a hoot?

# 17

I stared at Dex's prostrate body, watching, making sure he wasn't getting back up. Deep down I knew that was going to happen right before pigs started to fly.

The panicked horse seemed to sense a change in the air, as if the danger was now gone. He calmed, although he snorted a few times and his nostrils still flared. I didn't blame him. The large room smelled awful, like manure, throw up and blood. I approached the horse with extreme caution, keeping the phantom mare between me and the horse's hooves. Carefully, carefully I undid his lead and backed away.

I walked on unsteady feet over to the big doors, giving a wide berth to the horse and threw them open. "Here, horsie, horsie. Come on. You're a good boy. You did a good job, now run free. Go!"

A horse was much smarter than I ever thought. He saw that opening and went for it, leisurely walking out the doors and into the sunshine.

I looked around, found a phone mounted on the wall and, with shaking fingers, dialed 911. "I...I need help. A man horse tranquilized me and tried to make me his brood mare, which I really don't want to be, so I hit him on the head with an artificial vagina before he was stomped on by a horse."

I stayed on the line with the operator, most likely so he could confirm I wasn't a complete nut job making it all up for attention. "On top of that, he had someone start a fire somewhere in the national forest to kill my boyfriend! He's dead, I know he's dead!"

Ten agonizingly long minutes later the first cop car rolled up. I didn't know if he was the sheriff, police, SWAT or with the Royal Mounties. He came in a car with a light bar on top and had a gun strapped to his hip. Worked for me. The rest of the cavalry followed right behind and rescued me. But the horse had truly saved the day.

---

I WAS beside myself in the back of the ambulance. Dread and sheer panic over the possibility of Ty actually being dead made me a terrible patient. The paramedic probably had a less diplomatic word in mind to describe my demeanor. In fact, they threatened me with sedation if I didn't calm down.

By the time I got to the ER, I was seriously considering another sedative. The hurt and sadness overwhelming me would quickly be dulled by a little something in the IV now sticking out of my arm. I lay on a gurney, my clothes swapped for a lovely pale blue hospital gown. A flimsy blanket was pulled up to my waist. The air conditioning was set to tundra, the smell of antiseptic and rubbing alcohol permeated the air. Better than the scent of vomit. My mouth felt as if I hadn't brushed my teeth in a week, but at least my stomach was calm. No nausea, thank goodness. Wires attached to sticky electrodes stuck out every which way from me and into a machine that beeped quietly. What wasn't so quiet was the shouting coming from outside my closed curtain.

"I don't care if she's a hibernating bear. I'm going in there."

Ty. He was alive! His voice, all gruff with anger, sounded wonderful. Papers rustled, a grunt, the curtain ripped aside, practically pulled from the metal rod at the ceiling. Ty moved like a bull through Pamplona.

His green pants and yellow wildfire shirt were covered in dirt and black soot. Skin darkened by fire and sun. Eyes wild with...fear, anxiety. He stopped dead, still three feet away, his eyes searching my body, more intimately than the doctor's examination.

"Jesus, Jane." He ran a hand over his face, smearing the blackness that covered it.

Tentatively, he approached the gurney and placed a hand on the blanket, squeezing my foot gently as if afraid to touch me, of getting any closer.

I sat upright and held my arms out, words stuck behind the big glob of tears lodged in the back of my throat. He let out a deep breath and sat carefully on the gurney, pulling me to him as far as the tubing and wiring would allow. Once his arms were around me, I started crying. I couldn't stop for God knows how long, finally hiccupping to an unattractive finish while Ty held me, rubbing my back.

"I thought you were dead," he murmured, my head tucked under his chin. His smoky, sooty shirt smelled like a week-long barbeque and sweat, but I didn't care.

"I thought *you* were dead," I sniffled.

The curtain was yanked back once again. Goldie barreled in and over to the opposite side of the bed from Ty, all fluttering hands, teased hair and bad words. Her high-heeled mules click-clacked on the linoleum floor. She finally pulled herself together enough to speak. "I thought you were *both* dead. I can't believe it. I've been in Billings all day, talking to the...oh, for heaven's sake. Who would have thought that man...Are you sure you're...I mean really."

I'd never seen Goldie so flustered she couldn't complete a full sentence. So discombobulated she didn't have on any lipstick, her ponytail askew. She stroked a hand over my hair in a motherly way and plopped down on the bed on the other side.

She took a restorative breath. "I'm sure you're sick to death of answering questions, but will you *please* go over it again for me?" Obviously, she was desperate for details, but I could tell she didn't want to upset me.

Ty stood up and moved to sit in the utilitarian chair next to the bed. They didn't aim for comfort in the ER. I was cold without his body heat and I shivered. He looked much more relaxed now. Calmer, not happier. In fact, he looked downright angry. Wariness crept in. Angry at me?

"I haven't given much of a statement yet." I tucked my hair behind my ear, realized it was snarled and tangled. Good thing there wasn't a mirror around. I could only imagine what I looked like.

"A sheriff's been waiting for you to get settled to give a report. I'll just get him. Be right back." She dashed out, probably happy to have something to do.

I looked at Ty. He looked at me with those deep blue eyes. We said nothing, but I felt a lot. Knew I loved him. I was sure of it. A deranged lunatic had made things very clear.

He reached over and took my hand and held it until Goldie came clickety-clacking back with the sheriff. A middle-aged man with salt and pepper hair, crisp gray and blue uniform and a serious demeanor. He held a small pad and pen.

"Ma'am. Whenever you're ready."

Goldie returned to her spot at my side. No way was she going to miss out on the juicy, and morbid, details. I took a deep breath and recapped all that happened. When we came to Ty's text, he straightened in his chair as if shocked with a cattle prod.

"I didn't send you a text! How the hell could I do that when I was out fighting a fire? Besides, I lost my phone."

"You lost your phone when..." I darted my eyes to Goldie,

and then to the sheriff. I tried not to blush but I could feel my cheeks heat. "When we were in my kitchen the other night. It fell out of your pocket and went beneath the *kitchen table*."

Goldie cleared her throat. She was no dummy, but was polite enough not to embarrass me, at least not in front of the sheriff.

"What?" Ty was a little slower to catch on. When he did, he hid his own embarrassment under a whole lot of anger. He clenched his jaw as tight as his fists.

I went back to my story, glad to move past the sex-on-the-table portion. It wasn't really even part of what happened today anyway, so I was glad to get back on track. Away from my love life. Ty, Goldie and the sheriff remained quiet until I got to the part where Dex got his melon crushed.

"Good. Served the fucker right."

My mouth fell open. "Goldie!" I'd never heard her swear before. Sure, she'd said some colorful things, but never good old-fashioned bad words.

"I can't think of anything better," she replied.

"Asshole," added Ty angrily.

Goldie pointed a French manicured finger at Ty. "That's a good one, too."

"I could add a few but it wouldn't be professional," the sheriff added. A smile cracked his lips. "With the details you've provided, we should be able to close a whole slew of open and cold cases."

"Glad I could help," I said, although I didn't really mean it.

"What about that sweet horse?" Goldie asked, concerned. "Bless his heart."

That sweet horse had crushed his owner's skull but obviously all of us could overlook that small point.

"He's officially my new best friend," I said. "He even tops Kelly, but I figure under the circumstances she'll understand."

"Speaking of, did you call her?" Goldie asked.

I shook my head. "Can you do it for me? I don't want her to worry, but I don't think I can go through it all again right now."

Goldie looked between me and Ty. "Sure, sweetie. I'll walk the sheriff out."

Ty stood and faced me. Because of his height and my position on the gurney, I had to tilt my head up to look at him. He seemed even more furious than ever. "I can't believe you went off halfcocked to that man's ranch!"

Ty stood and paced the small space, slid the curtain closed for some privacy. Although if he kept shouting, nothing would be private.

My mouth fell open in surprise. "I...I—" Words clogged in my throat. Was I hearing him correctly or was ear damage a side effect of Ketamine? What gave him the right to yell at me?

"Why, Jane? Why the hell did you go there?"

I pointed my finger at him, livid. "Because you sent me a text."

"Right, the dropped phone. How did he know—"

He paused. I swear I saw a light bulb go off over his head. "Fuck, he watched us?" Ty placed his hands on his hips, stance wide. I had no doubt if Dex were there right now Ty would have killed him.

I nodded, but changed the subject. This was one topic neither of us wanted to dwell on. "What about you? He told me you were dead. He set that fire to kill you!"

Ty laughed sarcastically. "For such an asshole, he was pretty stupid. There were over fifty firefighters there. He clearly underestimated my abilities, and the people I work with. Besides, the guy he sent walked around with a can of gasoline and some matches. Once the wind kicked up and the fire got out of control, he practically crapped his pants. He all but climbed into the police car to escape the fire. Your criminal *friend,* Dex, should have stuck with meth."

I gritted my teeth. "Dex was not my friend."

"He was the guy at the restaurant."

Ty didn't make it a question, so I didn't respond. What could I say? I did have dinner with Dex. Reminding Ty I came home from that and had sex with him didn't seem like a good idea. Leaving one man to have sex with another didn't speak highly of me—out of context. Being with Dex that night made me realize I only wanted Ty. There was nothing I could say that would make him understand. Except one thing. "Ty, I lo—"

His words cut me off. "Goldie's here to take you home, right?"

Obviously, his mind wasn't in the same place as mine. I'd save the L word to share later. If there was a later.

"I thought..."

"What?" His voice was gravelly.

"I...never mind." I thought Ty would be the one to take me home, but I was wrong. I had a new feeling in my stomach and it wasn't nausea. And maybe the feeling was a little above my stomach, more in line with my heart. It felt like it was breaking. Tears I thought were over threatened.

"Just go," I whispered. I was impressed my voice didn't break.

He gave me a once over, from the top of my head to my feet beneath the blanket, then left. This time, when he yanked the curtain back, it ripped from the bar to hang down lopsided. Ty practically stomped off past the nurses' station. He talked briefly to Goldie, and then was gone. My heart went with him.

---

TWO HOURS LATER, with no long-term effects from the Ketamine, I'd been cleared by the ER doctors as well as by Paul, who'd been at the hospital for a woman in labor. When I described the projectile vomiting incident, they were reassured most of the drug had left my system. I felt foggy and had a few short dizzy spells here and there. Otherwise, I was back to normal.

If only I knew what normal was any more. Ty had seemingly breezed in and out of my life faster than I could change my sheets. I needed a good cry, but I wanted to hold off until I was alone, in bed with the covers over my head.

Instead, I sat on my couch with Goldie and Kelly. Wet hair from the shower, comfy sweats, hot tea with extra sugar in hand. I had no intention of drinking it, but its warmth felt good. I was dizzy from the drug, dazed from the insanity of the day. Numb from Ty's rejection.

Kelly was at the far end of the sofa, settled in for the long haul. Goldie sat on the coffee table, the two gnomes next to her, their beady little eyes and smiling faces practically shouting, "Ha ha!"

Both women were super upbeat and perky like cheerleaders, trying to pep me out of my funk. It wasn't working and they knew it. They were in funks of their own, upset about what could have happened. We were all out-of-sorts, circling around all the mine fields of conversation.

"I can't believe you want these things around," Goldie said as she picked up George, turned him around, waiting for more evil to pop out and do me harm. "All this nonsense because of a garden gnome." She shook her head.

"I made the sheriff get them from Dex's house before I went to the hospital. I don't have much interest in seeing them again, but I know the boys will when they get home."

She thunked George back down on the table. "You're right. They'd be devastated."

At first, the police wanted the gnomes for evidence. But they had Ty's cell phone which proved Dex had broken into my house. They couldn't press charges against a dead man, so they let me take the gnomes home. Besides, they had enough other felonies tied to Dex and didn't need a couple of garden gnomes as evidence.

Goldie glanced at her watch. "Oh, crap. I didn't realize how late it was. I feel bad leaving you right now after all that's happened."

"Go. I'm fine." I fake smiled.

She gave me the eye. "You're sure?"

I nodded.

"I'll stay with her," Kelly said, offering Goldie what looked like a reassuring smile.

She glanced at Kelly, considering. "Well, all right then." Standing, she leaned down to give me a kiss on my cheek. "I'm off, but I'll be back later. And sweetie, don't worry about Ty. He's just all confused right now."

*Confused.* Sure.

"Where are you headed tonight?" Kelly asked. Bless her heart for redirecting Goldie.

"Zelda Dinkleman's soon-to-be daughter-in-law's wedding shower. I can't wait to see Zelda's face when Arlene opens my present."

Goldie had that sinister look.

"What has that woman ever done to you?"

"She circled around Paul like a bee to honey before we married."

"That was forty years ago!"

"A woman scorned and all that." Goldie sniffed.

Kelly laughed. "Remind me to never cross you."

"So what did you get the poor girl?" I could only imagine the gift.

Goldie lit up like a Christmas tree. "His and hers slutty lingerie. Crotchless panties for Arlene and those new-fangled pouchless briefs for Zelda's son. Ha! She's going to think about her son, her *baby*, wearing pouchless briefs for the rest of her life. Can't wait to see her face. Gotta run!"

Kelly shook her head when the front door closed. "You know, that woman is nuts."

We watched a made-for-TV chick flick in companionable silence. I didn't have any idea what the movie was about. My mind was completely distracted with thoughts of Ty. I was relieved he wasn't hurt, hurt that he didn't want me, and I wanted him more than I ever thought possible.

There was a knock on the door. Kelly got up to answer it for me. From my seat on the couch I couldn't see who it was. Kelly spoke to the visitor for about a minute, quietly so I couldn't hear. Then Ty came into the living room. He looked the same as at the hospital. Dirty fire gear, sooty face. Angry look. Wide stance, broad shoulders, sexy body. I had no idea where he'd been, but it hadn't been near water or soap.

Zing! Damn. I hated feeling the zing for a man who didn't want me.

"Hi," I said weakly.

"I need a shower." He walked off and into my bathroom, shutting the door with a slam.

Kelly came over, gave me a quick careful hug. I held my tea out away from her arms. "It's going to be okay."

"Yeah, right." I laughed. "How can you say that? You weren't in the ER to see how angry he was."

"I saw the look on his face just now. He's hurting, too. Give him a chance."

"Give him a chance? He's the one who walked out on me!"

Kelly was unruffled by my anger. With seven kids, it was easy to stay calm. "I'm going to go."

"Fine, walk out on me, too," I moped.

Kelly laughed. "How about some cheese with that whine?"

I frowned. "Not funny."

"Like I said before, it's going to be okay. I'll call you later." She grabbed her keys and left.

I stared at the movie fuming and waited for Ty.

"You need more shampoo," he said when he came out of the bathroom. He wore a pair of gray cargo shorts and a ratty, but clean, farmer's market T-shirt. I hadn't noticed a bag of clothes when he'd come in, but he must have had one. His hair was damp from the shower, his face clean shaven.

I gave him the evil eye. "You've probably got plenty at your house!"

"I got so mad thinking about Dexter I squeezed the hell out of the bottle and shampoo shot everywhere." Obviously, he ignored my barb. "I want to kill him so badly I'm going to need anger management classes to get over it. But the fucker's already dead."

He moved to the far end of the couch where Kelly had been, lifted my feet, sat down and dropped them on his lap. Closed his eyes and sighed. "I'm so fucking tired."

This, I had not expected.

"What are you *doing* here?" Had he been wandering the streets looking like Smokey the Bear's sidekick?

He opened his eyes and looked at me. "What do you mean?" He looked completely confused by my anger. And that made me even angrier.

"You walked out on me!" I yelled.

"I didn't walk out on *you*." He gave my feet a squeeze. His hands warmed my skin. "I walked out of the *hospital*. I had to get the hell out of there. This day has been insane."

Duh.

"One minute I'm fighting a forest fire, the next minute a lunatic comes barreling out of the woods with a gas can in his hand. When he told us who paid him to start the fire, because clearly he couldn't come up with the idea on his own, I had a bad feeling. Got any beer?"

I nodded, completely baffled by Ty's disappearance, reappearance, shower. Everything.

He got up, got the beer from the fridge and returned to his spot.

After a few swallows he continued, "I play poker with one of the 911 dispatchers. He recognized your name from your call and thought I might want to know. I was tracked down on the fire and patched through the details. Driving back to town was the longest two hours of my life. He said you were fine but I had to see for myself."

Any interest in crying was gone, replaced by the happiness I'd felt early in the morning when Ty leaned over me in my bed and said he'd fallen for me. This day had been insane.

"I...I thought you walked away from me. From us."

Ty's eyes flared in understanding. He shook his head. "No. Never."

I bit my lip. "What about my dinner with Dex?"

Ty lifted an eyebrow. "I told you that night, you went with him for a reason. I know you're not a cheater."

I was still confused. "Then why were you so angry in the ER?"

He squeezed my foot again. "You just looked so fragile, so breakable, lying there. While you cried in my arms, I thought about what he could have done to you. What he had done to you. I was so angry, I had to get out of there. I was afraid in my anger I might hurt you, more than what Dexter had done. I'm sorry you didn't understand that."

As apologies go, it was a darn good one. I picked up George, cracks and all, his ceramic body cool beneath my fingers. "Who would have imagined my entire life would be turned upside down by two garden gnomes?"

"Never in a million years," Ty grumbled. He took George from me and put him back on the coffee table along with his beer. He lifted my feet off his lap and worked his way across the couch, lying on top of me, propped up on one elbow. I could feel every hard inch of him, some places much harder than others. His body heat seeped into me. He smelled like my soap and beer. I felt safe and sheltered, protected with him over me.

"Am I too heavy?" he asked, worried. He started to pull away, but I yanked him back on top of me.

"No, just right." I ran my fingers over the letters on his T-shirt, afraid to look him in the eye. "So, um, about what you said to me this morning in bed."

"Oh, you were awake." One tip of his mouth curved up.

"Only for the good parts."

"Good parts?" He tucked a curl behind my ear, studied my face, settled on my lips.

I pretended to think about it. "You said something about sex."

He smiled. "Sex is definitely a good part."

I pushed against him and laughed. "I also heard something about falling?"

Ty's eyes met mine. I could see so much in them. The fear from the day, the playful lust, the love. "Oh, I've definitely fallen."

He lowered his head for a kiss. Not just an it's-just-sex kiss. This was a love kiss and that made it all the better. Softened all the rough edges from the day. Lots of tongue didn't hurt either.

"I love you, Ty," I said, when we surfaced.

Ty smiled and exhaled. His expression was crowded with a mingling of relief and love. "I didn't think it was possible to care that much again after all the shit I saw in the Gulf. The first time I saw you, *bam*, I felt something."

I was reminded of the zing I felt when I first saw him at the pancake breakfast. The day we got the gnomes at the garage sale. "You felt a bam? I felt a zing."

He ran his hand over my hair again. His look, his touch was almost reverent. "A zing, huh? When I started feeling too much, I thought it was best just to walk away. But somehow you slipped in there. Just like those gnomes, in one day, you just changed my life."

"Now what?" I asked.

"I guess we just see what happens," Ty replied. "Without anyone trying to kill you."

"Probably a good idea." My heart lurched, forgetting the most important thing. "The boys. What about the boys?" What if he didn't want to take on someone else's kids? It was one thing to be in love with a woman, it was another to take on all her baggage, too.

Ty grinned. "You have to know how much they mean to me. The question is, what do you think they'll say to us being in a relationship?"

"Does this mean...does this mean no condoms?" I wondered.

Heat flared in his eyes. "I'm not ready for a baby, so we'd have to think of other birth control, but I'd love to take you bare, with nothing between us. I've...I've never done it before."

The idea of it had me squirming beneath him. "I'm on the pill."

He groaned, kissed me again. "The boys? You think they like me?"

Good question. I turned my head and saw George the Gnome and his friend staring at us again. Now their evil grins looked like smiles. Happy smiles. Maybe they weren't so bad after all.

"If you bring the gnomes to the airport when we pick them up, you'll probably be set for life."

"Done. Oh, Goldie called your mom to tell her what happened."

I nodded. "She told me. I'm glad because I don't want to go over all that again with my mom. At least right now."

"What you don't know is that your mom called me."

"Huh?" That was a surprise.

"I guess she believed Goldie, but wanted confirmation from someone else. Don't worry, I eased her mind and told her you'd call her later." He ran his fingers across my cheek. "I spoke with the boys, too. They're fine. Zach asked me a funny question though."

Ty smiled, kissed my forehead, my temple, behind my ear.

I melted. "Oh?"

"He wanted to know if I was giving you field hockey

lessons." He eyed me suspiciously. "Do you have any idea why he said that?"

I laughed until tears ran down my cheeks. Looked at the gnomes again before looking into Ty's eyes. Smiled. "Maybe I have to give you lessons instead." My hand slid down his body to grab hold of his *stick*. "Starting now."

# NOTE FROM VANESSA

Don't worry, there's more Small Town Romance to come!

But guess what? I've got some bonus content for you with Jane and Ty. So sign up for my mailing list. There will be special bonus content for each Small Town Romance book, just for my subscribers. Signing up will let you hear about my next release as soon as it is out, too (and you get a free book...wow!)

As always...thanks for loving my books and the wild ride!

Vanessa

## WANT MORE?

READ THE FIRST CHAPTER OF MONTANA ICE, THE SECOND BOOK IN THE SMALL TOWN ROMANCE SERIES.

## MONTANA ICE - CHAPTER ONE

When little girls played make-believe with their dolls, most pretended they were mommies or princesses or teachers. Had little tea parties with them, played dress-up. That was what my sister, Violet, had done with hers. Me? I played plumber with mine. I dressed my little Betsy Wets-Alot up in a pair of gray coveralls stolen from a male test pilot action figure I'd found at the toy store. He'd been tossed naked into the back of my closet until my sister had found him and used him for the groom in her pretend weddings.

Not only did I dress my self-wetting doll in menswear, I ran a straw down the pants leg to divert the faux pee away from her anatomically-incorrect little body. No potty for her. I'd been five and had known what I wanted to be when I grew up. I, Veronica Miller, had wanted to be a plumber. Just like my father.

Now, over twenty years later, I'd fulfilled my childhood dream. I was the plumber I'd longed to be, working with my dad. Soon to be working on my own. One last payment to my old man stood between his official retirement and my small business owner status.

I smiled to myself about this almost-upon-me momentous

occasion while lathering my hair in the shower. I squealed when the spray of water I was standing beneath went cold and quickly rinsed out the strawberry-scented shampoo.

"Stupid hot water heater," I grumbled to myself as I yanked back the plastic shower curtain and stepped out into the steam filled room. I longed to get back to my own house as Violet's plumbing system needed some serious work. Even in the thick humidity, goose bumps popped out all over my body as I quickly toweled off and snuggled into my ratty, yet wonderfully comfortable, flannel robe.

While I leaned over and rubbed my wet hair with a bright pink towel, I heard it. The sound of a key in a lock, the front door opening. I froze in place upside-down, staring at my knees between the edges of the robe, towel tangling with my long hair. Since I was a plumber, not a law enforcement officer, I lacked the training to keep panic at bay. That hot, adrenaline-induced fear rose up inside me between one heartbeat and the next. I could have sworn the little wet hairs on the back of my neck stood up.

Help. I needed to get help, but my cell was in my purse, which I'd dropped by the front door, one room away. And Violet had no house phone.

I stood up, flipped my dark hair back over my shoulder, held my breath and listened. Rustling and a little mumbling was all I could make out. Who was in Violet's house? Sure, they must have a key since I hadn't heard a window break, but the only other person who was *supposed* to have one was Violet, and she was in Utah.

I tiptoed over to the door, bit my lip and winced as I turned the knob and hoped it didn't squeak. I slowly opened the door as I held my breath. Peeking into the bedroom, I saw nothing out of the ordinary. Barely made bed, dirty clothes tossed haphazardly at the wicker hamper. Something heavy thumped onto the floor from the vicinity of the front door and I looked in that direction as if I had x-ray vision and could see through the wall to the person in the living room.

I squeezed through the small gap I'd made in the bathroom doorway, afraid if I opened it anymore, the old hinges would give me away. Breathing as quietly as possible, which was pretty hard in panic mode, I bent down and grabbed the first thing I could get my hands on to use as a weapon. What I held didn't register. I knew it was solid wood like a baseball bat and as good as I was going to get for protection.

Violet's house was small, with only one floor and a scary basement I rarely visited. Living room, kitchen, bedroom and bath. That's it. Which also meant there wasn't anywhere to hide.

For breaking and entering, the guy wasn't Mr. Stealth. It was the middle of the afternoon. He'd come in the front door and he was awfully noisy for someone being where they weren't supposed to be. Even if he was the worst robber ever, that didn't mean he wasn't dangerous.

My palms were sweaty as I peeked around the door jamb into the living room. His back was to me and he appeared to be looking down at something he held in front of him, probably his phone. It appeared he was texting, or reading one. Tall, around six feet, maybe a little more, and solid. He wore jeans and dark leather shoes. His black jacket was a lighter weight than one would expect for the dead of winter in Montana in the throes of a bitter cold snap. A gray knit cap covered most of his dark hair.

I didn't recognize him, but I wasn't in the mood to wait for him to turn around and see me. I decided to use the element of surprise. I tiptoed over to him and whacked him on the arm with my wooden weapon. Hard.

*Thwack!*

I'd aimed for his head, but nerves and slick palms messed me up and I hit his shoulder instead. The reverberations tingled in my fingertips.

"What the fuck?" Mr. Intruder said, his voice deep, full of surprise, the cell phone dropping to the floor at his feet. He raised a hand to his upper arm. As he started to turn to face me, I hit him again, this time on the back of the head.

*Crack!*

It wasn't the sound of his skull breaking, but my weapon instead. The wood broke into two, one of the pieces clattering to the floor.

Intruder grunted, fell to his knees with a thunk, then fell face first onto the floral area rug in front of the fireplace, his face turned toward me.

I stood there motionless, stunned, holding half of my broken weapon. Huh, varsity softball had paid off. It appeared I'd hit a home run. I looked down at the prostrate form on the floor. One leg moved a little, which, combined with some groaning, indicated I hadn't killed him. Even with his eyes closed, I instantly recognized him.

"Oh, shit," I whispered as I knelt down beside him. The thick wool of the carpet was scratchy against my knees. Why hadn't I known who it was before I knocked him unconscious? I should have been relieved an axe-wielding mad man wasn't trying to kill me, but I was too surprised instead.

It was Jack Reid. The guy I'd been in love with in high school who I hadn't seen in over ten years. Ten years where I'd often fantasize about him, about what could have been. I'd often dream about the moment he'd come back into my life, but this definitely wasn't it. Sure, when he'd gone out with Violet instead of me senior year I'd wanted to kill him, slowly and painfully for doing so, but I'd envisioned strangulation or a pummeling of some kind. Now that I'd possibly killed him, at least knocked him completely unconscious, with—I lifted my broken weapon—the Triple Smacker paddle from my box of sex toys for the toy party I was hosting tonight—I realized the anger and bitterness at his long-ago rejection hadn't gone away.

How dare he barge into my life again, unannounced, when

I wasn't the least bit ready for him! I wanted make-up, a killer dress, some fuck-me heels on, my hair done, with a hot guy in love with me on my arm when Jack saw me again. To make him see what he'd missed out on. Then I'd crush him beneath my stiletto heel before my lover shifted my attentions elsewhere.

But a ratty robe and tangled, wet hair? A sex toy paddle? Revenge and maybe a little payback would be nice, but a felony conviction for assault? Oh boy.

Dropping the broken paddle onto the floor, I leaned over Jack and gently probed the back of his head. No brains gushing out, no blood seeping from beneath his hat. One huge goose egg of a bump though. I winced, thinking about the headache —and maybe concussion—he might have.

Man, he smelled good. Woodsy, clean, male mixed with the fruity scent of my shampoo from my hair tangled about my face. His scent was sexy in an unconscious sort of way.

"Jack, Jack wake up," I said, gently moving his shoulder. "Jack!" He had to wake up because I couldn't live with myself being known around town as the woman who killed Jack Reid with a Triple Smacker.

After another groan and a few moans, he rolled onto his back, blinked his eyes a few times and stared at me. At first, unseeing, then with focus.

Boy, even knocked practically unconscious, he sure looked amazing. Ten years had done the man a lot of good. His face was more rugged, jaw more pronounced. It could have been the five o'clock shadow at two in the afternoon that helped with that. He had a fabulous tan. The kind you got from living in Florida. Lips I'd dreamed about kissing when I was sixteen still looked appealing now. His dark hair that peeked out of his cap had a little curl. His blue eyes, even unfocused, were just as I remembered. Longing, once forgotten, flared back to life.

He just stared at me, looking me over as if I was a space alien. A slow perusal from head to toe. I couldn't tell if he was confused or just addle pated. "Jack, say something."

He blinked. Smirked, but quickly winced.

"Um."

Oh God, had I caused him amnesia?

He cleared his throat. "Nice breast."

I glanced down at myself, one breast was definitely out there for Jack to see, my nipple hard. I yanked at the side of my robe that was glaringly open, my hand at my neck holding the lapels together.

"Is this how you treat all your boyfriends?" His blue eyes had cleared, weren't quite so foggy as a minute ago. "A kiss hello would probably be better, although maybe that's not your way." His gaze dropped to my chest again.

My mouth fell open as anger flared. "You're not my boyfriend. You lost your chance ten years ago," I said tartly.

Jack leered. The smile he gave me couldn't be described as anything else. "You flash everyone who comes through the door, or just me?" He lifted a hand and rubbed the back of his head, winced.

I felt my cheeks burn hot at the thought of my epic wardrobe malfunction. It was completely and utterly mortifying, and on top of that, he was being a complete jerk about it.

"Only ones I bash on the head first."

## ABOUT THE AUTHOR

Vanessa Vale is the *USA Today* Bestselling author of over 40 books, sexy romance novels, including her popular Bridgewater historical romance series and hot contemporary romances featuring unapologetic bad boys who don't just fall in love, they fall hard. When she's not writing, Vanessa savors the insanity of raising two boys, is figuring out how many meals she can make with a pressure cooker, and teaches a pretty mean karate class. While she's not as skilled at social media as her kids, she loves to interact with readers.

www.vanessavaleauthor.com

## ALSO BY VANESSA VALE

**Small Town Romance**

Montana Fire

Montana Ice

Montana Heat

Montana Wild

Montana Mine

**Steele Ranch**

Spurred

Wrangled

Tangled

Hitched

Lassoed

**Bridgewater County Series**

Ride Me Dirty

Claim Me Hard

Take Me Fast

Hold Me Close

Make Me Yours

Kiss Me Crazy

**Mail Order Bride of Slate Springs Series**

A Wanton Woman

A Wild Woman

A Wicked Woman

**Bridgewater Ménage Series**

Their Runaway Bride

Their Kidnapped Bride

Their Wayward Bride

Their Captivated Bride

Their Treasured Bride

Their Christmas Bride

Their Reluctant Bride

Their Stolen Bride

Their Brazen Bride

Their Bridgewater Brides- Books 1-3 Boxed Set

**Outlaw Brides Series**

Flirting With The Law

**MMA Fighter Romance Series**

Fight For Her

**Wildflower Bride Series**

Rose

Hyacinth

Dahlia

Daisy

Lily

**Montana Men Series**

The Lawman

The Cowboy

The Outlaw

**Standalone Reads**

Twice As Delicious

Western Widows

Sweet Justice

Mine To Take

Relentless

Sleepless Night

Man Candy - A Coloring Book

CPSIA information can be obtained
at www.ICGtesting.com
Printed in the USA
LVHW040103071020
668072LV00006B/593